Often compared to Nabokov and Borges, Ishikawa Jun (1899-1987) is one of Japan's most distinguished modern novelists. Winner of the Akutagawa Prize — Japan's most distinguished literary award — *The Bodhisattva* is Ishikawa Jun's powerful satire of Japanese intellectuals in the 1930s, and is considered to be his seminal work. Its sardonic humor can be seen as an antidote to the ultranationalist thinking pervasive in Japan at the time.

The Bodhisattva is the story of an impoverished novelist living in downtown Tokyo who is driven by a dream of the millennium. This dream is manifested in his commitment to writing about Joan of Arc and her chronicler Christine de Pizan, and in his love for a young woman involved in the political underground. The novelist builds successive layers through a series of parallels between "dust and flowers" — Japan in the 1930s and France in the fifteenth century — and the dream of divine intervention through Joan of Arc's Asian counterpart, the bodhisattva. Ishikawa Jun's beautiful layering of images from classical Western and Asian literature characterizes this remarkable work of modern Japanese resistance literature and metafiction.

THE BODHISATTVA, *or Samantabhadra*

MODERN ASIAN LITERATURE SERIES

THE BODHISATTVA

A NOVEL BY

COLUMBIA UNIVERSITY PRESS

or *Samantabhadra*

ISHIKAWA JUN

*Translated from the Japanese with an
introduction and critical essay by*
William Jefferson Tyler

91-142

NEW YORK

UNESCO COLLECTION OF REPRESENTATIVE WORKS
JAPANESE SERIES

This book is published with a contribution from funds-in-trust
deposited with Unesco by Japan.

In accordance with the regulations of the Unesco Collection of
Representative Works, the translation has been read by Kondo Ineko,
Professor Emeritus, Tsuda College, and Takeda Katsuhito, Professor,
Maseda University.

COLUMBIA UNIVERSITY PRESS
NEW YORK   OXFORD

The Bodhisattva, or Samantabhadra is a translation of FUGEN
by Jun Ishikawa, copyright © 1936 by Jun Ishikawa

English translation rights arranged with the author
through Iwanami Shoten, Publishers, Tokyo

Translation, preface, introduction, and critical essay copyright
© 1990 Columbia University Press

The translator and publisher gratefully acknowledge the generous
support toward publication given them by the Japan Foundation,
the Masuda Foundation, and the Wheatland Foundation.

Library of Congress Cataloging-in-Publication Data

Ishikawa, Jun, 1899–1987
    [Fugen.   English]
    The Bodhisattva, or Samantabhadra/Ishikawa Jun; translated
from the Japanese with an introduction and critical essay by
William Jefferson Tyler.
        p.   cm.—(Modern Asian literature series)
    Translation of: Fugen.
    ISBN 0-231-06962-6
    I. Title.   II. Title: Samantabhadra.   III. Series.
PL830.S5F813   1989
859.6'344—dc20   89-15856
                                        CIP

Casebound editions of Columbia University Press books are Smyth-sewn
and printed on permanent and durable acid-free paper

Book Design by Charles Hames

Printed in the United States of America
c 10 9 8 7 6 5 4 3 2 1

for Eva Margaret Jefferson & William Applegarth Tyler

Contents

Translator's Preface and Acknowledgments   ix

Introduction   xi

The Bodhisattva   1

Critical Essay: The Art and Act of Reflexivity
in *The Bodhisattva*   139

Notes to the Critical Essay   167

Translator's Preface and Acknowledgments

IT IS not uncommon to miss the point of an experimental work at first inspection. "A novel of manners," one member of the Akutagawa Prize committee called *The Bodhisattva*, notwithstanding a statement in the novel to the contrary. Doubtless its full import is not grasped in a single reading.

Moreover, *The Bodhisattva* is not a work that submits readily to translation. Aside from the problems faced by all translators, the complexity of the narrative, the density and recondite nature of its imagery, and the all-important matter of tone, especially an ironic or satirical one, oblige the translator to decide when, where, and why to impose a more incisive interpretative voice in order to insure that the overall thrust of the work, as well as its nuances, emerge in English.

First, in the name of readability, a major change in the physical appearance of the text has been introduced through considerably more paragraphing than exists in the original, and by setting off all dialogue passages. The author clearly meant to have the text look continuous, but the result in translation is an overly full, even forbidding, page.

Second, since many passages suggest one meaning or image only to switch promiscuously to another, the technique of apposition and parenthesis—as in "the endless tracings of my pen, the prolix and petulant limning of my troth" to capture the double meaning of "*memmen to kakikudokō*" for example—has been used to amplify and give expression to the full import of the original. Amplification also has the effect of reproducing the chatty rhythms of the Japanese.

Third, the focus of certain passages has been sharpened, spelling out in unobfuscated language what is stated less pointedly, e.g., "imperial realm" for *kokudo* or "imperial palace" for *kumo no ue*.

Japanese names are given in the Japanese manner, with the family name preceding the personal.

In undertaking this project the translator has had the support and advice of many institutions and friends. I wish to express my appreciation to Columbia University Press, Jennifer Crewe, Executive Editor; to the Japan Foundation, and to the Masuda Foundation of Yokohama, for subsidies to the press to defray part of the costs of publication; the former also supported summer research, as did the University of Pennsylvania; to Ishikawa Iku for many kindnesses, including the photograph of Ishikawa Jun; to Iwanami Shoten for its cooperation; to the Academic Computer Center, Amherst College, Betty Steele, Director, for without Betty's witty and patient instruction I should not have made of the computer screen a palimpsest for ease in revising drafts; to Henry and Jean Dunbar, for making summers at Blake Field possible; to Dale Saunders and Doris Bargen who offered much helpful advice concerning the critical essay, and the translation—each a stalwart champion of either the pros and cons of literal vs. free interpretation; to Howard Hibbett, for suggesting *Fugen* above all of Ishikawa's works for translation; to Izawa Yoshio, for his hospitality in Kobe—along with that of Noguchi Takehiko—and for corroboration of details through correspondence; to Masako Nakagawa Graham, for participating in the chore of checking the translation against the original; to Ken Kraft, and members of the Department of Oriental Studies, University of Pennsylvania, for assistance with terms in Buddhism, Chinese, and Sanskrit; to the teaching and clerical staff of the Inter-University Center, Yokohama, for "finishing touches"; and to Nadja Margolis, scholar of French literature, for information on Christine de Pizan.

I am especially indebted to Shimozato Masao for his sustained—and sustaining—enthusiasm during the time it has taken to bring this project to completion. When one wintry night we wondered if ever there would be other glorious days in the Valley, little did we know what seredipitious summers were yet in store.

Introduction

"I rise from my chair, and turning in the direction
of the popular refrain ... I shout 'NO!'"
—MARUSU NO UTA

WHEN ISHIKAWA Jun passed away on December 29, 1987, he was
at work on his twentieth novel, a tongue-in-cheek "banquet" of
love, power, and money in contemporary Japan. One can only
speculate as to the intent of this unfinished tale, but in entitling it
Hebi no uta (The Song of the Snake), perhaps he was harking back
a half century to thoughts of an early sally, *Marusu no uta* (The
Song of the War God), a denunciation of aggression abroad and
acquiescence at home that he wrote in the wake of the Japanese
invasion of China in 1937 and that constitutes one of the rare
instances of resistance literature written in Japan during the crucial
years before the Pacific War. Times change, but the salient feature
of this writer's life remained a rigorous anarchism, and of his
antiestablishment novels, a multilayered construction combining
literary parody, allegorical farce, and social satire.

BORN IN Tokyo in 1899, Ishikawa sought his literary roots in
the *bunjin* tradition of social iconoclasm and artistic epicureanism
developed by the *kyōka* poets, *sharebon* novelists, and *nanga*
painters of the late eighteenth century—Ōta Nampo, Santō
Kyōden, Watanabe Kazan to name, in his words, "the happy
few"—and that is transmitted to modern Japanese letters by Mori
Ōgai and Nagai Kafū. Especially during the war years, he decided
upon a course of inner emigration, and "through study abroad
in Edo ... discovered 'Japan's most modern age' in the decades
between Meiwa and Bunka [1764–1817]." By virtue of his singular
erudition, and his attitude of splendid isolation, he became the

tradition's contemporary heir, as well as its final practitioner—the "last of the literati" (*saigo no bunjin*) as the media phrase has it. Indeed, with his passing, there is no one to take his place.

At the same time, because of his overriding interest in modernity, Ishikawa grounded himself equally in the study and practice of modernist prose fiction as it has evolved in world literature over the last century. In his youth, he numbered among the first to translate French novels into Japanese: Anatole France's *Le lys rouge* in 1923; André Gide's *L'immoraliste* and *Les caves du Vatican* in 1924 and 1928. By his mid-thirties, he was writing and publishing his own *récits* and *romans*. More than any writer of his age— Kawabata Yasunari and Kobayashi Hideo were his peers, generationally speaking—he grasped the concepts that revolutionized Western art and literature after both world wars and set out to create what he called the *jikken shōsetsu*, or "experimental novel," contemporaneous with European innovators and well in advance of Japanese experimentalists such as Abe Kōbō and Ōe Kenzaburō. Because he never sought a popular following, recognition came only fleetingly at first—the Akutagawa Prize of 1936 for *The Bodhisattva;* a brief period of notoriety 1946–48 when he shared the *après-guerre* limelight with Sakaguchi Ango and Dazai Osamu—and substantially after the 1960s when he produced his best and most sustained novels: *Taka* (Hawks, 1953); *Shion monogatari* (Asters, 1956; translated by Donald Keene, 1961); *Aratama* (Wild Spirit, 1963); *Shifuku sennen* (The Millennium, 1965); *Kyōfūki* (Record of a Mad Wind, 1971–80); *Rokudō yugyō* (Playing in the Six Paths, 1983); as well as a series of essays written in the manner of Alain's *propos* and appearing under the penname, Isai ("the *kyōka* poet at his desk"). Looking in retrospect, we see that Ishikawa was an early proponent and creator of metafiction, fiction that uses itself to explore the meaning and potential of the fictive medium. It comes as no surprise to learn that in Japan his novels are often compared to those of Nabokov or Borges.

Fugen, or *The Bodhisattva*, as the title of this novella (Ishikawa considered it a *récit*) is rendered more broadly in this translation, first appeared in *Sakuhin*, a journal of progressive fiction, in 1936, and was quickly recognized, according to one of the judges of the Akutagawa Prize, for its success as "a novelistic novel . . . that penetrates to the core of the modern narrative." With the possible exception of the short story *Yamazakura* (Wild Cherries, 1936), which possesses the phantasmagorical and surrealistic elements characteristic of Ishikawa's mature fiction, no other prewar work anticipates better his experimental novels; and in none is the metafictional technique more apparent. Moreover, no subsequent novel rivals *The Bodhisattva* in demonstrating the blend of Ishikawa's modernist and literati tastes, a confluence that brings together first-person narration of the novel-within-the-narrative after the fashion of Gide in *Les faux-monnayeurs,* or Santō Kyōden in his *sharebon,* and the "illumination" of the text with *mitate,* or analog images, from Buddhist parable literature and the story of Joan of Arc.

The Bodhisattva asks a great deal of its reader. First, it requires an acquaintance with Buddhist iconography: of the paired image of flowers and dust, the beauty and ugliness of life, as well as its evanescence; of the concept of the bodhisattva, a being headed for awakening who acts to bring enlightenment to others. The bodhisattva forgoes nirvana, the repose of extinction, accepting the passions and frustrations of this world, in order to liberate others from suffering and ignorance. It asks for a knowledge of the legend of Han-shan, the eccentric "Cold Mountain" poet of T'ang China, and his sidekick, the lowly monk and broomsweep Shih-te; and of the Buddhist recension of the legend that identifies this pair of long-haired, laughing jackals as the incarnations of Mañjuśrî, the bodhisattva of the Buddha's wisdom, and Samantabhadra, the translator of this wisdom into practice. In the Garland and Lotus sutras, Samantabhadra figures prominently in the Buddhist pantheon as the bodhisattva who assumes the most activist and this-worldly descent into the mundane.

Moreover, *The Bodhisattva* asks us to suspend our usual expectations of the novel. Plot is, for example, minimal: a young man rushes to a train station to warn his love, whom he has not seen during the decade of her hiding in the political underground, that the police have set a trap to apprehend her. Meanwhile, style appears to be all-important: whether because of its garrulousness, after the manner that was fashionable in world literature of the 1930s, or the work's serio-comic tone and the narrator's perplexing manipulation of the text. We are called upon to look for an underlying literary metaphysic, and simultaneously, to be alert to the possibility—as the critical essay appended to this translation argues—of a hidden agenda, and to the clues that help us to read its message between the lines. Mystification in the face of political control and suppression was a technique practiced by the literati Nampo, Kyōden, and Kazan—all of whom came into conflict with the feudal authorities. Their lessons were not wasted on Ishikawa. It is important to recall that *The Bodhisattva* was written when publications were subject to censorship; moreover, the mood of the country was moving rapidly in the direction of militarism. The abortive coup, the famous "Two-Twenty-Six Incident" of February 1936 that is an important watershed date in the decline of civilian control, preceded the novel's appearance by only a matter of months. Open criticism in the press, not to mention playfulness in literature, was soon to be identified and prosecuted. The jingoistic chorus of *Katte kuru zo to isamashiku* (Oh so bravely, "Off to Victory") that stirred the air became the topic of parody in Ishikawa's dissenting *Marusu no uta,* but the story was banned, and he and his editor brought to court and fined.

One final word: *The Bodhisattva* is not a "Buddhist novel." Ishikawa's lifelong dream was a vision of an unfettered existence in an anarchial millennium. Accordingly, his fascination with Samantabhadra is as a literary vehicle, metaphor, or expedient. It arises out of the similarity between the bodhisattva's this-worldly activism on behalf of the unawakened and what, in a short essay of 1943, "On the Ways of Thought of the People of Edo," Ishikawa outlined as the genius of the Edo literary imagination, namely, the secularization (*zokuka*) of ideas—the insistence that abstractions pass the test of being made concrete and grounded in reality, thereby insuring their relativity to all. To employ the idiom used in *The Bodhisattva,* this is to *sewa ni kudaku,* "to break into the vernacular."

> "What I wish to do is set the world on its head by taking the mumbo-jumbo of the conundrums—'Difficult and Easy as Obverse and Reverse,' 'The Vision of the Washed Few and the Illusions of the Great Unwashed'—and put them into words people can understand.
> Because, I tell you, we shall never see the promised Buddhaland here on earth unless we are prepared to stand the world on end and upset the normal order of things. If there is

any hope of our protecting ourselves in these latter days of the
Buddha's law, it will take far more than a conventional mandala with Buddha seated in the middle, calmly catching forty
winks.''

鎌倉山　春葉書院にて   Wm. J. Tyler

THE BODHISATTVA, *or Samantabhadra*

CHAPTER ONE

JUST AS a bead of water upon a lacquer tray glitters and is gone before the hand that would hold it gemlike between two fingertips, so too the curious sparkle of Tarui Moichi dissipates when one considers him a potential character in a novel. He is nondescript; and one wonders, with the feeling somehow of being cheated, what had made him seem extraordinary. For the breezes that stir the pages of the novel are far different from the gusts of the mundane world, and Moichi too ordinary and insubstantial a subject—to pinch him is to crush him—should we, in taking him up as the topic of our tale, decide to scorn the earth and, by the sheer force of our soaring flight to the heights of seventh heaven, brush from our wings the dust of the floating world and the dregs of human sentimentality.

"Whoever said he was interesting, anyway?"

So ask me what recommends this fellow devoid of any apparent worth, and I would say it is his very worthlessness, the total lack of any discernible merit, that is the source of his appeal. Indeed, never was a man more constituted of nothing. But that I should champion this nonentity and press my argument, knowing full well there are no limits to how long one may argue the matter, reflects the chaotic state of my brain, suffering as I am from a hangover from last night's heavy drinking, as well as—and surely this is the more relevant point—the idle fantasies engendered by fidgeting abed until ten in the morning. When one further considers that the very mattress upon which I lie happens to belong to none other than the person in question, perhaps it comes as no surprise that I should think of him, but . . . enough of this.

"To hell with Tarui Moichi," I muttered to myself, kicking back the covers. I leapt from the bed, grateful to find the apartment equipped with a coldwater tap. Yet in the instant I flicked the spigot and began splashing my face with water, there came a knock at the door, and a persistent call.

"Mr. Tarui? Mr. Tarui? Are you there?"

I said nothing but was forced to reply when the visitor chose of his own accord to open the unlocked door and stick his head inside.

"What the hell?"

"I'm from *The Sunrise Press.*"

"What is it?"

"I'm here to collect."

"Tarui's not in, and I don't know anything about it."

"But aren't you Mr. Tarui?"

"No. I only spent the night. This is the first time I've ever been here."

"What . . . ?"

"He's gone to work."

"Can you tell me when you expect him?"

"I've no idea."

"He's already two months behind. Everytime I come to collect, somebody else is here."

"I wouldn't know about that."

"What am I going to do? He's never home."

"Why get upset? Try again some other time."

I succeeded at last in pushing the chagrined bill collector out of the apartment, but his parting shot—"Well, how am *I* supposed to know who lives here?"—delivered theatrically from the other side of the door, echoed, like the sound of his sandals as they flip-flopped down the corridor, the question that had been turning over in my mind. Though Moichi had made a nest for himself of this room, who, one wondered, was its true occupant?

Last night as I headed home from the cinema, walking down a back alley in Shinjuku, I had chanced on Moichi coming the opposite way. As always, he was dressed in Western style clothes of the latest fashion. Moichi was fussy about what he wore—and that alone.

"Oh, it's you ... I've been meaning ... "

The tightly molded shoulders of his fancy suit notwithstanding, Moichi seemed to shrink as he tucked in his chin and nodded with an embarrassed look. He forced a smile, reminded as he was, no doubt, of the wristwatch he had borrowed three months previous and had failed to return. His words hung in the air.

But he soon regained his composure, his voice taking on a lively tone. "I know just the place. It's right this way."

Moichi steered me down the street. He was not about to let me have a choice in the matter.

I could only ask myself if this latest sleight of hand was yet another display of the consummate art of this fellow who, incapable of sticking to anything, had made a virtue of inconsistency and turned it to his profit. Mercurial in all things, he had managed nonetheless—or at least until six months ago—to earn his keep by simply hanging about a vaudeville theater in Asakusa. Needless to say, he belonged to neither cast nor management, doing nothing more than running errands for one of the lead actors.

Although Moichi looked every inch the salaried type, in point of fact he has never held a steady job. And no sooner had we passed under the curtain over the door and into the bright lights of the drinking establishment than, spreading his wings like a gadfly, he was transformed into his true self. He flitted nervously about the bar flashing his calling card at the newcomers, and—"Yes, yes, how are you?"—halloed the regulars as though he were out for a stroll down the arcade at Asakusa.

Yet for all this facile display, little did it matter at what angle Moichi set the sail of his dapper brown derby because it never fully concealed a certain congenital earthiness that had no place in these urban waters. Nor could it hide the fact that the actor upon whom he had pinned his hopes had bolted the troupe and moved to Kansai, leaving Moichi with neither means of support nor a place to stay.

Where, then, should this rolling stone appear at the end of January but the second-floor apartment of a rooming house in Kurumazaka. The apartment belonged to the actor's friend who, it happens, was none other than myself.

"It'll only be for a couple of days," Moichi said, but two, three days became a week, and the week, a fortnight.

At first he was always out who-knows-where, but eventually he exhausted his list of people to visit. He stayed in, stretched out on the tatami, morning, noon, and night.

"Oh, how I'd like to be a whale. Bobbing on the surface of the sea, and sending up a spume of spray whenever I felt so inclined. How pleasant it would be! How carefree! Oh, to be a whale..."

"That's all very well for you, Moichi, but it doesn't do me any good to have a whale swimming about the apartment. Come on, how about finding yourself a job?"

"You know I've never meant to be an imposition. As a matter of fact, there's a boss in one of the political parties, and I've asked him to help me out. I should be hearing from him any day now..."

"It's not that I mind your being here. But with two of us crammed in this tiny room I suspect it can't be any more comfortable for you than it is for me. And then there's my work..."

"Oh yes, how's it going? Who did you say you were writing about? Chris...Chris...Christine what's-her-name?"

What need had I to tell Moichi that I was writing a biography of the medieval French poet and early feminist writer Christine de Pizan?

"More to the point is the question of your own work."

"Of course, that's important as you say, and that's why, uh... I'll be going out today."

Off Moichi went, not to return for a week and a half. When he reappeared he was wearing a stylish overcoat with a velvet collar, although judging from the creases where the coat had been folded and stored, it had been redeemed from the pawnbroker's shelf only recently. He presented me with a tin of Hope cigarettes for having put him up.

"And this," he said, producing an over-sized business card with the name and address of a financial establishment located in Kanda, "is what I'll be representing from now on."

The card from "Mutual Finance" gave a residential address as well: The Benihana Apartments, Banshū-chō, Yotsuya. There was even a telephone number.

"You've certainly come up in the world."

"Thanks to you, I've decided to make an honest living for myself."

"Splendid."

"By the way, would you mind lending me your wristwatch?

Don't worry, I'll have it back to you in the morning. I was planning to buy one, but suddenly they've called a big meeting for tonight, and..."

A good three months had elapsed since that conversation and last night when I ran into Moichi.

"It stopped running, you see, and I had to send it out to be fixed. You'll get it one of these days."

And when, after a few drinks at the bar, the time came to call for the check, he allowed that I need not worry on that score either. "This is on me—at least here it is. I'll take care of it," he said, putting on a bold front. But he had to step to the rear of the shop to arrange, in a whispered conversation, for future payment.

Once we were back on the street, Moichi was reminded of "another interesting place up ahead," and by the time we had been in and out of two or three bars, it was past one in the morning. I was about to take a taxi and go home, but he was insistent. The hour was late. I should spend the night at his new apartment.

"You ought to take a look at it at least. It's no distance."

The Benihana Apartments were located in a neighborhood just the other side of the red-light district in Shinjuku.

When we arrived at the apartment Moichi had to borrow small change "to get the gas turned on for tea." So reduced were his finances that upending the tea canister brought forth only a few loose leaves of the cheapest kind.

Nonetheless, the room was supplied with the basic furnishings and appointments that one expects of modern apartment house. There was, in addition to a built-in bed and a chaise longue, a small bookcase with five or six titles of a popular sort, coffee and tea cups—even a set of cordial glasses—in a glass-faced cupboard, and a bottle, albeit empty, of Johnny Walker scotch. On the table, a wilted peony had been arranged in a Kutani vase. A hand-tailored man's lounging kimono, lined and made of a handsome twill, had been put out on a hanger; over it hung a *hanten* jacket made of Yuki silk.

"You've set yourself up nicely this time, haven't you?"

"No, it's nothing much...."

"You have this place to yourself?"

"Friends drop in from time to time, but..."

That Moichi's otherwise voluble tongue should falter and go dumb suggested circumstances he thought best kept to himself.

Taking my cue, I crept into the proffered bed, and he, having collapsed on the chaise longue, became a host of snores. So it was that at the break of day, I found myself sprawled upon his bed.

"Take your time. There's no need to get up early. I'll put the key right here. Give it to the man out front when you leave."

Moichi was apparently employed after all, considering the way he passed up a cup of tea and raced out the door. One could also guess that his salary at Mutual Finance amounted to no more than forty or fifty yen a month. Given the fact that the room probably cost him at least twenty, maintaining the place must have been a precarious business indeed. Unless, of course, Moichi had come by a second source of income.

Why, then, as I started from the apartment—having driven off the man from *The Sunrise Press* only moments before—did I not consider it odd to find a second nameplate alongside the one marked "Tarui"? "Terao," it read, and without so much as a thought who this "Terao" might be, I headed back to my lodgings in Kurumazaka.

Now, I should interrupt my tale to say that everything I have said so far is true. I have not falsified or fabricated a single word. Yet I must admit to having avoided telling one part of the story. The reason is simple enough: I prefer not to discuss it.

As I said at the start, I did not jump for joy at the thought of talking about Tarui Moichi. And here I was back at my desk, ready to resume my work on the life and legend of Christine de Pizan, but I found myself rethinking the events of the previous night. Mere second thoughts, of course, considerations of taste . . .

When it comes to questions of like and dislike, the better part of valor knows to say nothing at all. But by merely saying what I preferred not to discuss, I had raised the subject, and, now that it has come up, what is the point of suppressing the rest of the story? I think it quite meaningless. . . .

First, there was the matter of the woman back at the bar.

But, no, before I go on about her, I had better wipe the slate clean and speak unequivocally of the unpleasantness that occurred later that night. Namely, that on our way back to Moichi's apartment, we were foolish enough to waste a half hour of our time at a brothel in the red-light district.

"How about this place?" suggested Moichi, stopping in the middle of the street. "Let's take a peek. It's even got a bar."

But what Moichi really had his eye on was the cash he had discerned to be hidden in my breast pocket. No sooner had he extended his hand and with an if-you-don't-mind extracted a yen note from me than he shot across the street and began talking in a low voice to a man standing in the entryway of one of the storefronts. In no time, he had his shoes coming off, and his hand gripped the railing of the stairway to the second floor. He turned and looked at me.

"Aren't you coming?"

Once upstairs we were served a drink, a dubious concoction passed off as coffee; and as for the bar, it was no more than a waiting room. It led to a series of cubicles that we were invited to use.

"Moichi . . ." I called after him, but he pretended to have gotten drunk all of a sudden.

"Aw, c'mon. What's wrong? We're not doing anything bad."

He turned a corner and disappeared, leaving me with no choice but to enter the cubicle reserved for me.

Fortunately the woman who showed me the room soon withdrew, and lying on my back under the light of a nightstand with a red shade, I gave myself over to the sound of a distant record player grinding out the lyrics of a popular ditty.

Suddenly a great commotion broke out directly across the hall. I could hear, along with the sound of entwined bodies crashing against a door, someone shouting and cursing. It was Moichi.

"You think you can cheat me, you goddamn bitch? You think a man could show his face on the streets of this town after he let the likes of you get away with this nonsense? Huh? What's that? Hell, bring 'em on. The more, the merrier. All you want. I'll handle the bastards."

"Don't be so rough. You're hurting me."

"Who's hurting who? I arranged everything with the guy downstairs, and the madam knows about it too. Say what you want, but I'm not leaving this room until tomorrow morning."

"But it's reserved for 'Short Time Only.' If you plan to stay the night, you have to pay full price."

"What are you talking about? Can't you tell time? What time do you think it was when we came into this joint?"

"Even with the special rate for after two in the morning, you'll have to take a room downstairs if you plan to spend the night."

"Don't put me on, lady. I paid to sleep in your room, not a reception parlor."

The woman ran across the hall.

"Mister, you'd better get up. Your friend's causing a terrible fuss."

"What's that?"

"Oh, you're no help. How do you expect me to handle him if you're just going to just lie there? Please come and help me."

I stepped into the corridor, thinking it was time for me to get out of the place.

"Hey, Moichi, what's going on?"

"Stay out of this, will you. Leave everything to me. I'll handle it."

Moichi had an old man in a sweater, probably a servant who worked for the house, pinned to the wall. Meanwhile, the madam had appeared, and tugging as hard as she could on Moichi's arm, struggled to get the old man free.

"Let him go, mister. He doesn't mean any harm. It's all my fault anyway. Let me have a chance to set things right. There now. Come with me. Over here."

She led us back to the room at the top of the stairs. Since I had nothing to say, I sat down on the sofa and watched. Moichi glowered at the woman.

"What do you take me for? A fall guy?"

"Of course not, young man, nothing of the sort. I didn't recognize you at first, that's all. Now, if you'll forget what's happened and leave quietly..."

"Look, we didn't come here to pick a fight, you know."

"I don't want to argue, so please keep your voice down. Here's a little something from me. If you'll agree to cooperate, it should take care of everything."

"It's still not right, but since you put it that way, we'll go."

Moichi prodded me with his elbow as we started down the stairs. He opened his fist slyly, letting me catch a glimpse of the half-dozen silver coins that glittered in the palm of his hand.

The pimps who worked for the brothel were at the entrance, their eyes glowing as though watching for prey. Groups of two or three more men—presumably members of the same gang—stood under the low-hanging eaves of the building across the street, or behind utility poles. I walked beside Moichi, who threw back his shoulders as he started to pass, perfectly calm, through the menacing scene.

From a few paces behind, one man demanded to know if we intended to walk by without "a word of greeting." He spoke of the etiquette observed among gangsters.

"Don't you two know how to say hello properly? Let's hear it from you boys."

Moichi walked unswervingly, throwing out his chest and letting the heels of his shoes ring against the pavement.

"Don't look back, whatever you do. And say nothing. Absolutely nothing," he whispered, his eyes set dead ahead.

Even as we rounded the corner at the main thoroughfare the men were still behind us, barking at our heels like a pack of dogs ready for the chase. Moichi broke into a mad dash, and following his lead, I fled with him. We ran recklessly, darting among the headlights of the taxis that thronged the street, slipping in and out of dark alleys, until we reached a quiet residential area that lay beyond the boundaries of the red-light district. We slowed our pace and caught our breath.

"You certainly ask a lot of a friend when you invite him for a night on the town," I said, my chest heaving.

"Sorry. I don't know what got into me. But look at the money we've made. It's enough carfare for a whole day, and just when I was feeling the pinch..."

—Ah, ah, what a curious, pathetic state of affairs! And to think I have lost all sense of proportion and let myself run on at such length about it!

Yet isn't it precisely because of this sordid landscape, a topography so spotted and stained, that I go on the way I do, forever issuing these inane reports, making pronouncements contrary to my own sense of good taste? As I sat at my desk, my head cupped in my hands, and feeling utterly disgusted and discouraged, I asked myself what was to become of this land, an imperial realm no less, in which such mindless breeds prevailed and proliferated.

Even the subject of the woman, the one whom I had meant to speak of in passing, the one whom I met at the bar where Moichi first took me last night, ceased to interest me.

In moments such as these, a spare moment that I was wasting shamelessly, wouldn't it have been far more salutary, and far more akin to my true nature, to reclaim my role as an investigator of history and get on with the manuscript I had started?

Shaking the weariness from my head and throwing open the window to contemplate the broad expanse of blue that comes on a day early in summer, I let my thoughts fly off to France in the fifteenth century, there to circle about the wizened head of the poetess of the Abbey at Poissy, the indomitable Christine de Pizan who, though exhausted by the advance of age and the havoc of war, her spirit nearly spent, perceived its final quickening, and in the last great beating of her wings of song, burst forth to sing *Le ditié de Jeanne d'Arc,* her magnificat in praise of Joan of Arc.

CHAPTER TWO

HISTORIANS MAY say what they will, but for my part it is not possible to write an account of the life of Christine de Pizan without speaking of Joan of Arc. That is to say ..., but my story gets ahead of itself. Let me speak first of Christine.

Christine de Pizan was born circa 1363 to Tommaso da Pizzano, a Venetian physician and astrologer. When she was five, her father was invited to serve at the court of Charles V of France, and Christine and her family moved to Paris. It is recorded she had many tutors and that she read exhaustively in the literature for the ennoblement of women. At the age of fifteen she married a French courtier, and as her father was much favored by the king, the House of Pizan prospered.

When Christine was twenty-five, however, her husband met an untimely death and left her with three small children. Thereafter, Christine's life became a path of thorns. Charles the V had died in 1380, and deprived of his sponsor at court, Tommaso soon went to his grave. The impoverished daughter, facing an uncertain future and burdened with the support of her children and her aged mother, saw no other avenue before her but the business of writing, peddling as wares the belles lettres of her avocation as a lady. Thus it is that we have come to see in this lady of several centuries past the first professional writer of her sex.

Her earliest works were love ballades and roundelays, but the record shows that her poetic affections were showered almost exclusively upon her children. For Christine, there was but one qualification: she needed only be a poet to speak of love. How different was her position from that later adopted by the critic Boileau who insisted "it takes little of the poet, one must also be a lover."

By and by Christine turned to prose, and in order to convert her sentences into cash, she chose not to await the patronage of the Church as was the custom of the day, but devised a means to have her tales copied for distribution to the general public. Indeed, when she writes, "And I, who once was woman, am become a man," she speaks of her success in bringing about the transformation—*La mutacion de fortune*—of her heart's pain.

The value of her works is a topic best left to the pens of literary historians. There is no question, however, as to what caused the world to spurn, to thrust mercilessly aside, the product of her assiduous labors. For, in addition to the reversals and privations that are part of life on this mortal plain, Christine found herself beset by a crisis that shook the land at its very foundations.

We need not dwell on the details. I speak of the agony and desolation created by the events that span the years before and after the beginning of the fifteenth century and that are known to history as the Hundred Years War.

In the several decades after Edward the Black Prince of England laid claim to the right of succession to the French throne, Norman shores had been subject to frequent attack by English forces crossing the Channel. Moreover, after the death of Charles V and the madness of Charles VI, the court was left in such disarray and the north of France so utterly trampled under the hooves of foreign cavalries that by the second decade of the fifteenth century even Charles VII could not find a safe abode within his realm. Given so precarious a state of affairs, and having lost all means to market her works, Christine sought refuge in Poissy, and cloistering herself in the abbey, vanished from sight.

For eleven years she lived thus confined, but when the triumphal news reached Poissy—the report of how, after a visitation from the archangel Michael two years earlier in May, 1429, a maiden, one Joan of the village of Arc, had raised the famed sword of Charles Martel, the standard bearer of yore; and of how she had lifted the siege of Orléans and taken the dauphin to Rheims to crown him officially king of France—this poetess, grown old but vital still, gathered the resources of her seventy years and began to sing the praises of "la Pucelle." History further records that Joan was executed at Rouen on May 30, 1431. Shortly thereafter Christine followed her to the grave.

Now, having run through these historical details, let me add that to my mind it is the tailend of the life of Christine de Pizan that marks the true beginning of her career as a poet, and it was from this point that I began weaving my version of her life and legend.

There is a time-honored form of child's play in which one draws different parts of a picture on six small squares of paper. By rearranging the pieces, it is possible to assemble the images in six different combinations. Accordingly, my particular portrait of Christine is—as it would be in the case of any woman I chose to depict—a thing unto itself, and at the same time, only one part of a potentially larger composition.

Because I am an old-fashioned type who is forever inquiring into the elements essential to the perfection of the larger design, I have found that, by introducing Joan of Arc into my account of the life of Christine de Pizan, by drawing an analogy between these women and touching upon the essence of their personalities—one, elevated to the divine, the other, brought low by the passage of time and near death yet still conversant with the spirit of the first—I have chanced upon an unexpectedly felicitous opportunity to speak of all womankind.

In fact, my vision of womankind is not so farfetched as it my seem. It has never been my wont to look upon Joan's manifestation in the life of Christine de Pizan as the sudden entrance of some wraith, floating footless across the stage in an easily dismissed bit of Kabuki or grand guignol. No, to the contrary, I have envisioned a scene far more complex and symbolic: an eye-arresting tableau of womankind as a garland of flowers, a wreath suspended in midair and formed from the powder of Christine's crushed bones, her dust commingling with all the other dust of the earth as it, rising and falling, tensing and expanding, dances in a shaft of sunlight. At the same time, I have sought to pluck from this garland the single blossom that is Joan of Arc in order to behold her as the embodiment of the beauty of all the diverse flowers.

To think in this way is, perhaps, utter nonsense, a silly juggling act on my part, but if I have chosen to write simultaneously of both women, to parallel the story of the Maid of Orléans with that of the Old Woman of Poissy, it is because I have longed to capture with my pen each subtle change fashioned upon the protean visage of womankind as she stands before the winds bearing both the dust and the blossoms of life.

My illumination of the tale of these two women is a palimpsest of my own devising, and as if that were not enough, let me erase the text and write of them in still larger terms. Albeit a slightly lame metaphor, the story of Joan and Christine has also become for me an analog version of the tale of that legendary pair of T'ang Buddhism, the long-haired, laughing jackels of Zen iconography—the besotted poet of Cold Mountain, Han-shan, and his sidekick, the broomsweep, Shih-te.

And, if this pair of Han-shan and Shih-te is, as legend has it, a manifestation of the tandem attendants of the historical Buddha, the Bodhisattva of Wisdom Mañjuśrî and the Bodhisattva of Compassion Samantabhadra, then let me call forth to center stage the broomsweep, this common simpleton who can never equal Mañjuśrî in wisdom yet whose kitchen scraps have nourished Han-shan's genius. Rather than the highbrow antics of the Cold Mountain poet who is forever howling and reciting before the wind, how much more fitting for one so inferior and dimwitted as myself to watch and imitate the humble ways of Shih-te! Let me seek my apprenticeship in the Way of Samantabhadra by following his example, and shouldering a broom, make a clean sweep of the earth.

But if, once I have taken up his broom, applying myself to the business of cleaning the streets of the city—of gathering trash from every corner—I find the task is not much of a challenge, nor the best use of my talents as a writer, then assign me the mission given to none other than Samantabhadra himself. Allow me to be the one to take the gem of Mañjuśrî's wisdom, and sundering it like a diamond into chips and pieces, translate its essence into the words of ordinary speech and publish them throughout the land. For without rendering his wisdom into everyday language, how can we hope for people to understand it? How else can we hope to see the day when the world is transformed to reveal itself in its true glory? To see paradise achieved on earth?

I have not flattered myself into thinking I am a manifest bodhisattva, but my life would be a total void were I to live without a particle of that conceit. And while it may be ludicrous for me to suggest that my humble words and deeds in any way approach the sublimity of Shih-te's, nonetheless I bear within my breast the singular desire to forge a link between my acts and the deportment of the fragrant Samantabhadra, to find some commonality between them and the compassionate and beatific ways of this bodhisattva who, in the wake of his celestial play, showers upon us the hundred treasures of the lotus flower. Indeed, because I am nourished by this desire, I have mustered the courage to stand before you and describe without the slightest trace of shame the events that took place last night at the brothel in Shinjuku. Such places are not unknown to Samantabhadra, and I do not feel the least inhibition in saying I have chosen him as my guardian spirit. There is none more appropriate: Samantabhadra is my bodhisattva!

Having thrown open the window, I sat upright at my desk and took out the manuscript I had neglected of late and began to write:

How dismal life would be were historical research to lead to the destruction of all myths. Therefore it is not my intent to add to the record a clever little interpretation explaining away the miracle of Joan of Arc's divine revelation. Nor do I hold with the popular thesis that it was on account of love that she lost her superhuman powers. The tragedy of romance lies not in the fact that a person is brought low by love but in the fragility of the human spirit which, riding the wings of love, cannot bear the dizzying heights. Had I written, for example, the Kabuki classic *Onna narukami—The Thundergod Woman*, I would have had the magical powers of the beautiful princess enhanced by love, not weakened. For what is love if its effect is to sap one's vital powers?

From the first voice in the sky at Domrémy to the pillar of fire at Rouen, Joan of Arc was every bit a chosen woman, and human history is made beautiful by it. Indeed to deny the beauty of her life would be to preclude not only the means by which women are beatified, but the coming of the day when the sâla tree shall blossom again—as it did when the Buddha, dying, passed into nirvana—and shower upon us the message of salvation here on earth. When all is said and done, and it is proven that the researchers are correct and the myths in error, isn't that precisely the moment we must call into question the validity of such investigations and take so-called "facts" cum grano salis? Now, as for Christine de Pizan...

But then the footsteps I heard mounting the stairs stopped outside my door.

"May I come in?"

Without permitting a second to reply, Kuzuhara Yasuko, the

proprietress of the lodging house, slid open the shōji and stepped into the room. She was dressed to go out, and with her middle-aged frame filling the doorway, she announced that she was ready for me to accompany her.

"What?"

"Well, I never. You mean to say you've forgotten our date?"

"What date?"

"You promised to introduce me to Mr. Sakagami."

"Oh, that's *right*. So I did."

"You're awful. Forgetting like that."

"It slipped my mind completely."

"What am I going to do with you? If you please, I'd like to get on our way. This is your business suit, isn't it?"

"There's no hurry. Sakagami never comes to the office before three, and the clock has just struck twelve."

"But if we don't go today..."

"I know, I know. I promised. Give me a few minutes."

Yasuko had put in an unsolicited appearance just as I was riding the momentum that comes when my pen warms to its material. In order to breathe a bit more life into my drab prose, I had been hovering on the brink, ready to launch into the colorful story of the Battle of Orléans.

But Yasuko had outflanked me and caught me off guard.

There was nothing for it but to put my pen aside, leave Christine and turn with considerable reluctance to the business of Kuzuhara Yasuko who has been pressing me for an introduction to an acquaintance, Sakagami Seiken.

Before I do that, however, I must explain something of the mechanism that lies behind the operation of this lodging house and, by the way, of my friend Iori Bunzō, who rents the other six-mat room adjoining mine here on the second floor. I must also explain the chain of events that will lead me to the subject of his younger sister, Yukari.

My heart leaps at the prospect of speaking of Yukari because the mere mention of her name is enough to make my head spin and leave me feeling as though my spirit will melt away.

I have even thought of jumping ahead, and was about to say... but the subject is too involved to permit cursory treatment. For the moment we shall have to ask Yasuko to go downstairs and wait.

CHAPTER THREE

IT WAS approximately a year ago that I took up residence in this room. I have lived in this lodging house longer than Yasuko, who became its owner only recently, but not as long as Iori Bunzō who has lived here a year longer than I. The order of things is such that for you to understand why the lodgers on the second floor should remain in place while the all-important landlord downstairs is subject to change requires that I go further back in time and begin by explaining the matter of the previous owner, one Tabe Hikosuke.

An exquisite vase is a thing of beauty that requires no complement. But take an ordinary pot and place it on a mantlepiece, and it never looks quite right. Only by finding its mate, by making it part of a pair, can it be given an air of respectability. Not that the vases become beautiful in themselves. It is simply that, whatever the arrangement, they manage to sink into an unobstrusive mediocrity that has an attraction of its own.

Alas, there is none of the marvelous contrast of Don Juan and Sganarelle, or Don Quixote and Sancho Panza, in matching Tabe Hikosuke with Tarui Moichi. Like two vases that, breathing with one accord, absorb the air of each other's mediocrity, Tabe and Tarui merely happened to appear side by side the day I first met them. Perhaps it was on that account that I came to see them as a matching pair.

But, to get on with Hikosuke's story . . .

One day four years ago when I spent my time loitering about the amusement district in Asakusa, the comedian actor and friend who now lives in Kansai asked if I knew anything about raising pet birds.

"Of course."

"Then come with me."

"Where?"

"Nippori."

"What do you want there?"

"To buy a pet bird."

"At a place specializing in pedigree breeds?"

"No, not exactly. There's an amateur bird fancier who I hear has a number of birds. 'Tabe' is the name. A friend told me about him. While I'm at it, I think I'll get a dog too."

"Does this fellow also run a kennel?"

"Well, no, he's not in the business, but supposedly he has two or three pups for sale."

Our destination was the corner of a neighborhood that we located after much inquiring up and down the winding and convoluted streets of Nippori. It was a smallish block surrounded by an ever-green hedge, with a set of row houses, each no more than a few yards wide, and each, a single story. Although they were cheaply constructed, the three that fronted on the street were semi-Western in style and had glass windows instead of sliding doors. Between the houses were narrow passageways giving access to a well at the rear—and to a fourth house, which had been squeezed onto the small plot of land beside the well. Its sole distinction was a fancy front door, a wooden latticework affair that slid open and closed. This was Tabe Hikosuke's house.

Later I learned that Tabe was born in the town of Kutsukake in the snow country of the Shinshū region. Although he was the second son of a man of means, now deceased, he had been unable to hold on to his inheritance. All that remained was this property in Nippori, his income deriving solely from the rental of the three houses in the front.

It was a warm spring day early in March, and what we saw as we entered the passage leading to the back of the lot was a man of thirty-five or six, dressed only in long underwear, happily whistling away, as though keeping time with the rustle of the breeze, while brushing aside a large airdale and a small fox terrier that persisted in getting underfoot. He had bent over and was using a pair of chopsticks to divide a mixture of leftover rice and miso soup into two bowls. He straightened up as he heard us approach, his plump, round body bouncing toward us like a rubber ball.

"Welcome, welcome. It's always a pleasure to have company. Step around this way, this way." His mouth and small moustache were kept in constant motion by the flow of words that poured from his lips.

"Go on now and eat your dinner," he added, patting the puppies on the back and pushing the bowls of food under their noses.

He put his hand to the pump by the well, cranking it vigorously and setting up quite a clatter as he washed the dirt from his bare feet.

"O-kumi! Where are you? O-kumi? Aren't you in there?"

A large glass window on the side of the house by the front door slowly opened as though moved by an enfeebled hand. From behind a faded curtain, a face appeared, ghostly pale, one calculated to send a chill down any spine. The whites of the eyes seem to stagnate in their sockets. The woman's body was thin and drawn, its life spent like an ephemerid surviving into the last days summer. Her dark, scrawny fingers clawed at the long, limp strands of hair that hung down both sides of her face.

"What now, Hikosuke?" The tone of voice was of utter calm. It seemed that nothing would be allowed to upset her.

"Why raise such a fuss?" she asked, casting an icy stare in our direction.

"Now, now, O-kumi, this is important. We have guests."

"Well, what's the matter? Why don't you show them in?"

We were taken into the house from the yard via the narrow veranda that skirted one edge of the living room. In the center of the room was a large table set over a footwarmer sunk in the floor. No doubt it was typical of a person raised in the snow country to have so large a footwarmer, and although it was already spring, to have it open and ready for use in anticipation of more cold weather. Hikosuke flipped up a corner of the ragged quilt that covered the frame of the table and began to stir the coals.

"Please, Mr. Tabe, don't bother on our account."

Despite the actor's suggestion, Hikosuke insisted on keeping us warm.

The southern exposure of the six-mat room that we had entered from the west side of the house was separated from the neighbor's yard by only a low fence. To the north, there was a kitchen and a space of three mats apparently intended for servant's quarters. The room by the entrance—the one with the large glass window that served as the sickroom for Hikosuke's wife—could not have been any larger, but since the sliding doors to both rooms were drawn, it was impossible to guess what lay inside.

The walls and mats of the room were caked with mud, the trackings of the puppies no doubt; predictably, a cat napped on the table over the footwarmer. There was a clock of the old-fashioned sort that struck the hours. To my surprise, arranged along the wall were several valuable Chinese plates, a red ware in the Sung style.

Still more surprising were the number of birdcages that, placed on shelves hanging over the dirt floor, filled all of the available space in the entryway. What an incredible variety of birds they contained: mynas, the popular Gouldian and Bengalese finches, roller canaries, robins, willow tits, chickadees, white eyes, avadavats—and even a nightingale, albeit of questionable distinction. The birds were crammed into their cages, each one vying for space and singing at the same time, so that our voices were drowned out by the chorus of chirps and trills and calls. It was scarcely a sight to be found in an ordinary household.

"Quite a collection, I must say."

Hikosuke parried the comedian's exaggerated look of amazement. "This isn't the half of it. I've gotten rid of most of my animals. Why, at one time we even had monkeys."

"Oh?"

"Right now I have the birds and the two pups. There was one more pup until the other day, but I had to let it go. And, of course, there's the cat ... "

"I'm impressed that he doesn't chase after the birds."

"Strange as it may seem, he gets along with them just fine. I do get complaints from the neighbors, though. He is always getting into their garbage."

"Oh?"

"Feel free to take any of the animals you like. While you're at it, you might take one or two of the humans you find lying about. There must be someone in the amusement district in Asakusa who could put them to good use."

"You have a large family?"

"No, there're only me and my wife, O-kumi," said Hikosuke, pointing in the direction of the sliding door on the west side of the house.

"She's resting and doesn't like to be disturbed. I hope you won't mind if she doesn't come out to greet to you. My apologies...."

"Is she ill?"

"Oh no, it's really nothing."

It was obvious from the tone of his voice that Hikosuke wanted to change the subject.

"No, what I meant to say is we get a lot of company. Friends, you know. Over there," this time he pointed to the sliding door on the northside of the house, "you'll find our latest guest. Landed here last night. He's still sound asleep.

"There's one more fellow who has been around for quite a while, but he stepped out a moment ago. He quit the university some time back, and ever since he's been living here. He says he can't find a job that suits him. I wouldn't know about that, but there's one thing I can tell you: he's got a hell of an eye when it comes to fish. Take him to the fishmarket, and he can tell by glancing at the trays that such-and-such a fish didn't come from where they say it did, or that it was caught by boats out of Misaki, or in the waters off the Bōshū shoals. Of course, he did rent a room over a fish store before he came to stay with us...."

Just then the fellow, dressed in dirty overalls, shuffled into the yard, humming a popular tune. He also entered the house from the veranda rather than the front door, and he carried a large bottle of sake and a wrapped package which he plunked down on the floor. His back was turned to us as he sat down on the veranda to remove his clogs.

"Hiko, you'll have to make do with canned crab. The boats didn't go out on account of high seas. Oh, sorry...you've got visitors. Excuse me for not noticing...well, it's nice to meet you."

This was the first time I met Tarui Moichi. He greeted us as though we were old friends.

"Your timing couldn't be better. How about a drink everybody?"

"That's certainly better than tea any day," said Hikosuke, his voice becoming animated. "You take care of the food, Moichi. I'll clean up here."

The actor and I sat in blank amazement, watching as the two men set about the preparations for an impromptu party. Hikosuke picked up a rag and wiped the top of the table, while Moichi disappeared into the kitchen, only to emerge moments later carrying several small side dishes on a large lacquer tray.

"There now. Sorry to have kept you waiting."

He sat down at the far end of the table, thrusting his feet into the footwarmer. He seemed very much at home.

"There's not much, but help yourselves."

"What about *him?*" inquired Hikosuke, pointing in the direction of the closed door.

"Still sleeping it off, I guess."

Now that Moichi had made himself comfortable, he was not about to get up and check. He lay back, and extending an arm, rattled the sliding door.

"How about it in there? Feel like getting up? Yes, I said, how about it? The booze is here...the sake."

We could hear someone begin to stir in the adjoining room, but when the unseen occupant allowed that he would be joining us, Hikosuke interjected there was no need to hurry.

"We won't mind if you don't want to drink with us," he said, smiling to himself.

The poorly mounted door screeched open. The man—shaking his drowsy head like an animal tossing its mane, and frowning at the brightness of the light—stood in the doorway, adjusting the two panels of his padded kimono. He was looking down at his clothes, his eyes directed away from us, but when he went to put on his glasses, shifting the tortoise-shell frames back and forth as he raised them to his face, I could not help emitting a short gasp of surprise. He too was taken aback.

"So it's you, is it?" he said.

"What a shock. I hardly knew you were alive."

"What do you mean? Think I give up that easily?"

"But where have you been all this time?"

"At home in the country. I got back to Tokyo just last night."

It was in this peculiar setting in Nippori that, quite by accident, I was reunited with my old friend Iori Bunzō. Rumor had it that he had died some time ago.

My friendship with Bunzō dated back a decade to the time when we attended the same private university and we met on campus. One day, during lunch, I had left my classmates in the preparatory course and gone for a walk on the sandy and grassy area beyond the school wall. In the far corner of the lot, seated on the ground, his legs thrown out in front of him, was Bunzō. He was engrossed in reading a book written in English.

Although Bunzō and I were in the same class at school, we moved in different circles. I had seen him before—he was tall for his age, and had a handsome, almost pretty face—but until that day there had not been an opportunity to strike up a conversation.

"What are you reading?" I asked at the risk of invading his privacy. He snapped the book shut and looked up at me from where he sat on the ground. He squinted as he struggled to peer through the thick lenses of his glasses. He was badly nearsighted.

"What is your opinion of George Moore?" he asked abruptly.

"You mean the novelist? I have nothing but praise for the way he dares to tell people what they don't wish to hear. Still, I can't believe he has much success in shocking people. He may rub them the wrong way, but it's a fairly limp wrist he uses in doing it."

However frivolous my answer may have sounded, at the time I considered it a mark of distinction to be able to reply to even the most unanticipated question in a manner indicative of total composure. Ease under fire, so to speak, was for me the height of all scholarship, of all art, of all the things I accepted for no special reason as high-minded and sublime, and that I considered to be mankind's noblest expressions, drinking them in yet understanding nothing. So that when presented with a subject about which I knew virtually nothing, invariably the blood would rush to my head and I would launch into a lengthy reply. In short, my so-called composure was nothing more than a disguise for a high degree of excitability.

It appeared Bunzō was of an equally excitable disposition. "I suspect," he said adopting a supercilious tone, "your opinion will require further qualification if it is to avoid the charge of being called an irresponsible bit of fluff."

"In that case, let us speak of an altogether different topic. How about 'sincerity,' since you think me insincere for failing to address your question directly?"

"Tell me," I said, relishing the occasion to hold forth, "what social convention requires people to screw up their faces and look unbearably serious when they go to talk of sincerity? It's as if one had to grow a forked tail in order to speak of the devil. Is sincerity so facile that it can be summoned simply by making a frown or flexing a muscle? In that case, the world ought to be a paradise for tax collectors and rickshaw men. But modern writers, or at least those worthy of the name, push a pen and not a cart....

"Nonetheless, how is it possible for the flower of sincerity to burst forth if the greasiness of the hand that holds the pen—the blue vein standing out on the author's forehead, the drop of sweat hanging on the tip of his nose, the anger in his shoulders, in sum, the whole fetid smell of his body—is transmitted to the tracings on the page? What a dreadful farce! One goes to read a novel but ends up seeing instead the big, fat face of the author.

"Not with George Moore, however. Now there's a mastermind of deception for you! Moore is one of those rare, amorphous types who is quite skillful at keeping himself out of his works. Yet he is also like a top, a top that spins not of its own accord but revolves about the axis of Walter Pater. Once you know that much—once you get a hand on Walter Pater—you've got George Moore at your fingertips. Now, as for Walter Pater..."

Bunzō broke into a high, raucous laugh.

"Take a look at yourself, will you? Your face is screwed into a terrible frown. According to your theory, it invalidates everything you've said. It proves you're being facetious, so I'll have to take what you say with a large grain of salt.

"What's more, you claim Pater is the key to understanding Moore. But I say, no, absolutely not. This Pater business is a joke. It's a joke that Moore has played on everyone. Forgive me for saying this, but because Moore has so many 'sincere' readers like yourself, he decided to have a little fun and dash off a few novels for them to read.

"I did learn one thing from him, though. If a person tries his hand at writing and produces a novel on a par with George Moore, he'd better quit before he starts."

I had underestimated Bunzō. At the point where I had decided he suffered from the same excitable disposition as myself, and possessed a temperament as volatile as my own, he systematically and coolly countered my argument and left me with no position to defend.

"Very well, go ahead and have your laugh. Goodbye."

As I kicked a stone and turned to go, he called after me.

"Hey, wait. Be a good sport and talk with me."

"What about?"

"How about the painter, Turner? Here, somewhere in this book, it says Turner knew if you looked at the limbs of a tree, they appear to be black. Especially if you examine them individually. But in order to give his canvas an overall impression of brightness, he painted the branches a lighter color.

"Good enough. Turner and I can agree on that point. Who cares whether the branches are black or not? I certainly don't, and I wouldn't want to be around the prig of an artist who prides himself on painting them as they are in nature.

"The point is the totality. The totality of the painting dictates the color, and it is for the sake of the larger work the individual branches are sacrificed. Likewise, it is for this—ah, how complex and demanding it all is!—that men become artists ... or writers.

"Take the case of the novel, for example. What a overwhelming proliferation of words it is! Balzac wrote so much that he left behind a mountain of trash, but what was it worth? Or even Moore—it depresses me to think he qualifies as a novelist. Tell me, why is it a writer takes up his pen at the precise moment he decides to relax his powers of concentration?"

"No wonder he can't resist a silly notion like the one that branches must be painted black, or any other nonsense for that matter," I said, chiming in.

"How right you are! It's as though an artist will have nothing to show for his work unless it assumes a prescribed form or shape. Most people are so narrowly constituted as to believe it's impossible to produce anything without a pen or a brush or a chisel. It's all in the equipment, they think."

"In that case, why don't you take up the task ... ?"

"Just a second there. Why don't I what? I certainly hope you're not suggesting I do something like take up writing poetry. Pity the poor poem, or what's more to the point, pity the poor fellow who writes it. I can hear him now, advertising himself like an attraction in a circus sideshow: 'Here I am, ladies and gentlemen, a good-for-nothing.'

"At any rate, there's no limit to the amount of time we could spend arguing about words. We'll never find the one that expresses completely what we want to say about George Moore, so let's drop the subject. Besides, it never mattered in the first place."

Such was the tenor of our first conversation, and thereafter Bunzō and I often went out to talk at lunchtime.

At coffee shops, he would order milk; and, at a restaurant, he refused to consider even the daily specials, insisting on only toast. When he finally sank his teeth into the meager slice of bread, it was with a look of pain.

"Don't you ever get hungry?" I asked.

"Is there any human habit more nasty than eating?"

"You think there's something despicable about food?"

"No, on the contrary, I feel insulted when I realize how much I enjoy it."

Time went by, and since we almost never went to class, neither of us was promoted. Finally, we decided to make a clean break of things, and announcing our intention to withdraw from the university, we moved to the center of the city and took up residence on the second floor of a lodging house.

Soon alcohol replaced milk as the chief staple in Bunzō's diet, and each night we took turns inviting the other to a succession of bars. At the same time, our interest in books shifted to clothes, and we had a series of eccentric outfits made up in accordance with our own designs. How we would let the red lining of our capes flap, releasing clouds of cologne! We were quite the sight, strutting about the city in the evenings, sniggering at the shocked passersby. I wonder now what mad passion drove us to expend so much time and energy on the singleminded pursuit of clothes and drink.

That I cannot begin to tell you of the conversations that transpired between us is not because of any diminution of my powers of memory. On the contrary, the recollection of every scene, of every vain pronouncement, is etched in the folds of my brain. Yet these fragments relate to no topic known to man. Or, shall I say, I could pull them together and produce something that would sound acceptable, but that will not solve the problem. These memories are, alas, locked in a secret code, unintelligible to anyone else, that Bunzō and I employed in speaking to each other.

I mean that in the course of our friendship we created a language, a special dialect for use in our own little world. What frustration we would have experienced, how we should have gritted our teeth, if in attempting to give shape and expression to our ideas and thoughts—to our philosophies—we had been confined to the language of everyday speech which lies so heavily on the tongue. Thanks to our special dialect, conversations could begin and end with no more than a single word. For either of us to say "aeroplane" was sufficient to bring on peals of laughter. Or "fireworks," a shower of tears. Could I but translate them here and now, but any explanation I might offer is in danger of sounding too longwinded to be meaningful. Our special expressions came into being because there were no equivalents, and it is for this reason that they will remain forever unique.

Even as I write, my long-standing impatience with words as they exist in everyday speech returns to me and, mounting to my lips, begins to stammer short-temperedly and set up static. I have no choice but to relegate this topic to the margin of the page and leave it there for the time being.

Now, let me think. . . .

Bunzō and I went on living in this manner for about a year. But then his father, who was an engineer with the government commission in Hokkaido, decided that Bunzō's younger sister, Yukari, ought to leave Sapporo and come to Tokyo to enter a prominent girls' school. He saw this move, moreover, as an opportunity to get his son out of the lodging house, and to put him and his sister under the supervision of a relative who lived in Yoyogi. Though Bunzō and I ceased to see one another on a daily basis, we continued to be close friends, one visiting the other regularly, and in the course of events, I came to know Yukari too.

—As for Yukari, what shall I say?

To speak of her, to mention her name, is to send a strange tremor through my entire being and leave me shaking all over. This feeling has persisted across the decade that has elapsed since Yukari first came to Tokyo and entered the mission school. Indeed it is an emotion so intense that not once have I been able to open my mouth and address her in the most conventional way, let alone go so far as to reveal my true feelings for her. Always the words have stuck in my throat—that is how earnestly I have kept this secret, and this secret alone. Not even Bunzō's sharp eye has been allowed to detect it. Moreover, I shall have to withhold it here too. It would be unconscionable for me to enlarge upon a subject likely to raise everyone's eyebrows at a time when I have chosen to keep the secret from my best friend.

There was another reason why my relationship with Yukari saw no further development. It was about this time that, due to certain circumstances, my family fell into the unhappy state of bankruptcy, and I was plunged into the depths of poverty. In order to keep body and soul together, I had to bestir myself, and through connections with my old acquaintance, the political commentator Sakagami Seiken, I was able to establish myself with the magazine, *Political Debate*, which Seiken edits.

I translated essays on foreign policy in Europe and America, and although my qualifications were dubious in the extreme, I wrote articles discussing social issues. I even generated a column—written on the basis of information supplied by Sakagami and appearing under a pseudonym—that dealt with the machinery of party politics, realignments within the Cabinet, and all other manner of political rumormongering. So overwhelming was this alluvium of manuscripts—a veritable trash heap—that it came perilously close to burying in its avalanche whatever literary creativity remained to me, the paltry inspirations left to be dispensed from my worn and depleted poem bag.

Meanwhile, Bunzō continued to do nothing. Perhaps it is the nature of the illness, but once he showed the first signs of having tuberculosis and began to cough blood, he chose to remain idle and indulge in drink. Finally, when he learned that his father was retiring from his government post in Sapporo and planned to return to the ancestral home in Hakodate, Bunzō decided to move back to Hokkaido. He ceased to correspond after two or three letters, and I had no further opportunity of seeing Yukari either.

But word reached me that Bunzō's penchant for drink had grown progressively worse. There were rumors that one day he wandered off into the highlands where the winds blow cold, or again, that one moonlit night he jumped into a small boat and rowed out to sea never to be heard from again.

No wonder I gasped in sheer astonishment when, after a lapse of more than three years and thinking him dead, I found Bunzō in the unlikely place of the house of Tabe Hikosuke, a man with whom I had neither previous contact nor karmic connection.

"Do you know these people?"

"Not until last night, I didn't."

Hikosuke interrupted Bunzō to explain.

"Last evening Motchan—yes, Moichi here—and I were having a drink in a Ginza café when along comes this one, weaving back and forth as he walked in the place dragging his suitcase. Later we learned he had just gotten off the train at Ueno Station. He was sitting at the table next to ours, when suddenly he said something crazy and began to pick a fight with Moichi. I wanted to smooth things over, so I proposed we all go for a drink. By the time we had been in and out of several bars, we were rip-roaring drunk."

"Wait now, I don't recall starting any fight."

"Well, let's say the alcohol was getting to you," said Moichi, picking up the thread of Hikosuke's story. "What really shocked us was around two in the morning. We got ready to leave the *oden* restaurant in Shimbashi and asked him where he lived. All he could say was 'Yoyogi, Yoyogi,' and if you didn't hold on to him, he'd collapse in a heap on the ground.

"What were we supposed to do? It would have been dangerous to leave him to manage on his own. So we got into a taxi and came here. No sooner were we in the door than he saw a bottle of alcohol sitting on a shelf, and without even asking, grabbed it and took a swig. I was so surprised I snatched the bottle out of his hand, but he kept shouting, 'Gimme a drink, let me drink.' I'm telling you, he's a real character!"

The vestige of Bunzō's once pretty face was still apparent, the outline of his sharp features not entirely gone, but his hair stood in dry, dirty tufts about the grayish complexion of his forehead. His cheeks were drawn, now dark, sunken hollows; and his eyes, glowing eerily behind his glasses, stared blankly into space. But because he clung to his long-standing habit—the vanity of using a stick of rouge on his lips—they were bright red, looking weird and slightly distorted, like a clam angrily clamping shut its shell.

I felt the muscles in my chest tighten. It seemed as though Bunzō was wandering lost and uncertain in the midst of a cold, damp fog.

"Say, Bun, how are you feeling these days?"

"Oh, fine."

"How are things up in Hokkaido?"

"Quiet as usual. But I was bored, and then there was this messy business here in Tokyo...."

"What are you taking about?"

"I mean Yukari."

"I don't see..."

"No, it's..."

Before Bunzō could finish, Moichi interrupted. "What a great stroke of luck for the two of you. Here, finish this off."

Moichi picked the sake bottle out of the disorder atop the table and forced it on us before I had a chance to ask Bunzō about Yukari. The actor, who had been discussing the subject of pet birds with

Hikosuke, announced that he had to get back to the theater. I decided to stay and talk.

Hikosuke was enjoying himself now that the actor had asked him to deliver a pair of canaries and a robin to his house. He suggested we have another bottle of sake to celebrate. But, as Moichi stood up to go to the store, O-kumi began calling Hikosuke from the other room. Hikosuke's brow wrinkled with annoyance.

"You'd best calm down."

"Get me medicine, I tell you."

"No."

"How can you be so mean?"

"Mean? I'm doing everything in my power to help you get well. You'll have to bear the pain."

"I don't care about my health...."

"What kind of answer is that?"

"I'm asking for a shot. Just one little shot, that's all."

"I told you to be quiet. Give me any trouble, and I'll tie you to the bed."

There was an alarming look on Hikosuke's face as he stood up and headed toward O-kumi's room.

"Is something wrong?" I asked.

"It's really too embarrassing to explain. The morphine, that's what did it, you know. It's to blame."

As Hikosuke spoke, a terrible clamor arose on the other side of the sliding door. It was the roar of the pain, the leaden striking of the clock at the cruel hour in which the drug, having invaded every cell, commenced its retreat, its stranglehold broken by the severity of the withdrawal treatment imposed upon the patient.

"Confound you," said Hikosuke, his eyes fixed on the invisible drug-demon he was about to attack and wrestle to the floor. He reached to open the sliding door.

Moichi stood up to intervene. "Hikosuke. Let me take care of this. Let me do it," and, opening the door a crack, he slipped into the adjoining room.

"What's happened, hm? Hush now, you'll have to be quiet...," Moichi began to speak to O-kumi in his dubious imitation of the Shinshū dialect. But then he lowered his voice, and we could no longer hear him.

"Yes, I understand you. I promise. No, O-kumi, I won't forget," he said finally, as he emerged from the room.

"I'll be right back," he said to Hikosuke, and looking thoroughly pleased with himself, rushed off to the store.

O-kumi had settled down by the time Moichi returned with the sake.

When the bottle was about finished, Hikosuke produced a deck of *hanafuda* gambling cards.

"Just a little indoor sport to aid the digestion."

Nothing particularly sticks in my mind concerning the sight of the three of us playing cards, nor did anything happen worthy of note. What concerned me throughout the evening, however, was the change in Bunzō's personality. Bunzō had never been one to pay attention to games of chance, but that night his bloodshot eyes were glued to the turn of each and every card. He became so feverish that at one point he shed the sleeves of his padded kimono, stripping to the waist, and taking out a coarse cotton handkerchief, mopped the sweat from the wet hair hanging across his brow. He began to raise his voice, and to shout in protest.

"No, no, that's not right."

It was distressing to see him petulantly and persistently argue over the most minute calculation of the score. Although he seemed to know the game was just a game, that it would come to naught, his efforts wasted no matter how hard he tried, the pointlessness of it all seemed to make him more determined than ever not to lose. His misspent passion was not unlike the abortive flower of a doomed love affair, and the more ardently he pursued it, the more intent he became upon proving the utterly meaninglessness of the moment.

Presently, it was Hikosuke's turn to deal, and Moichi had the last draw. Moichi appeared to have a system in mind, and when he went for the low card in the pile, Bunzō flew into a rage.

"How can you do that? How can you possibly pass that card to the dealer?"

"No fooling? I can do anything I want to. It's my business. I'm the one who has to pay if I'm wrong. Why should you care as long as I pay?"

Bunzō reached for his cup, and had I not stayed his hand, was about to dash what remained of the cold sake in Moichi's face.

Confronted with this madness, everyone fell silent—except for Hikosuke who was in an exceptionally good mood.

"Sorry, I shouldn't have started the game. But, you know the old saying, 'Rich men never quarrel.'"

Yet when, by who-knows-what turn of luck, Hikosuke began to lose after a winning streak—his fortunes collapsing noiselessly like a house of cards, the little wicker basket of his earnings now painfully empty—he sat upright where he had fallen on the floor and threw back his arms in a vigorous exercise.

"I think I'll take a break. My shoulders have gotten stiff. I can hardly move."

Hikosuke took Moichi's suggestion that he drop out of the game altogether. He stretched out on the floor, the three of us continuing to play beside him. He slept for a while, but suddenly he was on his feet, pulling on an old pair of trousers and a torn jacket that hung on a hook on the wall. He slipped into the straw sandals at the door and hurried out.

"Wonder what's gotten into him?"

Bunzō and I looked at Moichi in disbelief, but he assured us that Hikosuke "always acted that way. As long as he wins he's happy. Let him lose, and it puts him in a bad mood."

By now we had lost interest in the cards, which we left scattered on top of the table. Even the pretense of making small talk required too much of us, and we stretched out on the tatami to rest. But as we were about to doze off, we were awakened by the sound of hammering coming from the front yard. I pulled myself up far enough to be able to see around the corner of the veranda.

Hikosuke, seated crosslegged on a ground cloth of coal sacks, was banging away at the dilapidated doghouse, trying to nail it together. Out of a paper bag he had stuffed into his trouser pocket, he pulled a sweet bean-jam bun, an *Imagawa-yaki*. The bun had been mashed out of shape, but Hikosuke smacked his lips as he ate, lapping up with his tongue the contents that threatened to spill on the ground.

But if I go on in this manner, it will take forever to reach the part of the story dealing with the chain of events that led to Hikosuke's becoming proprietor of the lodging house in Kurumazaka.

Besides, for the last several minutes Kuzuhara Yasuko has been loudly and repeatedly calling my name from the foot of the stairs. The hands of my watch are close to the appointed hour of three, so now is the time for us to make a call on Sakagami Seiken.

CHAPTER FOUR

A WOMAN'S age is hard to judge in any case. How much more so
with Kuzuhara Yasuko who, on account of the ripeness of her figure
and the thickness of her makeup, appeared to be no more than
thirty-five or six but was in fact over forty. To be seen walking with
her, if only for the length of time it took to step outside and pick up
a taxi, was enough to make me blush and bring a look of embarrassment to my face. Try as I might to set distance between us,
she seemed determined, as no doubt she was with every man, to
brush against me and soil me with the lascivious odor of her body.

"What am I going to do with her?"

"With whom?"

"That woman from Nippori."

"Oh, you mean O-kumi?"

"She may be sick, but this nonsense happens all too often."

"She came to see you again?"

"Yes, late last evening."

"Same old story?"

"I could refuse if she asked for a whole yen, but when it's only
twenty or thirty sen, it's impossible to pretend I don't have the
money."

Because O-kumi suffered both from the severity of Hikosuke's
supervision and a desperate need for morphine injections, it was not
unusual for her to approach anyone, friend and stranger alike, and
ask for money. Of course, Hikosuke was supposed to be responsible
for her, but what he really supervised was not O-kumi but the
strings of his purse over which he held a tight rein. No matter whom

his wife bothered, he would merely bow repeatedly, ever the bobbing sycophant, and say he was terribly sorry.

"My hands are full, as you can see."

At least this was the attitude he assumed toward those he knew to have an adequate means of making a living. Moreover, perhaps due to some baseness in his character, he was not averse to humbling himself before strangers, even the most transparently poor, who managed to survive only by gathering the proverbial gleanings of the field. For his impoverished friends, however, he had no mercy.

"What the hell's the matter with you, lending her money? Didn't I tell you to turn her down flat? I don't want to hear about it."

Because he assumed such a high-handed manner, people's mild complaint with O-kumi often turned into vehement dislike of Hikosuke.

"He ought to watch her more carefully."

"I couldn't agree with you more."

"You see the shape she's in, but he goes around talking about how he needs to raise money for the observance of the third anniversary of her mother's death."

A taxi had stopped to pick us up, and I interrupted Yasuko to tell the driver to take us to Toranomon. It was, incidentally, the chain of events surrounding the death of O-kumi's mother that had led to the Tabes moving from Nippori to Kurumazaka, and then back again.

It was one day three summers ago. Bunzō and I were at Hikosuke's place in Nippori. It had become customary for us to spend much of our time there, and we had arrived to stay the night. Hikosuke had gone to the vaudeville theater in Asakusa, but Moichi was home. As usual, the three of us sat around a cushion—covering it with a white cloth and using it as a table—playing cards with a *hanafuda* deck. Except for the familiar flipping sound of the cards, the silence remained unbroken until the "peony" turned up, blossoming forth from the pile, and Moichi, who had been waiting for a suit in flowers, reached for it.

"What a way to go!"

Suddenly there was a voice, someone outside the locked front door, calling for the Tabes.

"Must be a bill collector," said Moichi, purposely speaking louder to drown it out. "This is no time to be asking for money. If there's any collecting to be done, it's my turn."

But the person outside the door persisted.

"Please, Mrs. Tabe, your old lady..."

"Listen, I'm telling you," shouted Moichi in the direction of the door, "the old woman isn't here."

O-kumi had worked as a geisha in the hot spas of Shinshū, her fateful addiction having its origin in the morphine injections she took to control the chronic gastritis brought on by heavy drinking. Just as the drug came to demand more and more of her, likewise the old woman—her mother—had attached herself to her daughter and refused to let go. According to Hikosuke, it was the old woman who was the crux of O-kumi's problems.

In contrast to days past when Hikosuke had his father to support him, and he had played the role of the gallant both as customer and patron to O-kumi, as soon as his parents passed away, the house in Kutsukake was taken over by a brother, one year Hikosuke's senior. Moreover, when the time came to divide the family estate, neither the brother nor a younger sister, who was married and lived elsewhere showed the least concern at incurring Hikosuke's displeasure, his cold stare having lost whatever chilling effect it may have once had on them. Indeed they made it abundantly clear how little they thought of Hikosuke, their low esteem manifesting itself in the size of his inheritance. Hikosuke's meager share was sufficient, nonetheless, to buy O-kumi's freedom and the four houses in Nippori, but it left no excess with which to care for O-kumi's mother.

For her part, the old woman was too infirm to continue her former profession as hairdresser, having lost the sight in one eye from a cataract and the full use of her legs. She was left to totter halfblind about the premises.

She was not without resources, however. Calling upon an inborn obstinacy, and summoning every drop of ire she could extract from her shriveled frame, she set about making life so miserable in the little house, and promoted such domestic contention, that finally even she could not tolerate the situation. She moved out and went to work babysitting the children in a residence nearby, the home of an army officer and his wife. Still, from time to time, she returned to the Tabes' house to assume her rightful position.

Words hardly describe her: this body, this thing of a human being, hunched over, and glowering at everyone from her corner of the main room. Without a doubt she was one of the ugliest sights in the world. It was as though in the midst of a bucolic scene in which birds sang and puppies frolicked, a fissure had open in the earth's crust, and out of the crack, a grotesquerie had emerged, rising slowly and immobile, out of the trapdoor of the stage.

Hikosuke too became something of a fiend, as he went about bleating and berating the old woman as "Babaa, Babaa." Consequently, there was no end to the arguments between him and O-kumi.

Yet even O-kumi disliked having it known the old woman was her mother, and she referred to her as her aunt. So, when on this occasion, as on many others, she wondered aloud from her side of the sliding door if something had happened to "auntie," clearly it was her mother that she had in mind. Her voice was weary, as though she preferred not to be bothered, but she did ask Moichi to go to the door.

"Damn," he said, clucking his tongue as he went.

The errand boy from the sake shop stood outside. He looked quite beside himself.

"It's the old lady at your house, sir."

"What about her?"

"Well, sir, it looks like it must be her."

"That's what I said. What about her?"

"Somebody was hit by a train at the railroad crossing. It looks like..."

Not even O-kumi could remain undisturbed. She slammed aside the sliding door to her room and stumbled out in her nightgown, still half asleep. Bunzō, Moichi, and I headed for the door.

"Please go and see. I'm in no condition."

"Yes, you stay here. We'll find out what's happened."

By the time we reached the railroad crossing, the crowd had grown so large that we had to push our way to the tracks. We saw a body covered with a straw mat, but it was the familiar set of clogs and the walking stick lying nearby that gave us a real start. We went up to the officer investigating the case, and turning back the mat, found it was the old woman. It was as though a pile of ashes had been wetted down and solidified into a gray mass. Her arms and legs were drawn up tightly against her chest. She looked more like a dog than a human being.

Whatever the old woman's final state, how can I speak such blasphemy? And have I the right? It is my loss that I should equate the demise of another human being with a dog's death, and I am diminished by it. Sadder still is the cavalier way, the absolute ease, with which I have taken the subject of life and death, and skimming over its surface, dispatched it in perfunctory fashion. There is a price to pay for blaspheming the dead, and there I was about to receive my comeuppance.

Namely, the endless stream of verbiage that poured from my lips revealed itself for what it truly was—mere empty talk. As the words began to resonate in my throat and rise to my lips, suddenly they became a heavy dross that, like lees sinking to the bottom of a cask, settled over me, and penetrating my brain, filled every fold, clogging the pleats of reason and leaving me no room to think. Furthermore, their cloying weight explained both the powerlessness I experienced and my inability to get to the core of human suffering. Indeed, only by taking up the pen can I hope to flush out this useless residue. It will only be by refining words, through dissociating them from the malodorousness of the body that...

But riding as I was in a taxi headed for Toranomon, and unable to put pen to paper, I found it far easier to use the tip of my tongue, and continuing my story, make short order of the tale of the old woman.

Learning of the emergency, Hikosuke hurried back to the house, and fetching a wagon, loaded it and carted the old woman home. After what passed for a wake, he took the corpse to the crematorium the next morning.

Take the details of that night—the hard-pressed state of Hikosuke's finances (the notice was due on the mortgage while the rents on the three frontal properties were in arrears) and the rathole down which O-kumi threw the money she pilfered for her injections; or, the volley of recriminations that ensued between husband and wife, their marriage ravaged, like sloughing flesh seared by the burning frustration of never having a spare yen for emergencies; or, Hikosuke's crapulence when those of us at the house scraped together enough cash to buy sake for the wake, and his feigned nonchalance under the influence; or, the dusty corner on the cabinet shelf to which the urn of the old woman's ashes was consigned, there being no money left after cremation to bury it; or, even the neighbors' gossip about the shabby way Hikosuke and O-kumi had treated the old lady. Were I to take these details, fit them into a peaceful setting replete with birdcages, and give them a clever twist or two, no doubt I would have the makings of a novel of manners.

Yet I have no interest in getting bogged down in anything so trifling. To the contrary, today brings a renewed desire to purify my mind, to sidestep, as one would the splashings of a mud puddle, the sullying memory of that night.

Nonetheless, the matter of the the negotiations with the Ministry of Railways remains to be told, and I must tell it even if the ending is hardly tidy, and the story worthy only of being thrown out with yesterday's trash.

Where money was concerned, Hikosuke had never been one to behave like a man born into a decent family. He would watch like a hawk the calculation of five or ten sen, only to lose all powers of comprehension—his mind drawing a total blank—when numbers exceeded ten yen. Thus it was on account of his mental arithmetic, his countless additions and subtractions concerning how much he might receive in condolence money that he spent every day in a terrible stew.

"What do you guess?" Think they'll give me fifty? How about fifty?" he asked, his face flushing.

Finally it came time to receive the young official sent from the government office. He arrived at the house dressed neat as a pin. Hikosuke began to stutter, the froth collecting at the corners of his mouth. Inching nervously forward on the tatami, he reminding the man cheekily that "this was a matter of a human life."

The official was unfazed and kept to his set, formalistic phrases. No doubt he had grown accustomed to seeing people fidget whenever the subject of death turned to money.

"The Ministry also has its standards. Were we speaking of the breadwinner and mainstay of a household, or perhaps of a child with a promising future, that might be one thing. Forgive me for asking, but the decreased was quite elderly, was she not?"

Polite almost to the point of being insulting, he bowed deeply and handed over a neatly wrapped packet, tied in the black and white strings required of an envelope used to present money to the bereaved. The numerals, "one hundred and fifty yen," figured prominently on the front.

It was now Hikosuke's turn to speak, and looking like a man who had been kicked in the shins trying not to show the pain, he leaned forward and bowed so deeply as almost to fall on his face.

"Now, this is very much appreciated."

He snatched up the envelope and tucked it inside his kimono;

and in an effort to hide the smile that began to spread across his face, he stood up and walked in a circle about the occupants of the room. It was behavior so transparent and embarrassing that O-kumi, who had not batted an eye as she sat with her nightgown folded primly about herself, felt forced to tell him to sit down.

"It doesn't look proper for you to be pacing about."

"I guess you're right," he replied halfheartedly.

Bunzō and I joined O-kumi in her suggestion that Hikosuke sit down and give some careful thought to the matter.

"Yes, Hiko, here's the chance you've been waiting for to rebuild your fortunes. Try to pull yourself together."

As a result of these deliberations, it was decided that the house at Nippori would be rented, there currently being a taker, and using the rental deposit and the condolence money as capital, the Tabes would move to Kurumazaka, to lease a larger residence and go into the business of running a boarding house. We too were to be pressed into service for the promotion of this venture, with Bunzō relocating from the relative's place where he had stayed since his return to Tokyo. He became the Tabes' first customer, and shortly thereafter, I, their second. Moichi was packed off to the theater in Asakusa where he would be looked after by the vaudeville actor. Except for the complications resulting from O-kumi's "illness," everything proceeded apace, and so much the better, because I am weary to the bone of speaking of the things of this world.

Yet, what should I envision now when at long last I had time to myself and could begin to compose in my mind the chapter on the Battle of Orléans?

Not Joan, but Yukari! (Yes, let me make a clean breast of it: the image of Joan of Arc that I am forever pursuing is invariably that of Yukari.)

—Ah, ah, Yukari, Yukari . . . what shall I say about you?

The taxi had reached Toranomon and was pulling up to the entrance of the building. Sakagami Seiken's offices were the corner suite on the fourth floor. Since someone was ahead of us, we sat down and waited by the screen that divided the reception room from the inner office.

Yasuko had come to solicit Seiken's services in placing a bid on some scrap metal that was about to be put up for sale by the Yamanoi Aircraft Corporation. And I had come as the person who was to introduce her to Seiken.

In all candor, I must confess that I knew very little about Kuzu-hara Yasuko, or her background. In fact, my insight derived from the conclusions I had tentatively drawn from observing her in this matter of the scrap metal. That I knew her at all was through my connection with Hikosuke.

Payment of outstanding debts falls due at the end of the year, and it was in late December that Hikosuke decided to sell the property in Kurumazaka. One reason was the muddle brought on by O-kumi's uncontrollable need for drugs. Not only had she carted off and pawned the few items of apparel and furniture that remained in the house, but she was borrowing money from everyone, even the errand boy from the sake shop and the girl at the cigarette stand.

Hikosuke was furious. His reputation in the eyes of the neighbors had been ruined, and as if that were not enough, now the finances of both the house and business were in jeopardy. He was sick and tired of continually paying off O-kumi's debts, of forever straightening out the entanglements she created, but then he too was overtaken by an equally feverish complaint—a minor form of addiction known as speculating in rice futures.

Needless to say, Hikosuke gave no forethought to the need to secure an adequate supply of capital, or to be licensed as a broker. No sooner did he have four or five yen in his sweaty palm than he was off to play this new game of chance, the results of which had a direct and immediate effect on each day's living expenses. Considering what it cost him, the game was no sport and certainly no fun. It was an obsession. So that while he may have whistled away each morning as he fed the birds and the one remaining terrier that he was determined to keep at any cost, as soon as these chores were done, he would rush up the stairs to the second floor to see Bunzō.

"How about it, Iori? How does it look today?"

He had been gullible enough to believe Bunzō once when the latter had spoken so self-assuredly of "the market" as he scanned the financial section of the newspaper.

"Hm, just as I predicted. Today's market looks good. If I had the money, I'd play it this way.... I'd shower 'em with a rain of gold and bring the entire country under my control."

Entrusting his hopes to predictions likely to confuse any other mortal, Hikosuke set off for the financial district in Kakigara-chō.

The result of this hit-or-miss proposition was invariably a loss. Thus, after having apologized for taking our next month's rent in advance, paid out in small increments each time Hikosuke appeared, it was not unusual for him to suggest that his shortfall at the end of each month was somehow our fault.

It was also not uncommon for the income from the rentals in Nippori to come in late. A property that develops the habit of not producing its rents is not unlike a house whose central pillar has been infested by termites. To tamper with it is only to make matters worse. Among the many tenants who had come and gone over the years, not one had paid on time. The worst offenders had taken to dividing the rent into fractions of fifty sen or a yen when pressed for payment. Moreover, the best tenant, a young, unemployed scholar from Shinshū, acquired a job and promptly moved away. Confronted with an impasse in which he could no longer afford to hold on to both properties—the one in Nippori and the one in Kurumazaka—Hikosuke still had the option of retreating to the house in Nippori since it entailed no expense to live there.

Yet not a word of this state of affairs was breathed to either of us residing on the second floor until just before the end of the year, when something had to be done and suddenly the property changed hands. It went to one Kuzuhara Yasuko whom Hikosuke knew only from his dealings in Kakigara-chō.

"How about it? I move out and you move in, taking the place as is."

There is no way to know what Yasuko originally had in mind in responding to Hikosuke's feeler that she take over the house, but it was clear that we were not to be consulted. Hikosuke signed us over to her along with the furnishings and other accoutrements.

Yet if Hikosuke thought he had moved with alacrity, he could never have matched the speed with which Yasuko, calmly and deliberately, assumed control of the place. Ensconcing herself in front of the hibachi in the main room on the first floor, she acted as though it had been hers all along.

"I understand you men are writers. I may not know much about books, but I do enjoy reading. Come sit down and have a cup of tea with me."

Not once did she give any indication of being prepared to hear, or allow to register, any complaint at the way we had been manipulated without our consent.

As a matter of fact, the long, wooden hibachi at which she seated herself had been brought to the house by Bunzō from his relative's place in Yoyogi, and when it proved too large for his own room, he installed it downstairs for the use of all. Along with the birdcages, it was one of the few items of value left in the house, the contents having been stripped by O-kumi's raids. Moreover, since to this day the hibachi is the sole ornament of the main room, one supposes that, aside from a body badly tarnished by the affairs of the world, Miss Kuzuhara arrived without possessions, moving in with nothing to her name, not even the vanity of a broken mirror stand. She made do with whatever of ours was at hand, whether it was the dishes and bowls for our meals, or the laundry buckets, the wash basins, even the brand of soap in the bath. As for clothes, she wore the same old kimono, with a flannel nightgown underneath when the weather turned cold.

Two dullards such as Bunzō and myself are slow to think of things monetary, but even we could not but wonder how Yasuko had raised the money for the move. Without a doubt, only the presence of some contrivance, some jack-in-the-box mechanism, could explain how she had gotten away with not paying the hundred-yen deposit required to assume the lease. Who knows what accommodation she had worked out with Hikosuke, but from the end of December through the first week of the new year, his nameplate continued to be posted outside the front door and all callers were greeted with the information that "Mr. Tabe has returned to the country to visit his family. I'm watching the house."

About the middle of the month, however, it was changed to read "Kuzuhara," and when a policeman called to officially register Yasuko as a new resident in the neighborhood, she announced, "I'll be running this lodging house from now on."

"My late husband," she added, "was in the Army, you know ... "

But then the holder of the deed on the property began to realize something suspicious was afoot, and he hurriedly sent over a proxy, a man of about forty who wore dark glasses. He questioned Yasuko as best he could, but her reply was always the same.

"Mr. Tabe is handling the arrangements. I don't know a thing."

Meanwhile, back in Nippori, Hikosuke had bolted the front door, and in order to avoid inquiries, spent his days and nights in a neighborhood mah-jongg parlor. Callers found O-kumi alone, confined to her broken bed and stealthily turning the pages of her copy of *King* magazine in the hope that no one would detect the fact that she was home.

This left only Yasuko to bargain with. How she accomplished the feat I shall never know, but she succeeded in delivering five crisp ten-yen notes to the proxy on the last day of February.

"I've never said I won't pay, but the rest will have to come latter."

The dispute with the proxy over the money continued these last four, going on five, months, but Yasuko has yet to pay the monthly rent, to say nothing of the balance on the deposit money. Nonetheless, she has not been evicted, a fact that testifies to either a weakness in the landlord's position—the house can hardly be used for any other purpose, despite the fact that it is in a neighborhood unlikely to attract boarders—or some sort of exceptional appeasement policy hammered out between Yasuko and the go-between in the dark glasses.

Still more mysterious is the presence of a thin, white-haired gentleman who appears downstairs from time to time. As to what role he plays, one can only guess. The entire business is fraught with riddles that I cannot hope to understand.

Although I take ignorance as bliss, there is *one* thing about which I cannot remain disinterested. Bunzō and I had paid Hikosuke only rent, and for meals, we made do either with bread we kept in our rooms or by going out to eat. But since the change in the management, Yasuko has insisted the arrangement worked an undue hardship upon us.

"It must be terribly inconvenient for you men to have to go out like that. I don't pretend to be much of a cook, but I can come up with a little ordinary fare . . . "

Yasuko cooked for us each morning and evening, using whatever materials were readily available. But if it was a service designed to provide meals at cost, we were shocked to receive an itemized tab at the end of the month, its figures filling out every line of a ruled sheet of paper. Five sen for tea. Fifteen sen for miso soup with a fish cake. Thirty sen for a green salad containing the most startling of vegetables—finely chopped squid legs.

The sheer tenacity with which the small sums were written out seemed to speak of Yasuko's determination that not a day pass before payment was received. We could only look on in dumbfounded amazement as she planted herself on the floor in the corridor outside our rooms and unblinkingly presented us the bill. No doubt it was by similar means of squeezing cash out of people that she had managed to raise the money to pay the proxy.

Why didn't we react quickly and move elsewhere? Why did we choose to exist in this ignominious state? These are really larger issues that extend beyond the topic at hand, but it would be correct to say that in staying behind, we became quite literally Yasuko's prisoners, having been powerfully seduced by the force of her determination to survive. In fact, we remained on the second floor, as though nailed to the spot, our mouths gaping in disbelief; and we did so out of shock and surprise. It was a feeling that bordered on admiration.

What did leave us truly exasperated, however, was the unfeeling complexion, a certain chilly whiteness, that characterized Yasuko's personality.

"Please don't cook for us anymore. Neither of us cares what we eat, and we don't like food forced on us. So thanks, but no thanks!"

"Besides, we find it very annoying the way you are consuming our money. How can you victimize us like this? And to think you can be so causal about it. It sticks like a bone in our throats to think you could do this to us. It really makes us choke."

"You say that because you spend too much time in the house. That's why you don't enjoy your food. You ought to go out every now and then."

Doubtless Yasuko was the one most exercised over her actions. Yet it would be going too far to suggest that her response stemmed from the cunning of devising a strategy or the pleasure of seeing it turned to her advantage. Unlike a device with a false bottom—a thermos bottle, or a box within a box, for example—Yasuko was not equipped with the insight that would have allowed her to extricate herself from her own skin in order to examine why she acted as she did. With complete disregard for how others might respond, she merely lined up her chess pieces and pushed them blindly across the board using whatever irregular move was necessary to win at the game. Or, again, she was like a blind masseuse who, with no regard for his customer's wishes, insists on massaging a pulled muscle.

Monomania was her normal stage of mind, and because she was

forever caught up in the excitement of her little plans, she chose to ignore our reaction even though it had taken her by surprise. It was only natural her cool, brazen face should appear to us as that of a masked bandit. We found ourselves—"ahem"—clearing our throats at what she had to say.

"What kind of answer is that, Yasuko? How can you treat us like this?"

"I always feel I cannot do enough for the two of you. I know I should do much more but, as you see, I'm all by myself.... Things will get better. I promise they will. As a matter of fact, I've heard of a little moneymaking scheme, and if all goes well.... I'm embarrassed to tell you this, but it has to do with the disposal of excess government scrap metal, five thousand tons to be exact, at a bargain price. I think I want to take it off the company's hands. Now, what was the name of the firm that's handling the sale? Oh yes, I remember, it's the Yamanoi Aircraft Corporation..."

"Oh, Yamanoi."

I foolishly let slip the fact I knew the name.

By being alert and picking up on what I had said, Yasuko inquired whether I knew Mr. Yamanoi, the president of the corporation.

"Not personally."

"Then you know someone who does?"

"Well, yes, a man named Sakagami."

"I wonder if I could persuade you to introduce me to him. You know how much I would appreciate it. And if you could arrange for him to introduce me to Mr. Yamanoi, that would be even better. All I have to do is meet Mr. Yamanoi."

Yasuko's eyebrows shot up at the prospect of having landed the parvenu Yamanoi who had made his fortune during one of the recent national mobilizations and who now ranked among the top members of a leading political party. I reeled away from her hot breath, averting my eyes in the direction of the veranda and beyond —to a woman's summer kimono hanging on the clothesline. It was made of faded cotton hand towels that had been pieced together.

The towels were not of the kind given out by business establishments as souvenirs for patronage; rather they were of a special, far more suggestive type, dyed with the designs of ivy tendrils or swirling pools of water and printed with the words "Spring Feels Better in Hakusan" or "The Eternal Pleasures at Tenjin." They seemed to suggest that what Yasuko chose to air in the bright light of the sun was not only these faded phrases but also her whole past which heretofore had been presented to us as the abstemious life of an army officer's wife.

Although Yasuko's manner of dress would never have been mistaken for that of a former geisha, could she have been trying to say she had numbered among the scullery maids who keep body and soul afloat by passing from one kitchen to another among the houses in pleasure districts? That being the case, her life was like the residue in a tea cup, the fur that remains after the water has evaporated. There was no reason why she should have been susceptible to any subtleness of feeling or goodness of heart.

Yet as I sat beside Yasuko in Seiken's office, the more I studied her and the improbable manner in which she handled herself, the more impressed I became. First of all, her outfit was markedly different from her usual attire. She wore a lightweight *haori* jacket over a kimono of sheer silk crêpe (albeit a bit worn with age), and everything was set off with touches of gold—a bit of gold stitching on her kimono collar, a heavy gold ring incised with a peony design, a stylish pair of gold-rimmed eyeglasses. I had no idea how she had obtained it all, but that was not information one so unconversant with the ways of the world as myself was likely to extrapolate, no matter how discerning my eye or how hard I stared.

Let me add that the word I had let slip concerning Sakagami's connection with Yamanoi was not idle chatter. In fact, there were two plaques by the door to Seiken's office, "*Political Debate,* Inc." and "The Yamanoi Association." As head of the association and principal backer of the magazine, no doubt Mr. Yamanoi, Esq., Attorney-at-Law, was the milch cow for the prominent commentator on political affairs, Mr. Sakagami Seiken.

"Oh my, sorry to have kept you waiting," said Seiken as he emerged from the other side of the screen dividing the room. "How are you these days? Write anything?"

"No, my life seems to be taken up with too many commonplace errands."

"That so?"

"Actually, it is one of these errands that brings me here today. This lady is most anxious to meet you."

I introduced Yasuko to Seiken. No sooner had she said how-do-you-do than Yasuko set aside her freshly lit cigarette and launched into her story. I sat listening half-heartedly to the garrulous stream of words that issued from her mouth as she explained at length the nature of her business. Not one to be immune to such matters, Seiken listened intently.

"I see," he said sitting back in his chair and letting his vest, draped with a platinum and gold chain, ride up on his ample stomach. The rim of his glasses caught the light and shone with a brilliance rivaling that of his balding pate.

"In other words, you want to meet Mr. Yamanoi, and from there you'll take care of everything."

"That's right. I'd really like to try and do this. Whether the introduction's done in my name, or whomever's, is immaterial to me."

"You'll excuse me for asking, but what about capital?"

"If we can come to terms, I'm prepared to pay."

"Hm. But you realize there are many other bidders. Whether things will go as smoothly as you wish depends on the bidding. I see no harm in my approaching Mr. Yamanoi on your behalf, but I must also tell you that knowing him makes it, in a sense, more difficult. Everything is predicated upon further examination of where you stand. Of course, by that I mean your investment capital, things like that. Then perhaps something..."

It was like someone had taken a stack of copper coins and was shaking them beside my ear. No longer able to tolerate being in the room, and wishing to get back to the continuation of my chapter on Joan of Arc, I stood up.

"Excuse me, but I have other business to attend to."

"Really?" replied Yasuko. "In that case, I'll stay a bit longer."

She was now firmly glued to the seat, and leaving Seiken to tend to her, I hurried out of the building.

I felt as though I was covered with a layer of dust, and as soon as I reached the street, I gave myself a dusting from head to toe.

—Ah, ah, what ineptitude! How could I have been so foolish as to abandon my own work to be dragged about by the likes of Kuzuhara Yasuko?

Yet at the critical juncture when the best course of action would have been for me to jump into a taxi and return home, I allowed myself to be seduced by the fragrant breeze that stirred the sun-splashed row of trees lining the street. Caught up in a lighthearted mood, I turned from the streetcar tracks, and heading in the direction of Karasumori, I ambled along the broad avenue that led to the rear entrance of Shimbashi Station.

Often when I announce I shall settle down and get to work, a feeling of exhaustion overtakes me, and to do anything becomes a chore. In what is admittedly a bad habit, I take a break and have a cigarette in order to dispel my feelings of ennui. The upshot is I fail to seize the opportunity to take up my pen, and despite my good intentions, I let myself be enveloped in the stuffy affairs of the world. Yet that I should find myself continually in this predicament, gasping for air in the midst of a swirling cloud of dust, is not entirely the fault of my disposition. It appears that for some time now I have been operating under the formidable influence of an unknown but malevolent curse.

CHAPTER FIVE

AS I sauntered along I reached the entrance to the grounds of the Karasumori Shrine. I observed a couple standing by the side of the street half a block ahead of me. They were intent on their conversation. The woman was dressed in a kimono, her hair done in an abbreviated version of the "ginkgo" style. The man wore a Panama hat with the brim turned down in front. His kimono consisted of a single layer of a coarse Satsuma weave over which he had tied a "soldier boy" obi, a silver-gray crêpe silk dappled in white. Entwined about his delicate fingers were the strings of a small cloth purse, which hung limply at his side.

I could tell from his profile that the man was Terao Jinsaku, son of the owner of the "House of the Roan Steed," a shop in Atagoshita that handled rare and expensive antiques. Jinsaku taught the art of chanting for the Nō theater, giving lessons in the style of the Kanze school. I have known him for many years.

Just as I felt relieved that he had not seen me and that I would get by him unnoticed, Jinsaku suddenly turned around and looked up the street. I had no choice but to stop, and to exchange a few words of greeting.

"Oh, it's you!"

Now Jinsaku's companion had spoken and was thanking me for last night. She was the woman I had seen in Shinjuku—at the first bar to which Moichi had taken me. As I said before, I have lost all interest in talking about her. In fact, she had slipped my mind completely.

Yet there she was, and since she has gone to the trouble to remind me of her existence by putting in an unsolicited appearance, it becomes my turn among the many ineluctable twists of fate to back up a bit and speak of our original encounter.

That is, of course, more easily said than done, but suffice it to say she was a rarity among the girls who hosted the bars of Shinjuku. What caught my eye was her manner of dress and the finesse with which she handled her customers; in short, I was impressed by everything that set her apart from the hot and heavy style of the average barmaid. Nonetheless, she did not appear to be the owner, or the one who managed the shop. It is really quite curious; odder still was the degree of familiarity with which Moichi greeted her.

"It's certainly nice to see you again. Where've you been? We haven't seen you here lately."

"I took a week off because I wasn't feeling very well."

"That's too bad."

"It's why I didn't get around to your place either."

"Never mind me. What about the other party?"

"I haven't seen him since the last time the three of us were together. Have you?"

"No, but I plan to drop in on him in a day or two—at the *house*."

"Tell him how angry I am when you see him."

"Ha! You can't mean that?"

"I most certainly do. I'm really upset with him."

Who could fathom what they were talking about? Even if they were to repeat the conversation for me now, I doubt I could guess whom they meant by "the other party."

But the fact that I acknowledged the woman's thanks, however perfunctorily, appeared to have upset Jinsaku. He became quite agitated.

"You know this fellow?" he queried, his voice faltering even as he sought to interrogate her. "Where did you meet?"

"Last night at the bar. He came in with Moichi."

"Oh, I see," he said, his face turning pink with embarrassment.

"I meant to tell you before," he said addressing me. "But, well, I let it go because we don't seem to run into each other these days."

"Tell me what?"

"You mean you don't know? I have no idea what Moichi may have said to you about my renting the apartment, but I did it to help him out. I give lessons to a pupil in Shinjuku, and since I come all the way from Atagoshita, I thought it would be convenient to have a place where I could stop and rest before I started home. Usually, Moichi..."

"So that's it. Hm..."

I recalled the nameplates I had seen by the door to Moichi's apartment.

"So you're the 'Terao'? I figured Moichi couldn't have pulled off the trick of renting the place by himself. It never occurred to me to think of you, though. And Moichi didn't breathe a word about it."

"No, he wouldn't."

Jinsaku bit his lip, frustrated in his attempt to keep his secret to himself.

"You know, Moichi turns out to be an honest chap, after all. You told him not to talk, and he hasn't."

"You're joking. Whoever said I told him not to say anything?"

"Let's not argue about it. Whatever's happening, don't worry. I'm not the type to go rushing off to the house in Atagoshita to report on you. I have no desire to get into that kind of business."

Jinsaku's father was a distant relative, and Jinsaku's wife, Hisako, an old friend. Hisako was in poor health of late. Having contracted pleurisy, she stayed in bed much of the time. Naturally, Jinsaku preferred that I not know what he did in private while he was away from home.

"For my own sake I'm glad Moichi didn't go into the details. If the apartment really belongs to you, I'm willing to bet it's the setting for some sort of off-color production you're planning, and that Moichi has only the smallest of parts to play in the drama you've concocted."

"Of all the..."

His thumbs thrust into his obi, Jinsaku gave an exaggerated lift to his shoulders. It was as if the matter could be excused by shrugging it off.

"Since I have you here," he said, flashing a smile, "how about if I invite you out for a few drinks on the town? I can't do it now because I have business to attend to for the shop, but what about this evening? In Shinjuku? That would be perfect for me. Meet me at the place you went last night with Moichi. Around eight?"

"I don't know if I can make it."

"Of course you can. What could be wrong with having a drink together?"

"If I get there, I get there."

"Good. I'll be waiting."

As I started once more in the direction of Shimbashi Station, I could not help puzzling over my conversation with Jinsaku. One might understand Moichi's reluctance at having to explain about Jinsaku's involvement in renting the apartment, but I found it strange that in almost no time he and Jinsaku had become close friends. To the best of my knowledge, they had met only once or twice, and it had been at my instigation.

Yet hadn't Jinsaku started to say what Moichi "usually" did? The matter-of-factness with which he addressed the entire proposition seemed to suggest that at some point, and by means unknown to me, Moichi had made himself an indispensible part of Jinsaku's private life. Still it was hard to understand what motive Moichi had in keeping the information secret.

What of it? The entire matter is too ludicrous for words. As one who is as weary with the traffic of this dusty world, how much better not to be counted among their number, and to be treated as an outsider. Who cares how Jinsaku and Moichi came to know each other, or how their interests coincided? Enough of these absurd entanglements. Isn't it far more important that I get to my desk and take up my pen?

Yet as I was about to enter the station with every intention of going home, I was distracted as someone approached from behind and brushed against me.

"Where are you off to?"

I turned around to find the woman who had been with Jinsaku.

She was handsomely dressed. The design of her outfit involved the interplay of blue and white, and it gave her a chic, almost mannish look, that complemented the tightly wrapped bun of her hairdo. Diagonal stripes of pale indigo had been woven, as though applied with a brush, into the white crêpe de chine of the kimono; here and there irises of the same color were superimposed on the brush strokes. Tied about her waist was a Hakata obi, a single band of silver thread running horizontally along the center of the stiff, navy-blue fabric. The straps of the sandals, as well as the felt covering the insteps, were the same shade of blue. The sole concession to a bright color was the red of the tie-dyed sash that was tucked in along the top edge of the obi to hold it in place.

Her face, her breasts, her hips were full and shapely. As she stood in the entryway to the station, she was like a figure who had stepped out of a Kaigetsudō print. The dust in the air mingled with the powerful aura that radiated from her person, a combination so overwhelming as to take away my breath. To be approached in public by such a beautiful woman, by one so conspicuously well dressed, and in terms so cordial, was...an embarrassment. I blushed and involuntarily stepped back, as though to get away.

"I'm going home," I announced.

"To Kurumazaka?"

"How did you know?"

"I hear about you every time Moichi and Jinsaku come to the bar."

"Where's Jinsaku?"

"He said he had business to take care of. Who knows what it is, though."

"Well, goodbye."

"What's your hurry? Why don't you come with me?"

"Where?"

"How about a place where we can have a drink together? At least that's what I'd like to do."

"I'm not a drinker like Moichi, you know. I really haven't time to waste."

"Why say a thing like that? Come along and keep me company."

"No thanks. I've work to do."

"How awful, working on a gorgeous day like this. Come to my place."

"Your place?"

"Yes, why don't you come over for a while?"

I grew more and more uncomfortable as people began, first, to cast curious looks our way and then to stare quite openly. What in the world did this woman see in me, a bookish intellectual? Was I someone with whom to talk and pass the time? Or was there a deeper motive, one in which I would be used as leverage in her relations with Jinsaku? I had no time to think.

"Have a stiff drink and then set to work. That's how it is with writing, you know."

"I never expected I'd be taught how to write by you."

"Humph."

As I turned to go, she hailed a taxi, and quickly slipping to the far side of the back seat, called to me to get in.

"Come on now."

—Ah, ah, what lack of dignity on my part! How could I have allowed myself to be drawn into the vehicle?

"Where are we going?"

"Be quiet and leave everything to me."

The taxi passed Shōwa Avenue and headed toward Kayaba-chō. Crossing the Eitai Bridge over the Sumida River, it followed the streetcar tracks that led to the heart of the Susaki red-light district. When the driver came to the broad thoroughfare running east and west through the district, the woman told him to turn left and stop just beyond the corner. The taxi pulled up in front of a small house, squeezed between two large establishments that offered rooms for rent by the hour or the night.

The packs of Shikishima cigarettes suspended on strings made of twisted paper and the dolls sitting on their balsa wood boxes—in fact all the neat and pretty prizes that decorated the storefront—identified the house as one of the attractions found in red-light districts, a shooting gallery for amateur archers.

"I'm home," said the woman, addressing the matron who sat in front of the shop. She addressed her as "elder sister"; the sister's hair was done up in the kind of a chignon worn by a married woman.

"O-tsuna, you're back early."

"Is everything straight upstairs?"

"Yes, but the gentleman...? Oh, I see, I didn't mean... Please go on up. Please."

At the top of the narrow flight of stairs, there were two rooms. The second story had greater depth than one would have supposed from the outside, but the ceiling was low—my head almost brushed against it.

I sat down, leaning against the windowsill of the four-and-a-half mat room that overlooked the street and attempted to relax and make myself feel comfortable. Meanwhile, from the adjoining room I could hear the sound of drawers being opened and closed as the woman, going through her dresser, pulled out a change of clothes. When she reappeared, she was dressed in a cotton kimono. The design on the fabric was of interlocking wheels. As though perfectly timed, the sister entered the room with a pot of tea.

"Aren't you the quick one?" she remarked. "Changed already, I see."

"Don't we have any beer? It's so hot today."

"You drank the last bottle, didn't you?"

"You're right, I did. In that case..."

"I'll be happy to take care of it," I said, reaching into my pocket. "I'm embarrassed at having come empty-handed."

The sister accepted the note that I took from my wallet and, without making any fuss, simply thanked me and disappeared down the stairs.

Soon the makings of a small party were arranged on the table. Leaving a young girl to tend to the shop, the older sister joined us. The two women chattered away as I raised my glass of beer and, succumbing to my bad habit, the illness I have nursed across the years, I commenced to drink.

—Ah, ah, the image of Joan of Arc appeared to fade away, receding further and further into the distance.

"He's making a fool of me, you know."

"What are you talking about, O-tsuna?"

"Who else but Jinsaku."

"That's strange. Where did you meet him? I thought..."

"I phoned him from Shimbashi. At least he had the decency to come out and see me. But he kept saying how busy he had been and how he couldn't get out of the house, or that he wouldn't be able to see me for the time being. You and I both know that isn't the case."

"If he says he's busy..."

"I don't understand it. I mean, this foolishness about whether he is going to set me up in business or not. Doesn't he realize he's delaying everything?"

"You're right about that," the sister replied, turning to me to explain.

"Jinsaku told O-tsuna that she should go ahead and open a restaurant and bar. One of my friends—she used to be in Shitaya—has a place in Shinjuku, and O-tsuna has been going over nights to, well, learn the trade. But all of a sudden Jinsaku, the key figure in all this, won't let us know what the next step is to be."

"He's much too vague. Moichi is in a bind too. Of course, he's on Jinsaku's side, so there's no point in counting on him."

"What's happened with the apartment?"

"Same as usual. But since Jinsaku hasn't been going there lately, it appears he's not paying the rent. That's why I say Moichi is having a hard time."

"*He*'s having a difficult time? O-tsuna, you've got to think of yourself."

Why this beautiful woman, now known to me as O-tsuna, should have become involved with Terao Jinsaku was beyond my comprehension. I felt certain, however, that Jinsaku had calculated the costs of such an affair, and having mentally rehearsed the scenario beforehand, had settled upon a modern-style apartment as the best and least expensive location for staging his contemporary romance. But once the apartment was of no more use, and he ceased to frequent it, the responsibility for looking after the place had been shifted to Moichi. Moichi became no more than a watchdog or a doorman; no wonder he was hard pressed to pay for the newspaper subscription. Nor did it take much guesswork to understand why Moichi, knowing how calculating Jinsaku could be and in order to maneuver him into paying the rent, spent so much time traveling back and forth to Jinsaku's house in Atagoshita.

"Moichi's a tremendous help, isn't he? He even takes care of chores here. The other day he came over and helped me set up shelves and repaper the shōji screens. What's more, I've never known him to appear without a gift. He always brings a little something, a box of kelp cooked in soy sauce, or a small bag of *monaka* cakes."

I managed to contain myself at hearing the sister speak extravagantly of Moichi, but it came as a real surprise to know what she and O-tsuna had to say about Tabe Hikosuke.

"Whatever became of that fellow they call 'Hiko'?"

"Oh, he went off to Katsuura in Chiba Prefecture to keep his sister company."

I was so astonished I could not resist asking how they knew Hikosuke.

"Haven't you heard? His sister has been staying at the Benihana Apartments for a few days. She had the children with her."

"At Moichi's place?"

"That's right."

Hikosuke's sister had been married to a doctor who died and left her with two small children. Unlike Hikosuke, she had held on to her share of their parents' estate, and her late husband had left her a sizeable income from his medical practice in the Shinshū region.

Given these resources, she treated her elder brother like a subordinate, and whenever she and the children came to Tokyo, Hikosuke was obliged to go to the train station to meet them, to carry their baggage, and to appear for their excursions to the department stores. While the sister shopped, it was Hikosuke's job to tend to the children, pushing them along or carrying them on his back. Matters had reached the point where, in order to realize the occasional gift of a little pocket money, he was constantly at his sister's beck and call.

Recently, the sister had closed the house in Shinshū and moved to the Bōshū Peninsula in Chiba Prefecture, which she chose for its proximity to Tokyo. The country air would be good for the delicate health of her children; at the same time, they would be close to reputable schools in the metropolitan area when the time came for them to begin their elementary education.

I had known about the move to Chiba, and Hikosuke's going off to Katsuura to visit his sister, but this was the first I had heard of the sister staying at Moichi's apartment. Clearly there was good reason for her to avoid the complications of the house in Nippori, but one could also imagine a widow's ingenuity—the special talent for working out the accomodation that best suits her convenience— was at work in this latest maneuver. By throwing a little cash Moichi's way, she had found the means to save on the high cost of staying over in the city.

But where was Moichi supposed to retire in the meantime? Or, for that matter, who was doing what, when, and with whom in the confines of the small apartment?

"It must be hard for Moichi to get any rest with so many people coming and going."

"I really feel sorry for him. O-tsuna told him not to leave when she was there with Jinsaku, but apparently Moichi didn't feel right sticking around."

"What do you mean? I've never stayed in the apartment. I just drop in now and then."

"Supposedly Moichi would go out and take a turn about the block, and if O-tsuna and Jinsaku were still there when he got back, he'd wait in the corridor, pacing back and forth, back and forth."

"I haven't any idea what you're talking about. How can you make up such a preposterous story?"

"But isn't that what happened? You told me how funny he looked."

"You're terrible! How awful of you to say such a thing. Now stop it."

O-tsuna was in such haste to clasp her hand over her sister's mouth that she reached directly across my lap, her body collapsing on mine.

"Careful there. I'm not Terao Jinsaku, you know."

"Oh, let's forget him. No doubt he's dragged some new number to the apartment already. Moichi won't tell me, but I know. Anyway, Jinsaku can do as he pleases."

"Hey, get off me, will you."

"Aren't you the sissy?" O-tsuna smiled, burrowing her elbows deeper. With her arms propped on my lap, she let her body slither across the tatami like a tangle of seagrasses undulating in a wave.

"For some reason I feel terribly sleepy," she yawned.

My face is already bright red at having revealed this much. I haven't the audacity, let alone the time and energy, to go into further detail.

Make one mistake, and how true it is there is no end to the trouble it begets. That I had fallen into the trap of a most serious and irreparable error became apparent when the older sister retired from the room, and O-tsuna and I spent several inglorious hours together.

In retrospect I ask myself if, and at what point, I might have broken off this ignominious association and set myself free. Was it when we arrived at the shooting gallery? Or at Shimbashi Station? Or, still further back, when I left the house in the company of Kuzuhara Yasuko? Furthermore, I wonder if the problem is of such a deep-seated nature, having put down its nefarious roots long before I was aware, that no amount of pulling and tugging at this weed will eradicate it. Hadn't I resolved to perform a bit of radical surgery on myself the instant I stood up and walked out of Seiken's office?

But little by little I had let the ground give way beneath me, and before I could cry out, I found myself sinking into the muddy sea of desire. Only after having immersed myself in its tossing waves did I come to the painful realization I was drowning and did not know how to save myself. I can talk all I want about spiritual zeal and abstinence of the flesh, but what is the point if I remain woefully ignorant of the means whereby one mortifies the body and quickens the spirit? Without such knowledge, what hope is there of ever seeing the day of the flowering of my spirit, or the fruit borne of its labors?

—Ah, ah, to what end do I speak of zeal and abstinence? To what end...?

If only I knew. At any rate, of this much I am certain: my madly rushing about is a waste. These errands and excursions on behalf of the world have weighted me down. They have becomes the dregs of my existence, and I, the detritus of my own meaningless and wasted efforts. I have failed, and I am tempted to take an obvious failure of will and see it as the work of a malevolent spirit that has cursed me with bad luck. It is all too easy to think this way, but far too dangerous for my own good.

Keep company in life with ill fortune, making it the excuse for all that goes wrong, and one has only to heave a great sigh of relief and put his life in the hands of fate. Yet in that instant, in the moment one surrenders to the rationale of bad luck, the last particle of the will's power to resist is blown away and one falls into an imbecilic state. There shall be no salvation, no release, for me in this vale of tears, until I put the lash to my enfeebled spirit and drive it forward.

Yet I fear my personality is so consituted that, however severe the lashing, the aftereffect will not be repentance but mere remorse. In the end, I hardly know what I had willed in the first place. Consider the paving stones or the stand of trees across the way—as a human being I may think I have been set apart from them, but to what purpose?

There, at the heart of the metropolis and its great roar, all I could see on the horizon was the shadow of desolate clouds piled one on top of another. Night had fallen and entered the room. As I sat there looking out the window, I felt utterly oppressed by the darkness that hung so heavily, layer by layer, over the lights of the city. I felt crushed by its weight, pinned down and unable to move. The woman slept silently beside me, covered in a light quilt that assumed the contour of her womanflesh, adorning it with an array of fans scattered across a turquoise background. But I was filled with shame. So great was my humiliation, and so hard did I bite the nail of my thumb out of frustration, that it turned an incandescent blue and white, burning like the hottest of flames....

Suddenly I got up, and leaving O-tsuna to sleep, I ran down the stairs. The sister bade me goodbye at the entrance, but I hardly acknowledged her as I jumped into a taxi that came cruising along looking for a customer. I returned home straightway. The thought of Jinsaku and my promise to meet him did not cross my mind.

The hour seemed late, but it was only a little after nine o'clock. The fact that the front door was locked from the inside suggested that Yasuko had yet to return. Entering by the kitchen door, which is never bolted, I went directly to my room. I sat down at the desk, as though to chain myself to it, and grabbed my pen. The desire to get back to work was like a great thirst, and I intended to give my slackened throat its due of cooling waters.

"Now, what shall I write?"

I sat there, my pen stiffly poised over a sheet of paper. What a fool I was to think that a body aflame could burst forth as a gurgling spring.

A voice shouted from the other side of the wall.

"Hey, is that you? You home?"

It was Bunzō. He had disappeared three days earlier saying he was going to visit his relative's house in Yoyogi.

"So you're still alive?" I shouted back.

"Sure. How were things in my absence?"

"More and more chaotic."

"Why don't you come over here?"

Judging from the way Bunzō slurred his words, I could guess he had consumed his usual amount of cheap spirits and collapsed on his sagging mattress. He would lie languidly stretched across the bed, dozing on and off through the night, lifting a book and then tossing it aside. At times he would talk to himself, his monologue droning on and on, as he stared at the ceiling.

Yet if Bunzō and I are to engage in one of our lengthy conversations, it is of equal likelihood that my manuscript will lie white atop the desk, the blankness of its pages an unspoken complaint against the pitiful manner in which it has been cast aside not only tonight but on many other occasions.

CHAPTER SIX

"YUKARI, YUKARI."

Each time I have intoned her name and started to speak of the object of my secret love, the petty affairs of the world have intervened, and in responding to their call rather than addressing the topic at hand, I have continued to let my story go astray. Someone might see an artful bit of camouflage in this tendency of mine, and no doubt there is ample evidence for such an opinion. Yet ultimately the problem arises because, when it comes time to speak of her, of who she is and what she does, I am quite ignorant; aside from my secret longing for her, I have virtually nothing to say.

Indeed the Yukari that I know is the Yukari of a decade ago, Yukari the schoolgirl who commuted each day from her relative's house in Yoyogi to the mission school. Thereafter I lost all contact with her. Not until my reunion with Bunzō at Hikosuke's house was I able to learn even a part of her story. What I have to convey here is, therefore, extremely brief.

Namely that Yukari continued to live at her relative's house in Tokyo after she graduated from school. But then one day the relative was shocked to find his charge had taken up with a certain young man and run away from home. It was for this reason that the family sent Bunzō to Tokyo to investigate matters.

The young man with whom Yukari had run off was a member of the outlawed communist party, one of the embattled few who fought on behalf of the one party of the proletariat, or at least until he fell into the snares of a police dragnet and was imprisoned. Eventually he was released on bail, but no sooner had he regained his freedom than he vanished without a trace. Being a fellow travel-ler and his companion in all things, Yukari was also thought to have gone underground with him. Even to this day several years later, no one, not even the police, knows of her whereabouts. I have often wondered if the day will ever come when Yukari will respond to my secret call.

Whenever Bunzō returned from a visit to his relative in Yoyogi, my heart was stirred by the vain hope that he might have news of his sister. It was with this expectation that I perched on the edge of his bed—which occupies fully half the room—and with a glass of cheap whiskey in one hand, waited for him to broach the subject.

He startled me by sitting upright.

"That woman downstairs is indefatigable," he began, turning the conversation in an unanticipated direction.

"Why is that?"

"She says she's looking for a patron."

"You mean in connection with the scrap-metal business?"

"No, although that's part of it. She seems to think her body is marketable too."

"Why should you find it odd to hear her say that? Even in summer her blood runs cold, so she could use somebody to keep her warm. You heard a rumor or something?"

"Hm."

"Who from?"

"Tabe."

Bunzō had stopped by Nippori on his way home. The story he related was of how Hikosuke had set out to find a job. Hikosuke's financial situation was worse than ever—as if keeping up with the mounting costs of O-kumi's habit were not enough of a strain, he had fallen behind in paying the ground rent on the Nippori property. The landholder had assumed a belligerent attitude and sent a lawyer around to the house. Hikosuke was forced to sell the terrier, his last pup, and to cut back on the number of birds he kept. Now that his speculation in rice futures had turned out badly, he had begun to clamor about the need for work—"A job! A job!" he shouted—but it was hard to believe that a middle-aged man lacking any specific trade or talent would find a position easily, let alone one that was tailor-made to his needs.

But Hikosuke had set about contacting whomever he knew, and among the various people he approached was a Mr. Tsuruta, an acquaintance from Kakigara-chō, the president of the sightseeing company, Famous Places of Japan, Ltd., a man in his sixties—or at least that was the impression we had, because Tsuruta turned out to be the same elderly man Bunzō and I had seen downstairs calling on Yasuko from time to time. There was good reason, moreover, to believe it was Tsuruta whom Yasuko had relied upon in trying her hand at the lodging-house business, and he who had put her on to the idea of investing in the scrap metal.

At the same time, perhaps it had been reluctance on Tsuruta's part that explained why Yasuko had found the logistics of opening and operating the lodging house difficult in the initial months. He had held back the necessary funds, according to Hikosuke, who, enjoying his self-appointed role as an authority on the subject, rambled on and on in talking to Bunzō.

"Look, Tsuruta has to think of himself, so I'm sure he had his reasons for backing off."

Insofar as the old man's principal line of business was usury, and he had set his sights on Yasuko's hide—a hide no less the equal of his own in its oily greediness—it was perhaps only natural Tsuruta would be cautious about advancing money, or at least until Yasuko became more forthcoming and her body inclined to prove its "sincerity." Likewise, Yasuko insisted on a display of fidelity from Tsuruta, but one done in accordance with her terms.

So long as "sincerity" remained untranslated into its true meaning of hard cash, there would never be an end to their jockeying back and forth over the question of who was truly sincere. But Yasuko had a slight advantage. She was unlikely to regret the loss of the one thing that she had to offer. In the end the standoff became a test of wills in which Yasuko grew more and more anxious about where the old man's endless suspicions were leading him. She was on the verge of giving in, and not unsurprisingly, this was due to a dwindling confidence in her ability to use her physical charms to continue to lure Tsuruta. Yasuko was frantic, her eyes figuratively bloodshot from the strain of being constantly on the lookout for whatever cash she could raise to ease her day-to-day financial pinch, to squeeze whatever she could from whomever she chose.

And yet, while the sight of her may appear laughable, the two of us on the second floor were the truly ludicrous ones. For what was to become of us? Here we were, worrying ourselves to the point of exhaustion over the rubbish of this trash heap. Whereas we ought to have been able to walk on by—unconcerned whether it was Tsuruta or Yasuko who would sustain a loss, or whether Hikosuke would become a tour guide with Tsuruta's company, or what compromise Jinsaku and Moichi would reach concerning the apartment, each thinking he had bested the other—instead we had stepped into a quagmire, and unable to extricate ourselves, flailed about like the other lost souls.

It was no laughing matter, and as I lifted my head, my eyes seemed to cloud over. Everything became vague and indistinct, but I could still see Bunzō, his thin frame resting on the bed like a dead body committed to the waves, his tongue numbed by the daily intake of cheap liquor, his eyes staring at the ceiling as though transfixed by who knows what specter. All talk of Hikosuke had vanished into thin air, and he had slipped into an incoherent monologue.

—"I, Iori Bunzō, what am I . . . ?

"Yes, for the record, put me down as a 'defect.' I am a defect. I am a misfit ill-suited to living in this day and age when one is obliged to fight and continually push oneself forward. I'm a defect in the social system.

"We could delve into the reasons why, but since you and I know right from the start that the world is to blame, why bother? I'm certainly not interested in pretending to care, and on top of that, what difference would it make? What I mean to say is my defect is of such a deep-seated nature that it will always be there, and I'll always be defective, no matter how much society changes.

"Given the last several thousand years of human history, and the way people act today, you can't tell me that, by taking the whole motley crew of the human race and shaking it up a bit, we can hope to see any fundamental change in the make-up of the average human being. That's why I say 'No thanks' to having to associate with the likes of my contemporary fellow man.

"Actually, I think it's really rather humble and gracious of me to say the problem has its origin in what's wrong with me and not in what's wrong with the world. But what else do I have to offer people? Now if folks out there want to talk about how they're going to change for my sake, of how they'll try of accommodate me, that's all very well and good, but you and I know it's really out of the question and won't happen anyway. Certainly the world would be a far better place, and nothing would be more valuable, were there a crucible in which people could be melted down and recast, but we all know that's not possible.

"Creatures like Yukari are different, of course. They're so zealous by nature they go up in flames by themselves. But Yukari is Yukari. She has her way of doing things, and I mine.

"Strange as it may sound, I am still deeply attached to this world. Only recently I thought of trying my hand at writing again. I was in a whimsical mood, so I took out my pen, but it was no use. I had forgotten the words and the characters. No, 'forgotten' isn't quite right. I realized I no longer had the faintest notion what is meant by 'characters' or 'the written word,' or what they stand for.

"Words are truly curious things, you know, and I have never fully understood why we want to write in such odd squiggles. I tried writing the character for my own name. Iori. I drew a mark. Then a line underneath it. But I couldn't remember what came next. No, I think I knew, but I couldn't believe in what I wrote.

"'Is this right?' 'Is this the way it should look?' I must have asked myself a hundred times, and then I began to panic out of a sense of utter helplessness. When you write words down, they are supposed to mean something. But have you ever stopped to ask yourself what a strange convention writing is?

"So now I have alcohol instead. I bought the cheapest and foulest brand I could find, and I plan to use its bitterness to cut away at the vitality that keeps me alive—my all-too-human desire to stay in this world and cling to life. Booze. That's the key to my reincarnation. I have only to invoke its name . . . but, no, this is a secret I shall keep to myself. At last I have succeeded in becoming one of the evil spirits of Chinese mythology, those creatures that live in the rivers and mountains and that come out disguised as tigers and boars to wreck havoc on human beings.

"Yes, Kuzuhara Yasuko is the lowest of the low. Why should I ever have to move from this room? But, then again, what does it matter where I move? All rooms are sordid—any room, on any second floor. So what if Yasuko feeds me potatoes and takes my money? You'd think people would be smarter, that they'd be cleverer than to spend their time stealing the little money I have left. It's such a waste.

"I went to Nippori. Hikosuke begged me to go with him to the police station. He had to get O-kumi out of jail because they said she had been rounded up with a bunch of drug addicts. She must have been doing something wrong someplace. But Hikosuke was too frightened to open his mouth in front of the police, so I did the talking. We got O-kumi out and took her home.

"Hikosuke was furious, but no matter how angry he got, O-kumi remained as calm and collected as ever. What a sight!—that composure of hers. But then, she has her equal in me when it comes to maintaining the pretense of a cool exterior. How could I have sat there, quietly drinking my glass of sake while Hikosuke slapped her around? I kept asking myself if it was me sitting there, doing nothing. The whole affair was an illusion, as though I were living in a world of my own in which my actions, and those of the others in the room, took place on opposite sides of a thick wall of mist.

"I became invisible, like a fish floundering about in a pitch black sea, a fish oblivious to any kind of questioning, blind to any sort of reflection on the meaning of the self, or about what passes for good or evil, or noble or base. At the same time, I was touched to the core by each and every slap, by the sheer senselessness of what I watched, and I was filled with a terrible sense of poignancy. It was as though the pain I felt was the sole outlet for the frustration inherent in my view of the world. That is, if I have any philosophy worth calling a worldview ... "

Bunzō's monologue went on, but my brain ceased to register what he said because I too had launched into a soliloquy of my own. For some time now Bunzō and I had ceased to really converse with one another. Our conversations have been replaced by mutterings, mutual parts of a dialogue spoken in delirium, that take on the semblance of a normal exchange on the rare occasion when we hit upon the same subject. We are like two cogwheels—cogs meeting and wheels spinning relentlessly—but each propelling wheels in other directions.

"'Defect?' So what?" I said, challenging him.

"You say 'defect,' but I say the only way to deal with defects is to turn them into flowers. Arthur Symons—or somebody or other —once said: write so as to make flowers bloom on paper.

"Do you think the average yokel who's been licked into shape by a bunch of slobs and who is considered perfect by every pig in the sty can pull off a stunt like that? You think I'm impressed with the fellow who is faultless? Not I. What terrifies me is the man whose life is like a huge, black hole, but who makes flowers bloom out of the void in himself.

"When I write . . . no, let's not talk about me . . . although I must confess there is a curious parallel between the way I have allowed myself to get involved with writing about a glamorless old hag like Christine de Pizan and the curious asceticism you practice in using cheap booze to whittle away at the source of your physical health. There's a resemblance, all right, but that's about as far as it goes. The circumstances behind your kind of asceticism and mine appear to be quite different in nature.

"Don't get me wrong. I'm not promoting any of the esoteric nonsense—'the tradition outside the teachings'—that the religious talk about. That's not for me. What I want to do is set the world on its head by taking the mumbo-jumbo of the conundrums— 'Difficult and Easy as Obverse and Reverse,' 'The Vision of the Washed Few and the Illusions of the Great Unwashed'—and put them into words that people can understand.

"Because, I tell you, we shall never see the promised Buddhaland here on earth unless we are prepared to stand the world on end and upset the normal order of things. If there is any hope of our protecting ourselves in these latter days of the Buddha's law, it will take far more than a conventional mandala with Buddha seated in the middle, calmly catching forty winks.

"O happy Buddha, I beseech you: You must be among the very first to drive yourself mad! My Samantabhadra is already out in the universe, doing his whirling dance in the sky. Shih-te stands in the midst of a cloud of dust wielding his broom and brushing up a storm. Send for Han-shan. Doubtless he's in a bar somewhere, dead drunk. Yet, I ask you, isn't this spectacle exactly the right iconography for illuminating my version of the miraculous life of the bodhisattva Samantabhadra?"

"*The Life of the Bodhisattva? A Chronicle of the Works of Samantabhadra?*" Bunzō broke into my monologue, skeptically repeating my words as though he were testing them for the title of a book.

"How could you possibly be proud of yourself? Think how silly you look, kneeling at your desk and listening to your pen scratch away at the composition of a dirty old mandala. You think that'll qualify you to say you've seen it all, that you are now enlightened about everything? It's only by dropping dead like me that a man becomes a bodhisattva. So where will that leave you when I die, and laughing a high laugh, I hop on a cloud and wing my way off to the heavens? Ha! That'll teach you!"

"You can be any old bodhisattva you like, but let me straighten you out about one thing: if you think the only place Samantabhadra resides is above the clouds, in some sort of imperial palace in the sky, you're dead wrong, and, what's more, you're looking in the wrong direction. I can't make myself any clearer on this point: it is because my bodhisattva manifests himself here on earth that he is a true bodhisattva."

"No, let me straighten you out. Your so-called wisdom is frivolous and impudent crap."

"What you mean is, instead of being impertinent, I'd be better off to go out and drop dead. Well, drop dead yourself. If you want to turn into a buzzard and fly away, that's fine with me."

"Nothing would make you happier, I'm sure. But you're crazy if you think I'll give you the satisfaction of seeing the sweet smile of my dying face. If there's any dropping dead to be done, I'll do it on my own. Hell, no. You drop dead first, you ass."

Bunzō leapt from the bed, and putting his hands round my neck, tried to strangle me. "*You* drop dead," he shouted, applying more and more pressure.

My neck seemed wrapped in cotton. I felt nothing. When I seized his wrists and pulled them away, his brawny arms flew back looking white and forlorn in the air as freshly pulled teeth. I realized that, no matter how much strength Bunzō might have once possessed, there no longer existed any task to which he might indenture his hands, and by putting them to work, get a grip on life again. I blanched, my being iced to the core.

"What's happened, Bun? Hey, pull yourself together," I said, shaking his shoulders.

His body, which had collapsed against mine, suddenly straightened upright, but his eyes stared vacantly ahead, seeing nothing. He continued to let his lips move, delivering their senseless monologue.

Presently I heard a car stop at the end of the alley. The sound of footfalls at the backdoor signaled Yasuko's return. Bunzō, still reeling, excused himself for the night, and collapsing on the bed, pulled the quilt up to his chin.

This quilted robe of his, with sleeves into which he can slip his arms, speaks more than anything else of what Bunzō's life has become in the last few years. On warm nights such as tonight it serves as his blanket, and during the cold months of the year he wears it about the room as a padded gown. Since it is a rarity for him to go out, he spends most of the day in bed; and given the position of his bed in relation to the window, the sunlight pouring into the room falls directly on the left shoulder. This has caused the part of the robe exposed to the sun to fade to the point that the original design is no longer visible, while the right shoulder retains its dark, variegated pattern. Even Bunzō remarked about the contrast, joking about it in a cryptic way.

"You know, people think I'm lazy, and that I took the easy way out, spending my life basking in the sunlight, warming my shell like a turtle. But nobody gives me credit for the considerable trouble I've expended in getting the moss to grow on the other half of the robe."

What, pray tell, did this dangerous game mean? What was the point of Bunzō's lethal sunbathing? Although the brutal heat of the sun and the whimsy of the changing seasons had eaten away at its fabric, the robe had become a living thing. Wrapping itself about him, its sleeves clutching his resistant frame more and more tenaciously, it was like a family of maggots that had set up house in his flesh. It warmed him and kept him company, but it would bide its time and watch for the unguarded moment when it could establish its lockhold and bring him to the ground.

—Ah, ah, a stick of incense burns slowly, the length of its ash like the sand in an hourglass, as it measures out in a thin column of smoke the remaining hours and minutes of this wrestling match. But to what heaven has its scent been offered? To what god was this contest given as the flower of his festival day? What remained before my eyes as I looked at Bunzō was the bluish black profile of his face, a face that, as it withered away, became a charred branch, and crackling, a dying ember.

I decided to let him sleep, but as I was about to slip from the room, I heard him say:

"I found out about Yukari."

"What?!"

"Or maybe I should say the police found out. But my contact tells me she had already gotten away by the time they went to arrest her."

"What happened after that?"

"I don't know. An investigation is still in progress at police headquarters. At any rate, I thought I'd try to contact her. She is my sister, after all. I gave out this address."

"To whom?"

"A fellow I know who's connected with the political underground. I left word with him. He'll probably let her know about me."

"But how in the world are you going to be able to see her? When? Where?"

Without thinking, I had pressed too many questions on him at once. His eyes closed, Bunzō kept muttering something as though he were delirious with fever. He fell into a deep sleep, his breath drawn in low, even measures so peaceful and inaudible as to be disconcerting, but I had no choice save to leave him. I returned to my room discouraged and flopped on the floor.

Yet I could not sleep because an image of Yukari continued to float before my eyes. The vision of her, of when I had seen her last as a young girl, raced about my mind and haunted me with frightful persistence.

Why was it, I wondered, that the thought of O-tsuna from whom I had parted only hours before, and the memory of the inglorious act we had shared, now seemed to have quite fled my mind. She was like the illusion Bunzō described, the property of an unknown world that existed on the other side of a thick wall of mist. Still more perplexing, why did I resist the idea of trying to remember her, and instead, by coolly setting her aside, chose to make her seem unreal?

CHAPTER SEVEN

THE NEXT day I was fully resigned to being harassed by Yasuko, for how could anyone as garrulous as she not deliver a report detailing all that had occurred in her interview with Sakagami Seiken? She was restless and flitted about the house, but contrary to my expectations, her manner suggested a desire not to talk with me and to avoid the subject of Seiken altogether. I took this as a stroke of good fortune, and since Bunzō—who woke often in the course of a night—typically slept through the day, I was able to turn to my desk and think of getting to work.

But as I picked up my pen and congratulated myself that— "today at last!"—I had an uncommon opportunity to settle down and collect my thoughts, I found I could not muster the slightest enthusiasm for my work. As a general rule, the inspiration to write derives not from anything anterior to the act of writing but from the act itself. Though I reminded myself of this truism, it was equally apparent I was about to accomplish nothing. If one cannot write, one cannot. It is as simple as that, but when I was at a loss to know what to do with myself—"What now?" I thought—I made two unexpected discoveries about myself.

The first relates to a habit of mine. Although I experience great enthusiasm at writing the parts of a story that interest me, I tend to set aside the ones I do not enjoy, and to make matters worse, not to return to them. While such an approach may be acceptable in recording a series of random impressions, in the case of a biography it has the effect of leaving gaps here and there, giving the manuscript an overall spotty quality. As I reread my life of Christine de

Pizan, I could see what a jumble it was—scattered passages but not much in the way of continuity.

The second discovery has to do with the nature of my continuing attachment to the world. The image of Yukari that I have secreted within my breast and that floats before my eyes from time to time has always been a vision in and of itself pure and unsullied. Yukari stands high above, and I, far below, catch an occasional glimpse of her through rifts in the pristine clouds. Yet I would be less than candid to suggest that there have never been wayward fantasies or that it has never been necessary to drive them from my mind in order to protect the sanctity of this vision.

After last night's inglorious act, and having plummeted as far as I could in the direction of sheer wantonness, my mind had suddenly cleared. Nary a murky thought remained, neither cloud to cast a shadow nor mist to dim the light, so apparent was the true object of my desire. To be able at last to devote myself singlemindedly to the adoration of an innocent maiden was to experience an emotion not unlike that of opening one's heart to a new and vast horizon, and feeling reassured, I saw no need to remonstrate with myself over the matter of O-tsuna. Growing expansive, I became convinced that, should I apply pen to paper and should the pen move of its own accord, surely it would be with a lightness bordering on the poetic.

Yet, cursed fate, by giving myself to these silly discoveries, my pen ceased to function at all. There was nothing for it but to end my day's labors as early as possible. I stretched out on the tatami, unable to resist a congenital tendency to laziness, and randomly turning the pages of a dictionary of poetic terms for seasonal and special occasions that happened to be close at hand, I came upon an entry for early summer: "Verdure or green leaves." As I repeated the words—"green leaves, green leaves"—to myself, they began to take shape in the form of the seventeen syllables of a haiku. Soon this trifling sport designed to while away the time ran to some twenty or thirty forgettable verses that formed in my mind and then vanished like bubbles rising to the surface of a pond.

By now it was late afternoon. Bunzō rose toward dusk, and inevitably the hour for drinking was at hand. There would, of course, be no resisting his entreaties, and so it was writ that this day, like so many others, would end in idleness.

Soon it was midnight. The day was about to come to a close without bearing fruit and with nothing to record, except that toward evening there had been a letter from Jinsaku and a visit from Hikosuke.

Jinsaku's letter had been mailed the previous night. After several sarcastic remarks about my failure to appear at the bar in Shinjuku, he announced the completion of his modern adaptation of the Nō drama *Semimaru—The Legend of the Blind Musician of Ausaka*. The letter went on to say that as he had been working on the manuscript for quite some time, he wished to show it to me and to hear my criticisms. Would I be so kind as to call at his house in Atagoshita the next day?

Concerning the matter of Jinsaku's adaptations for the Nō theater, the story is roughly as follows:

IT COMES as no surprise to find that people behave differently at home and away. We know, moreover, this hypocrisy is often a simple matter of expediency. But not so in the case of Terao Jinsaku. Indeed even a long-standing acquaintance like myself is unable to divine which of his two faces is the true indicator of his single layer of skin. For so untheatrical and uninspired is Jinsaku, his looks lacking in knowing wink or revealing gag, that both facades appear to be the indiscriminate and legitimate expression of his innermost feelings. Who is the real Jinsaku? The man at a bar or elsewhere, the bouyant, lighthearted chap who tends to become intoxicated with himself and the sound of his voice? Or the Jinsaku at home who hardly speaks to a soul, certainly not to his wife Hisako? Apart from the lessons he gives to the handful of students who come to his house for instruction in chanting texts, he spends his time seated taciturnly at his desk. He is at work, feverishly writing what he refers to as "new works" for the Nō theater.

Whatever his true facade, clearly Jinsaku has his opinions concerning the Nō. Namely, that the dramas performed today are, for the most part, fairly exact replicas of those performed by Zeami and other early practitioners. But, even though the Nō is currently popular, to continue in this fashion is to court the danger at some later point in time that the theater will be largely abandoned and the art relegated to a status not unlike that of the court music preserved by the Imperial Household Ministry. In order to insure the perpetuation of his craft, Jinsaku conceived the idea of creating new dramas—adaptations—that would be more in keeping with the times.

His view is the antithesis of my own. When we speak of a perfected art like the Nō, we recognize that, except for extinction, it has exhausted any further potential for development. At the same time, as a truly consummate form, it is open to multiple levels of interpretation. The spirituality that lies at its heart continues to manifest itself in many ways—the general and the particular, the highbrow or the low—but it is not something that can be copied. Thus, not only are all contemporary inventions doomed to reveal themselves as hopelessly inadequate, but also we need only examine, as actual examples, the case of the "new works" created for the Nō in the Edo period. Of them, *Kiku jidō—The Chrysanthemum Page of the Chou* alone has survived into the modern repertoire. In more recent times, masters of modern Japanese literature such as Takahama Kyoshi and Yamazaki Gakudō have tried their hand at the genre and produced two or three passable works. They are, nonetheless, the triflings of dilletantes.

When we examine the historical record, we find that creating new works for the Nō is a waste of effort. Furthermore, since Jinsaku writes from the stance of a performer rather than a playwright, I have warned him repeatedly that there is considerable risk his peers will view his efforts as the tamperings of an actor-heretic rather than as the work of a contemporary composer in the medium. I have stuck to this line of argument, refraining at all times from bluntly stating my opinions that neither is the Nō capable of producing the burst of flame required of a modern art because it is so staid a genre, nor are Jinsaku's talents sufficient to the task since he lacks the requisite literary background.

Yet Jinsaku has been heedless as a deaf-mute, so intent is he on this business, and so crabbed is his nature, he has clung all the more stubbornly to his monstrous notion of the "new Nō." He is almost beside himself with excitement when he reads to me passages from his completed pieces, making pronouncements as to how this dance will be choreographed or what cries and shouts are to interpolated into the incidental music. I know whatever I say to the contrary will be rendered meaningless, and having no desire to point out step by step how paltry his versions are in comparison with the originals they no longer resemble, I have let him carry on, interjecting—"hm, hm"—only the most innocuous sounds of consent.

But then there is the matter of his most problematic revision, the one based on the drama *Semimaru*. Because this drama includes, both in its dramatis personae and its dialogue, a number of references to the imperial family and points that may be construed as lèse majesté, the Kanze school has hesitated to present it for a number of years. More recently, officialdom has called for its prohibition. As Jinsaku despaired of ever seeing the work performed again and simultaneously lamented the disappearance of a classic from the repertoire, he decided to bring it back to the stage in a new, revised version that excludes the offensive passages. Jinsaku's motivations notwithstanding, I have no interest in his campaign, and I had succeeded in ignoring it until tonight when I sat holding his letter in my right hand. The thrust of the letter is he will give me no peace. I am about to be bothered once more with the *Semimaru* revisions.

Now, let me say that Hikosuke's visit was of no particular importance. It took place during Yasuko's absence—she had gone off some place or other—and at the hour in the evening when Bunzō and I had settled down to some serious drinking. We heard a voice at the front door, and peering down the stairs, we saw Hikosuke standing in the doorway with the hem of his striped kimono tucked up into his obi. He looked rather sheepish as he stood there asking to come in.

"What is it? Why don't you come on up?"

He climbed the stairs, sat down, and leaning against the wall, let his legs and feet, dirty with the dust of the street, sprawl across the tatami. With a handkerchief he wiped at the sweat that formed in big drops on his brow.

"Phew! I'm exhausted."

Although he accepted a drink quite readily, he only held it in his hand. Instead he continued to shift and fidget in his seat, his eyes seemingly drawn to the pile of small change on the edge of my desk, a few coins left from buying cigarettes.

"What's up?"

"Nothing. I just walked all the way here."

"From where?"

"Oh, on my way back from some place else. I had to crop tails."

"What's that?!"

"Somebody's terrier had a litter of pups. They asked me to come by, so I went to crop the tails. After calling on them ..."

Given the way Hikosuke lowered his voice to a barely audible level, there was not much point in asking him where he had been.

"You're sure you haven't run out of carfare? I've got that much, if it's what you need. There, take it."

Hikosuke seized the pile of loose change and stuffed it into his kimono sleeve with such speed that one would have thought he had vacuumed it up.

"Thanks so much. Er, that's one reason why I stopped by. You can't get on the train if you're short a sen, you know. There's nothing like small change!"

His voice took on a renewed liveliness, and emptying his glass in a single, deep draught, he grabbed the liquor bottle and liberally poured himself another round. He bolted down one of the dried, grilled fish set out as appetizers.

"Thanks for this too," he said, smacking his lips as was his habit and talking as he chewed.

Bunzō stared sullenly at Hikosuke, but suddenly he turned in my direction, and looking as though he were about to snap at me, launched into a fiery tirade.

"Valéry once said something to the effect that a work of literature is nothing more than a piecing together of an author's unending, but interrupted, efforts. While I couldn't agree with him more, how can anybody make such an outrageous statement? You mean to tell me all a writer has to do is crank out a work like *Monsieur Teste* and after that everyone will accept what he has to say? That all you have to do is something vaguely resembling work and then you can say anything you damn well please?"

"Here we go again," interjected Hikosuke sarcastically. "Arguing for argument's sake." Although he looked as though he wanted to join in, he was soon squeezed out by the torrent of words that Bunzō and I, paying him no heed, began to unleash upon each other. He drank the last few sips from his glass, and unable to bear sitting idly by, stood up and seemingly vanished into thin air.

What should I have written down, what entry should I have made, if for the sake of conjecture, we pretend that I kept a diary by my side and noted the daily events of my life? Moreover, because today was no exception but came at the end of a long chain of such days, I wonder what I might have recorded on those occasions as well. I have only my monologues, but no one is more bored with their repetition than I.

As I lay in bed staring at the ceiling, I happened to recall a passage I had read in one of Tolstoy's diaries: "Given my present situation, the best thing is to do nothing and to say nothing, isn't it? It is essential not to disturb anything, just as it is necessary for me to understand fully that I require nothing. This is what I clearly understood today."

Had I written this passage, no doubt it would read: "Given my present situation, in which I do not know what this thing is I call 'myself', I have nothing to do. Lacking anything to do, I chatter aimlessly. I have lost the key to the destruction of the predicament I find myself in, and as a result, I am like a person who has wandered off into the clouds. I now realize I have never truly understood what was essential, or nonessential. That's the problem. Moreover, this is not something I realized only today. I have understood it for some time, but what is the worth of saying, simply, '*I understand*'?"

The meaning of "to understand" ought never be construed to refer to some sort of vapid comprehension, and I would be humiliated to find myself having recorded any questionable remarks like the above. That is why I have chosen not to write, and I resort to simply chattering away. Even this solution runs contrary to my wishes, but I keep talking, and so long as I manage to do so, I tell myself I have not gone completely to rot. Prattling is my last resort.

But there is one phrase that shall not cross my lips. No matter how confused I may become, I hope never to be accused of having said the "I-know-nothing," the "I-understand-nothing," that is considered the smart thing to say in certain quarters. For what could be more frivolous and irresponsible than the fellow who, having delivered himself of such a line, sits back sulking, resting on the laurels of his proclaimed ignorance? How much better to bite off one's tongue, and, silencing oneself, refrain from the use of words altogether.

Since my tongue continues to function, however sluggishly, let me take this opportunity to be completely frank and admit there have been moments late at night when I have thought I would be better off not living at all. I have kicked back the covers and leapt from my bed to shout, "I shall die!" Bunzō, who has heard me cry out like this before, has latter jokingly asked, "Not dead yet?"

I know I run the risk of being thought a fool, but perhaps the reason I am alive today lies in the very nature of my cry. It is as though the vitality of the words "To die!" breathes new life into me.

In fact, when I sit silently contemplating death and when the darkness before me seems unfathomably deep, in the moment I lift my voice and raise my troubled cry, flowers fall from heaven and the earth is filled with incense. It is the fragrance of the transcendently beautiful bodhisattva Samantabhadra who rides forth mounted upon his white elephant. In that instant, I know *words* are my true bodhisattva. *Words* are my Samantabhadra.

CHAPTER EIGHT

IT WAS nearly noon when I awoke the next day. Although I am seldom an early riser, I find there is nothing more miraculous than the experience of waking in the morning. As I lay in bed, massaging my hands and feet in the warm light of the sun, I could not help marveling at the way they had come back to life. Here was this body of mine, and it was still alive. I examined myself as I would some small organism I had picked up and held tightly between my fingertips.

As I smoked several cigarettes, taking long, leisurely draws, I let my mind drift back to the shadowy realm of sleep from which it had just emerged, my thoughts caressing longingly the pale, gossamer curtain that separates dreams from reality.

The hour of waking is for me the most lustrous of the twenty-four. In a recounting of the mythical origins of the sun, for example, what fascinates me is not the celestial body itself but rather the twilight of sunrise and sunset, the interregna of Dawn and Dusk who rule its coming and going. By immersing myself in the interplay of light and dark, by allowing myself to be enveloped by the nebulous consciousness of a person hovering between life and death, I have come to feel I am able to participate in the dark secrets of the soul.

I have adopted this notion, and as a result it will be difficult to persuade me that what the practitioner of Zen calls the "clairvoyant eye" is anything so simplistic as to see through to the other side of reality on a day when the firmament is crowned by a crisp, blue sky. To the contrary, it is the stroke of genius, the flash of insight, that knows the fragrances not of this world are to be found by wandering off in the mists . . . and by using one's nose to sniff them out. Or at least that is the conclusion I have come to.

Doubtless the Buddhist will not share my lugubrious view. Because for him awakening exists as a possibility for all human beings, it is a light at the far end of the Way, and he is saved from the boundless gloom that is so much a part of my world. For him, the Way is posted with a signboard closing it to the traffic of anything depressing or gray.

But what do I care about smart-assed contrivances like awakening or enlightenment? They are the product of small-minded men, a device thought up to make them look clever. As far as I am concerned one can take the entire monastic routine—all those endless questions of whether to take to the hills or go down to the sea, the whole show of how to bestir oneself and renounce the world— and leave it to the good ole boys of the Buddhist faith. I want no part of it. Even the labor of lifting the tip of one finger in the manner of Master T'ien-lung is too much of an effort for me. I prefer to spend my days lolling about the back alleys of this dirty city, getting covered in its dust yet whistling away at the breeze without so much as a single care. How nice it would be! Better still, if I might have my wish fulfilled—my long-standing prayer answered—I should see myself transformed into the spirit of *prajñâ*. Translating wisdom into action, my brand of religious zeal would assume the form most natural and inevitable for me, namely, total inactivity!

Could I but maintain this morning's indolence for a day, or even two or three, what an incredible feat of magic, what a miracle of Taoist intercourse, it would be! I might even flatter myself into thinking I had become a true master of the way.

Yet my present state of ataraxia was destined to last only as long as it took several cigarettes to go up in smoke, and while the ephemerality of anything, even a cigarette, is the sort of topic likely to set me prattling, going on and on like a shrewish wife admonishing her husband in a curtain lecture, this morning there will be no time for it, no such leisure having been granted. Before I could achieve the perfect equanimity of finishing my last cigarette, there was, alas, a rattling sound at the shōji and into my room marched Yasuko, bursting the bubble of my pleasure without the least compunction.

"Are you awake?" she inquired, asking the obvious and planting herself by my pillow. I could guess from her demeanor that she was about to unburden herself.

As a general rule, self-centered people do not hold with great ambition. It is typical of them to spend their days pursuing hither and yon this little device or that small fancy. But let them stumble upon some singular plan, a one-way street far from their usual paths, and they become like something bewitched, the insistent look of "I-must-have-this" writ large on their faces, their physiognomies revealing telltale signs of a fox possession.

Because Yasuko's expression was fixed, her eyes set unflinchingly on a goal seen only by herself, she did not notice how I sat bolt upright in bed, the hairs on my flesh bristling at the sight of this middle-aged woman who, as she inched on her knees closer to my pillow, looked more and more like an expectant mother, the small lines and wrinkles round the edge of her nose turning a pale blue. Her voice shook so much she could hardly finish the sentence she had started.

"That, that Mr. Sakagami, what sort of man is he . . . ?"

"What sort?"

"To tell the truth, I went to see him again yesterday. About the scrap metal."

"Well then, I don't see why you need to ask me about him."

"No, I know it's rude to ask, but what can you tell me about his standard of living, his home life . . . his wife . . . his children?"

Despite my many years of association with Seiken, I had never paid the least bit of attention to such matters. All in all, I am not interested in the personal affairs of others. Yet Yasuko had succeeded in arousing my curiosity. Not that I desired to know more about Seiken. No, what fascinated me was the discovery I was to make about her.

Heretofore, I had decided that people like Yasuko drew no distinction between the world of the living and the realm of dead. They lived as though the two were one and the same, letting their hair turn to snakes, their bodies become infested with lice, their black blood dripping, as it oozed from their pores, into the great sea of mud that lies at the bottom of hell. To their way of thinking, there was no such thing as a crack in the hard surface of reality, nothing so unworldly and errant as a dream or a vision that might sneak its way in. Yet what did I perceive in the stare of this woman who trained her eyes on me, her gaze fixed as though frozen in place, but the face of a dreamer? Now, what could Yasuko's dream be?

Since she and her ilk possess no other abode but the bottomless pit of this world, the dream they dream is but a clutching at straws, of seeing the dust that dances about their heads as the flower of their lives. Not for them the enormous lust for wealth as in the case of I-tun of the ancient land of Lu, nor the insatiable thirst for power as in the case of Empress Wu of the T'ang dynasty.

No, Yasuko's dream was nothing of the sort. Rather than a grand ideal that shook the soul to the core with its greed and ambition, it was a short-term affair, an instant intrigue that extended no further than the end of her nose and that asked no more of her than to dig in her fingernails and cling tenaciously to the reckoning of how to convert ten yen into a hundred, or a hundred into a thousand. If all proceeded apace, so much the better. But let the distance between the the the tip of her nose and the achievement of her goal measure more than an inch, then it gaped before her like an impassable abyss. Rather than struggle to find the means to cross it, she would as soon cast her dream aside, like so much cheap goods, the unwanted remnant of an ideal.

Indeed Yasuko had never done a thing so charming as to press her hands together and bow her head in supplication before either the gods or the Buddha, and she had gone on record as saying, "Why, superstitions are silly." But of late the drawing of a fortune or the lispings of a streetcorner fortune-teller had become sufficient cause to not only set her heart apatter but also make her hands fly across the beads of her abacus. Who knows what diviner's prophesy had brought on this latest attack of monomania? Still, I could not help being moved at the thought that even Yasuko could embrace the romance of life.

—Ah, ah, though the autumn leaves may fall from their branches, the seed of the tree will not perish!

And yet it was premature of me to call romantic anything associated with Kuzuhara Yasuko, the sheer weight of her derrière being force enough to break down the bar to any door standing between her and the fulfillment of her dreams. Unable to contain myself as she pressed still closer, I gave vent to the anger rising in my throat.

"What is the point of asking me? Yes, it's true I know a little bit about whatever it is you want to know, but damn it, I'm not interested in this nonsense. It really makes me angry to think I know anything at all. So, why ask me?"

My anger had no effect. Yasuko looked at me as intently as before and began to repeat: "What is his standard of living ... his home life ... his ... " It was a litany offered to who-knows-what god by a witch of the swamp pursuing the will-o'-the-wisp. To follow the line of her vision was to run headlong into a solid wall, one that, albeit gray and peeling, stood high and formidable. And though the sun shone through the window and made my room feel warm and bright, I could not help gnashing my teeth at the gloom I perceived as filling every corner. Certainly no one could have hoped to detect in such a place a whiff of the sandalwood fragrance of a bodhisattva.

Realizing I was unwilling to entertain her questions, she grumbled, "This is terrible. You're no help at all." As she stood up and turned to go, she snapped her kimono sleeve briskly and let it slap me across the face.

Something leadish gray, the color of cat fur, hung in the air after she had left the room, and like the morning that had been so cruelly spoiled, it seemed to condense into an asphyxiating gas. Abandoning both my indolent fantasies and my unfinished manuscript, I leapt out of bed and charged down the stairs. I rushed from the house, not even casting a sidelong glance at the tray on which Yasuko had set out breakfast.

Now where?

In no time I had walked as far as the main thoroughfare in Ueno, where I entered a coffee shop and sat down. But the waitress was too countryfied, the tea too lukewarm, the voice emanating from the record player too shrill. In short, everything was designed to nurture the seeds of my discontent and send me flying into a rage. For me to fuss over such trivia is evidence of an illogical mind, and ample reason for me to be ashamed of myself, but once I throw a tantrum, I hardly know what I am doing. Slapping down the money I owed, I stalked out of the shop only to have a taxi brush perilously close by my side.

"Watch out!" shouted the driver.

That I was fool enough to angrily shout back, "Hey you ... " might have been forgivable, but I insisted on flagging him down, and as I was about to say: "No, buster, it's you who ought to watch it," the words that issued from my lips were altogether different from what I expected.

"Take me to Atagoshita."

Had Jinsaku's letter of the previous night lurked in the back of my mind and had its unconscious effect? I told myself that to become involved in this business of assisting him with his "new Nō" would only fuel the fires of my discontent, but I sank into the seat of the taxi feeling stupefied by my own behavior. Dolt that I was, I could not save myself. The taxi accelerated and headed off to Atagoshita.

The House of the Roan Steed, the antique store owned by Jinsaku's father, was located on a back street, but it was identified easily by its shingle, the distinguished name of the shop carved into the wood of the signboard in the style of the Ming dynasty calligrapher Wen Cheng-ming. To the rear, at the end of a walk bordered by stones and bamboo, was the Terao residence.

As I stood at the doorway, I could overhear the chanting of a passage from the Nō play, *Senju*. Jinsaku was in the midst of giving a lesson. "*'though at the distant end of the east, how deep do our affections run. Though remote from the refined life of the capital, the distance in no way diminishes our compassion. We too are no less moved to tears by the blossoms in spring, the maples in autumn . . .'*"

A maid came to the door, but instead of conducting me to the family room, to which as a close friend I was usually taken, I was led to Hisako's bedchamber. Even as I stood in the entryway I had detected a stuffy, medicinal smell in the air, and fearing Hisako's illness had taken a turn for the worse, I soon found myself moving as quietly as possible, silently treading the corridor that gave access to her room at the far end of the house. Hisako was in bed, stretched out on her back.

"Come in," she said, barely able to lift her head and speaking in a frail voice.

"Hisako, what's happened to you? Have you let your condition get worse?"

"This time I'm going to die."

"No, you can't mean that."

"Even if I didn't, this is probably the last time you'll see me as a member of this household."

Although Hisako seemed unable to go on, her face flushed, and her color improved a bit. Perhaps the sight of a friend in whom she could confide had brought a release of tension. It allowed her to relax and unleash all at once the anger she had bitten back and kept inside. There was even a look of joy on her face, as though she had stepped outside and been invigorated by a breath of fresh air. But for her to say such things, to speak of death, or to intimate divorce, indicated the depth of her mental strain. I was at a loss to know how to assuage her and quickly looked away. My silence served only to make her more overwrought.

"I may as well die," she announced in a high-pitched, defiant tone, "since Jinsaku treats me as if I were dead. It'll be better for him that I go quickly."

She tried to pull herself up in bed, and I, not knowing what to do, suggested she had better rest.

"There's nothing to worry about, Hisako. I'm sure Jinsaku ..."

"No, he says he can't wait for me to die."

"That's nonsense."

"No, it isn't. I'm certain that's what he thinks. He already has some young, modern thing picked out. Do you know her? The one he calls O-tsuna?"

"What?"

"She came here, you know. Yesterday, she did."

"Oh..?"

"What do you call it ... the way Chinese girls wear their hair? Anyway, she was here, her hair plaited into a long braid and wrapped around her head, putting on airs like an actress, dressed in bright colors and reeking of perfume. 'How do you do?' says she. Not only did she have the effrontery to introduce herself but also to tell me how indebted she was to Jinsaku for his kindness and generosity!"

"You actually met her?"

"Jinsaku wasn't home, so I.... Of course, I wasn't in any condition to deal with her given the way I feel. She's a well-dressed crook, that's what she is. She said there were reasons why she was entitled to receive money from Jinsaku."

"The nerve of that hussy."

No doubt it had been on account of O-tsuna's visit that Hisako had taken to her bed again, but what good would it be for me to spend time, even for Hisako's sake, nodding agreement to her every statement of righteous indignation? I know I am cold and indifferent when it comes to dealing with others' problems, but in this instance I could feel the anger welling inside of me, and I wanted to reach out and smack O-tsuna across the face. Yet I was preplexed by the source of my emotions. Had I become jealous of Jinsaku and the hold he exercised over O-tsuna?

How specious is this long-standing petition of mine, this eternal longing after Yukari. Though I may intone her name and try to call her to my side, she had become a lofty and unapproachable goddess, an apotheosis. On the one hand, the fragrance of her rose still had the power to intoxicate my soul, but on the other, ever since my ephemeral tryst with O-tsuna the reek of O-tsuna's body had clung to my skin and began to enter my blood. I was aghast at the thought of how this poison—a toxin almost too lethal to combat—had attacked me and taken me unaware. I was the source of my own downfall, but ironically, the more shocked I became at the prospect of being dragged about by O-tsuna, the greater fixity she assumed in my mind. Unable to hear a word more of what Hisako said, I pursued, first, the face of Yukari shrouded in mist and, then, the fiery bosom of O-tsuna as she burned in hell. It was a nightmare that came in alternating flashes.

Since I continued to stare absentmindedly at the ceiling, Hisako abandoned the subject of O-tsuna and turned the conversation in a different direction. Either the force of her complaint had been dulled by my attitude, or her tongue had been lightened by its exercising.

"You know, Mr. Tabe came to see me last night. He's back from his sister's place in Katsuura."

"Tabe? Here?"

"Yes, our pet terrier had pups a while back, so I asked him to crop the tails. I asked him to come quite some time ago."

"You don't mean to tell me Tabe comes here too?"

"Oh, I thought you knew. The first time he was with Mr. Tarui. You known, Mr. Tabe is such a nice person. He's so kind. In fact, both of them are, Mr. Tabe and Mr. Tarui. Just before New Year's they came over and helped with the annual cleaning."

"You don't say."

"Last night Mr. Tabe went to the trouble of coming over, but Jinsaku wasn't home. I felt bad because I couldn't receive him properly, but I had gone straight to bed after that O-tsuna woman was here. I did offer him a little sake before he left, though."

Considering the fact that Hikosuke had stopped by our place to pick up carfare, could it have been he had resisted the urge to ask

Hisako for money even though he was short on change? And that he had walked all the way from Atagoshita to Kurumazaka, scuffing along in his clogs? The story struck me as comical. But why hadn't he said something?

Truly, whether one speaks of Hikosuke or Moichi, they have no other god but the illusory figure called money. Should anyone appear on the scene vaguely resembling this deity, they will endow him on the spot with the power of the thunderbolt and install him on an unapproachable throne above the clouds. He need only lean back in his seat, and Hikosuke and Moichi will begin to bow and bob their heads although they have yet to receive his blessing or broach the all-important negotiations for money. Often in situations where they had a perfect right to expect remuneration, the words have stuck in their throats and they failed to ask for payment.

Moreover, each kept his little money god hidden away, and though each spoke ill of the other's parsimoniousness, when it came time to calculate debit and credit with each other, they were equally prepared to argue about the smallest sums, down to a sen or two.

I was about to lament that there was no predicting what this pair might do, when I was reminded of the unpredictability of my own well-being. Whatever image I had entertained about Yukari or O-tsuna had vanished, snuffed out by the eddies of dust slowly circulating in Hisako's stuffy, unventilated room. Fortunately, as I sought to stifle the cough that rose in my throat, the maid appeared to announce that the chanting lesson was over.

"Let me show you to the study on the second floor."

When I entered the room, Jinsaku received me formally, seated on his knees, the skirt of his kimono carefully folded about him. He bowed and then looked up at me, his expression drawn and pale.

"I have a serious favor to ask," he began solemnly.

"What's the meaning of all the formality? I'm resigned to helping you, if it's the *Semimaru* revisions you're worried about."

"No, this is more important. It's difficult to explain, but..."

"What is?"

"Actually, it has to do with O-tsuna. You know, the woman you met the other day?"

"Oh, the one Hisako said was here."

"So you've heard about it?"

"Yes, just now."

"That's why I'm in trouble. I never intended to hide the business about the apartment from you. I didn't think to tell you, that's all."

"Don't worry about it. So what's the favor you want to ask?

"Well, it's ..."

"If the woman comes all the way over here and forces her way in, it must have something to do with money."

"Well, yes, I mean ... in the first place, I have good reason to stop going to Moichi's apartment."

"Oh?"

"It's because O-tsuna ..., " Jinsaku pursed his lips, "appears to be involved with another man."

"Hm."

Surely word of our indiscretion could not have reached him this quickly. "What makes you say that?" I asked, drawing a deep breath.

"I don't have evidence, but it seems ... no, there's no doubt about it, I can tell."

"Do you have any idea who it is?"

"I know this sounds ridiculous ... in fact, it's so preposterous it doesn't make sense. It's ... Tarui."

"Moichi?" My surprise must have been obvious from the tone of my voice. "That can't be. Not Moichi. No, O-tsuna's not the type to get involved with him. She's in an altogether different category."

"That's what you'd expect people to say." Jinsaku's voice assumed a calm, confident tone. "At least at first. But initial impressions are just that—first impressions. It's when you say to yourself, 'Oh, no, he's not the type, it could never be him' that the person turns out to be a traitor."

"Wait a second. Am I going to have to listen to a lecture on this?"

"No. But it's true. I'm telling you the truth."

To any other ear the list of suspicions and charges that Jinsaku enumerated would have sounded like the babblings of a madman. The more he spoke, the more fire he seemed to breathe. His eyes became bloodshot, his jaw firmly set, his fists clenched. The veins throbbing at his temples made his receding hairline stand out all the more prominently.

While it was hard to believe Moichi could be involved with O-tsuna, the idea was unsettling, and like Jinsaku, I too began to get upset. My face turned red, my throat became dry, my voice, husky. An unseen specter had grabbed the two of us by the nape of the neck, and however much Jinsaku and I wiggled and squirmed— the firm, fragrant tatami suddenly becoming soggy and spongelike under our feet—we were hoisted into the air like a pair of rabbits that had been injected with the same lethal dose. Indeed, the more we thrashed about, each writhing with the pain of having been branded by O-tsuna, the more the bright afternoon seemed to vanish into a fathomless haze.

"The nerve of him, that bastard Moichi," I shouted, but my voice lacked conviction. Instead of an angry protest, it became a tiny whimper that echoed faintly about the room. I was angry, nonetheless, and I almost went so far as to unburden myself and share with Jinsaku the story of what had happened at O-tsuna's.

But when I considered the fact that Jinsaku and I were two strange birds, the latest issue of rara avises born on this barren island, a land too sterile to water and nourish the seeds of a taste for naked sentiment or directness of speech, I realized there was no point in telling him. Because of our upbringing, what we say to each other has a hollow ring. Words lose their meaning, and what is left is the empty shell of formality. Indeed, they become useful only to fumigate the air, to drive away insects or ward off the inauspicious, as when one puts a match to a bundle of pine needles and it bursts into puffs of acrid smoke.

"The nerve of him," said Jinsaku, his voice echoing my own. "That bastard. There's no doubt about it. He's the one who put O-tsuna up to coming here and asking for ten thousand yen."

"Ten thousand yen?"

"That's right. That's the amount O-tsuna tells me I have to produce. But I can see she hasn't concocted this scheme by herself. I'll bet Moichi is behind it. He's the one pulling the strings."

"You really think he's capable of it?"

"Of course he is. He kept you from knowing about the apartment, didn't he? That must have been part of his plan too, now that I think of it."

"What do you intend to do?"

"That's why I said I have a favor to ask."

"You don't think *I* can bargain Moichi into taking less, do you?"

"No, no. That's not it at all. It's not Moichi, or the money. It's none of that."

"Well, what is it?"

"It's O-tsuna. I don't want to lose her. Even if it costs ten, even twenty, thousand. I want her."

"But you're the one who's been trying to break things off, aren't you?"

"Until yesterday, yes. But this nonsense about Moichi makes me furious. When O-tsuna came here yesterday saying we had to break up, suddenly everything became crystal clear. I realized I couldn't go on without her. Even if she needs Moichi too. Even if it means I'm going to be swindled."

"I still don't see what I'm supposed to do. You're not making sense."

"I know it's crazy, but I can't keep from doing it. Even if it sounds absurd, you'll have to help me."

Each time Jinsaku repeated O-tsuna's name, I felt a stabbing pain. I could hardly manage to sit still. I wanted to jump up, but I bore it as best I could, clenching my fists so tightly that my fingernails bit into the palms of my hands. I knew at any moment I might spring at Jinsaku and try to strangle him.

Jinsaku too was shaking, unable to contain himself. Suddenly his hands flew across the table and seized a stack of handwritten papers neatly threaded together and bound into a small book. Written on the cover in large, block letters were the characters, "*Semimaru,* An Adaptation," and spitting out the words, "Take this, take this," he ripped it into shreds, stood up, and threw it against the wall. The scraps of paper flew into the air, momentarily suspended, before they fluttered about our heads, falling silently to the floor like bits of cloth. Meanwhile Jinsaku had collapsed in a heap. I did my utmost to control myself as I sat there staring at him. I strained to keep every limb and muscle in check, fearing any movement would set in motion the one and only act my hands were ready to commit, namely, to strangle him.

After a long, painful silence, Jinsaku managed to speak. His voice faltered and threatened to fade away.

"I know I'm going to die. Someone is going to kill me."

"What makes you say a thing like that?"

"Hisako is going to haunt me until I drop dead. She's the one, I'm certain."

He grabbed my hands and squeezed them tightly. "Please save me. I can't help myself."

"What are you talking about?"

"It's the truth."

Jinsaku brought his face so close to mine I could see every pore. He breathed heavily as he spoke.

"Do you believe in wraiths? Do you believe that living human beings can assume apparitional form?"

That Jinsaku should babble in this fashion was proof he was possessed, and no amount of common sense could cure so strange a patient. Similarly, to answer his question was to find myself caught in the same net, to share his fate as a miserable insect caught in the sticky threads of a spider's web. Moreover, to be trapped in this web was to sympathize with him, to understand the meaning of his cries, to respond to the secret code sweet to the ears of all disembodied souls who wander in the crepuscular light dividing life from death. Convinced that a wraith must be present in the room, I clutched at Jinsaku's hands just as he had clutched at mine.

"Is it true?"

"I know it is. You saw yourself the terrible state Hisako is in. Until now she has given her tacit consent whenever I've been involved with another woman, but this time things are different. She probably offered Moichi a drink, and you know him, one glass of sake and he tells everything. No doubt it was part of his plan to get her upset. And, wouldn't you know, along comes O-tsuna just when I knew Hisako had figured things out. Hisako's been carrying on ever since about how 'that O-tsuna woman' is going to 'devour' her. 'She wants to eat my dead flesh,' she keeps saying.

"But now Hisako has decided to take her revenge by devouring *me!* Oh yes, I'm sure of it. Last night when I came in late—and she was as cold as the ice pack on which she had propped her head—I asked what was wrong. She said, 'You're quite pleased with yourself, aren't you? But I'm going to be nice and die for you.' I told her not to say such things.

"Then she says: 'Even if I wanted to go on living, that woman won't allow it,' whereupon she told me how O-tsuna had called at the house. 'Why, she looked like she was about to celebrate some sort of sacred rite. I suspect she has already sucked my blood and is using it to paint her face. Look how my arms have withered away.'

" 'I want you to sleep with me tonight. We'll sleep together, I'll hold you in my arms. And if you're really good, I'll give you something special. I'll take these pale and purple lips of mine and press them all over your body. C'mon. Get into bed with me.

"'So you think you'll run away to your study, do you? What a coward! Do you think for a minute I'll let you go upstairs and sleep alone, dreaming of your O-tsuna? In the middle of the night you'll find I'm right by your side. You'll be as surprised as if someone dashed cold water on you. I'll be lying right next to you with my arm crooked about your neck.'

"Even as we sit here talking, Hisako knows what I'm saying. She's downstairs lying in bed and looking at us through the ceiling. Ah, those eyes!"

Stumbling to his feet, Jinsaku began pointing here and there at the sliding doors, shaking his finger. "Those eyes... there they are, there they are... no, over there."

As he stepped into the curtain of dust floating in the dim light of the window, he looked like a stick figure in a shadow play, the skeleton of its detachable limbs visible only through the opaque screen behind which it is manipulated.

"Jinsaku, get hold of yourself. Pull yourself together."

I tried to restrain him from behind, but as the sweat beaded on his nose and he sought to squeeze a final ounce of strength from his thin frame, I was sucked into the motion of his hands and feet. There we were, about to go dancing around the room together. But I made a last effort to hold my ground, and in that instant, he lost the will to resist. His body went limp, collapsing into my arms not unlike a piece of hard candy that suddenly cracks and melts in one's mouth. I, too, staggered and fell to my knees.

"What's the matter with you?" he chided. "Pull yourself together."

Jinsaku was on the floor, his back propped against my knees, his legs sprawled out underneath him. Except for the sound of our labored breathing that came in waves, the room was completely silent—not even the buzzing of a fly could be heard. Unwittingly I had become his accomplice, a part of a set of bells to be rung in tandem. But now that my partner had broken down, I had no choice but to listen to the sound of his groans which tolled woefully out of tune.

Mounted on the wall was a framed piece of calligraphy copied from the Chinese classic *Shih ching—The Book of Poems*. "Eternal as South Mountain," it read, and our spastic thrashing seemed ridiculously out of place in its presence. Indeed, for a moment I thought I heard it guffaw, however inaudibly, and have a good laugh at our expense.

Jinsaku appeared to have recovered at long last. "I'm going to be all right. Thank you, but I'm all right now."

He stood up, his face flushed, his body shuddering as though a seizure had past and he were shaking off the aftereffects. He straightened the folds of his kimono and sat down, looking much as he had when I entered the room.

"I'm terribly sorry," he said. "I never meant for you to see me this way."

Gradually his voice regained its composure.

"I can't keep this up. I've got to do something. Fortunately, Father isn't around. He and Mother left two days ago on a trip to Osaka and Kyoto—a little business combined with pleasure—so during their absence, I must.... Oh well, never mind. Let's have a drink. I realize I'm imposing on you, but if we could have time to discuss everything over a drink..."

Jinsaku was about to continue when the overcast lifted outside, and the sun poured through the window. Feeling like a fish that had swum at last into the light, I leapt at the thought of getting out of the stuffy room. I stood up, and though Jinsaku asked me to stay, I brushed his entreaties aside and headed out the door. I broke into a mad dash, not knowing how or where my legs would carry me. In time their pace slowed, but not until I was startled by the sound of passing streetcars did I come to my senses and realize I was standing at the main intersection at Toranomon. I looked up at the building and saw the gold letters on the windows that spelled out the name, *Political Debate*.

—Ah, ah, Sakagami Seiken. "And as to his standard of living, his homelife, his...." I could hear Yasuko's questions of earlier in the day ringing in my ears.

"Do you suppose...?"

In a flash of intuition, I considered for the first time the possibility that Seiken and Yasuko had struck up an affair, but no sooner had the thought been spun in my mind than its thin thread snapped, there being no room left in my brain to accomodate idle speculation.

Yes, enough of this. I should be thinking about Joan of Arc. It is imperative that I get back to my manuscript and write as much and as fast as I can! I had no other hope than to throw myself upon the infinite mercy of the bodhisattva Samantabhadra, hop in a taxi, and head for Kurumazaka. I tore down the alley to the house and was about to throw open the front door when it was pushed aside from within. Out stepped Bunzō.

"What's wrong? You drunk?" he asked.

"No, I am more than drunk."

"What have you been up to?"

"I haven't done a thing, but I'll be damned if everybody isn't conspiring to make my life miserable."

"Well, speaking of 'the floating world' and all its travails, you'd better come with me."

"Where?"

"Nippori. Moichi was here. O-kumi's dying."

"What...?"

"Ever since that trouble with the police, she hasn't been the same. Her condition has gotten worse, and the life seems to have gone out of her. They say she wants to eat ice cream once more before she dies. I thought I'd buy some and take it to her. How about coming along with me?"

"I'll come later, if I can. I've had more than my fill of the human race. I can't face going there right now."

"Sounds like a overdose of bad luck to me. Why don't you go upstairs, climb into bed, and try a little of our favorite medicine for forgetting the world? Maybe that'll do it. But, then again, maybe it won't. I can't tell anymore. Lately Saint Alcohol hasn't been able to work his miracles for me."

CHAPTER NINE

I MIGHT have wished to think of the foregoing as a faded photograph or a dated farce from the distant past, but judging from the play of sunlight on the windowpane, less than an hour had elapsed since I passed Bunzō at the door, rushed upstairs, and collapsed on the tatami. I was exhausted; and now that the fatigue had hit me full force, it was not for my pen, but the liquor bottle, that I reached. I set my teeth on the edge of my cup, and biting at the lip of the glass, I sipped the brew as though taking a bitter medicine.

Doubtless there is no better remedy, its bitterness a fitting antidote that rivals the unhappiness of my present state of mind. In which case, my tongue has become an impediment, hampering the effect the booze, interrupting its free flow to complain of the taste. And if my tongue is an encumbrance, how much more unworthy are these deliquent hands that will not hold a pen. They will be the first to be chopped off, for what need have I of their prosaic members? Crippled, blind, deaf—I shall become all of these things.

The ear was a noble and precious instrument, the petal of a flower, to George Sand in her ministrations to Chopin. But having been deprived of the elegant music of this world, its waltzes and its serenades, to say nothing of the ethereal harmonies, the esoteric music of the spheres; and having been tormented for no good purpose by the roar of the city, its noise like static on a radio, my ears have become pathways to hell, holes in my head opened by devils as they beat their tails going back and forth.

Thus, on account of the hushed voices I heard downstairs break into a loud spat, I emitted a mournful groan and clamped my hands to my head. What had commenced as a whispered conversation became a shouting match, and then a pitched battle, Yasuko's skirling voice rising still shriller and making the paper on the shōji rattle. As I had surmised, it was Tsuruta, the president of Famous Places of Japan, Ltd, who was the object of her recriminations.

"Why don't you keep voice down? Someone upstairs will hear you."

"Don't tell me what to do. This is my house. Yes, that's right. So long as you won't talk about money, it is. So keep your opinions to yourself. What's that? You're telling me I'm the one who's been avoiding you?"

"I never said that. You're putting words in my mouth."

"So what is it then? Yes, I'll admit it. I was out walking with him. Indeed I was. So what are you going to do about it? You say you have a witness and that you've investigated. Whoever heard of such nonsense? Bring that busybody of a witness to see me. I'll set him straight. I'll tell him to his face what I think."

"Then you were with him?"

"I told you. It had to do with the scrap metal. Of course, if you had a detective on the case, you'd know that much. His name is Sakagami. Of *Political Debate*. But if you think I'm going to tolerate your getting jealous over him taking me out for lunch, you have another thought coming."

"Did I say anything...?"

"You're jealous! Yes, you are. Why, the other day you were carrying on about my having two young men as lodgers."

"That's enough now."

"No, it isn't. I'm going to call them downstairs, and we can discuss it once and for all. You talk big, but what do you buy me? Look at this crock of a teapot. Here, take it, since you're so unhappy with me."

"Watch what you're doing. It'll break. What do you think you're doing, damn it?"

I felt like a drop of water on a hot skillet as I jumped up, and for the second time that day madly rushed out the front door. As I stood in the gusts swirling about the corner of the street, I wondered where to go. I have found that in the "burning house" of this world, human beings are a clamorous lot. For one such as myself who has lost sight of the ladder by which he might scale the heights of heaven and thereby escape the world, where can I go but the grave? Is my only choice to take up the company of the whispered tones of the dead?

Such was the sigh of despair that registered within me, and it began to take shape, albeit at first vague and indistinct, its pattern a muddied puddle that rippled and assumed the outline of O-kumi's pallid face. She looked like a stagnant cesspool, her soul escaping its putrid flesh like a gas seeping to the surface. For some reason I am inclined toward such images, to reach out and grasp at bubbles, or smoke as it smolders but does not yet burst into flame. Without so much as a second thought, I found my feet carrying me in the direction of Nippori.

Moichi was on the opposite side of the platform when I alighted from the train.

"How's the patient?"

"Not good. There'll be a wake by nightfall if her condition remains the same."

"Where are you off to?"

"I promised to go out with friends. One of the bosses at the office is celebrating the completion of his new house. I was invited."

"Better a party than a wake, huh?"

Moichi laughed nervously, but he looked thoroughly pleased with himself, his nose already twitching in time with the music. He looked as though he were about to break into the nasal twang of a popular ditty—just the sort of song one sang at a house warming. He hurried to board the departing train, his footfalls ringing on the concrete platform like the sound of a hammer driving nails into a coffin. I felt I was about to be pulled into a hole in the ground. The slithery tentacle of Death that hovered over O-kumi was now coiling itself about me.

Oh, the sight at the Tabes'! How shall I catalog the list of miseries? If it was not the shredded edges and worn surfaces of the tatami mats, frayed and looking brownish red in the twilight, then it was the gray film that covered the surface from the spilt sake and dirt tracked in by the puppies that no longer romped through the premises. It was on this worn and dirty floor that a single, soiled layer of bedding had been spread, and O-kumi lay asleep, looking chilled to the bone in the sunny, even steamy, room. As I knelt by her pillow, all words of comfort froze on my lips, and I felt my skin crawl. I found myself in the unpleasant position of having to watch a person die.

The wall that had once been decorated with Chinese plates was stripped bare, the plaster gouged and scratched; the bird cages, now empty, sat atop the shelves blackened with soot. There was not a stick of furniture left in the place, and the object that was stretched out before me scarcely qualified as human. "Nothing but skin and bones," may be a commonplace expression, but O-kumi's wasted flesh did indeed look like chaff winnowed from grain, her skin a tanned hide stretched tautly over each and every disintegrating bone. Her eyes were like the carved intricacies of an ivory netsuke, her parched, half-opened lids revealing dark pools of mucous within the sockets. Only the joints retained their obstinacy. From the ribs to the extremities, they protruded, each bone rasping as it turned in the desiccated hollows of a body to which the flow of blood has gone dry.

From what medieval collection, what scroll depicting the hideousness of death and disease, had this portrayal been derived, so bizarre and horrific was the sight of her? Though I dislike human suffering as much as anyone else and grit my teeth at the thought of having to see someone in pain, why had I been singled out to have thrust before my eyes this strange reproduction, the superimposition on O-kumi's face of the Buddhist depiction of the nine stages of the decomposition of the body? It was small comfort to know she was alive—a real human being in contrast to a mere painting—yet why, and worst of all, did the breath of life continue to reside in the cracks and marrow of her bones and persist with ruthless tenacity to cling to this world? By protracting her death, it made her seem all the more miserable.

The irrelevance of the bright summer kimono to its wearer, the pathetically twisted shape of her body as it appeared here and there from beneath the robe, the movements of the throat accompanying the short, wheezing gasps for air, the dull light that lay trapped in the shrunken pupils of the eyes—all spoke of the nether world, whose messenger was now darkly passing under the ridgepole of the house.

—Ah, ah, what terrible deed had preordained that, even as she lived, O-kumi should endure the punishment of having her body put on display, exposed like that of a common criminal, for all to see? And by what elemental, physical heaviness of her anatomy was the catalytic effect of death held in check and she not allowed to evaporate into thin air? I had no choice but to sit as erectly as possible, praying all the while that my bodhisattva Samantabhadra would cast upon us a single petal of his royal diadem and make sweet the bitter grasses of this earth. Would that he grant us even a droplet from his water bottle to sweeten our foul mortal breath.

Unable to tolerate the silence that ensued as Bunzō and I sat on either side of O-kumi biting our lips, Hikosuke began to lament.

"Look at her. She's lost, she's gone for good."

"Lower your voice, will you."

"What? Do you think she can hear me? She kept asking for ice cream, but she didn't even respond when Bunzō went to the trouble of buying some and bringing it to her. I held the spoon to her lips, but she wouldn't take it. It's not everyday a friend brings an expensive gift like ice cream. At least this time you'd think ... "

Even Hikosuke's glib tongue was checked by the ungiving silence against which his voice reverberated. His words were like an echo in an abyss. Who knows how much time passed in the space of those interminable minutes? O-kumi's life was measured out by the insistent ticking of an alarm clock.

Suddenly, as though possessed by who-knows-what force and moved by an unknown instinct, the body lying before us began with a great bending and creaking of its bones to sit up in bed. Along with the lewd glint that appeared in her grey, protruding eyes, O-kumi raised her voice and rent the silence with a ghoulish cry. Turning toward Hikosuke, she spread her arms and legs.

There are no words to describe what happened next, nor shall I venture a description. Who knows what law of human nature, what rationale of natural philosophy, can be applied to explain this unanticipated turn of events. But it was an indisputable fact that O-kumi—or the physical being known by that name and that now stood at the brink of death—turned to her husband, and in a most flagrant gesture, made a display of her desire to be possessed physically.

So arresting was the sight, we could scarcely believe what we saw. It was as if the normal functioning of the eye had been reversed; that secrets of several thousands of years of human history encoded within our bodies had been called up to the retina which then projected the bizarre cinematographic image into the visible world. The memory of a lost age, a time when apes roamed the forests of hoary antiquity, was forcefully transmitted to the physical object that was O-kumi, its uninhibited carnality taking control of her. Such madness, such scandal, is not of this world.

For me it was not a question of aesthetics, or even incredulity at O-kumi's behavior, but the dread, the fear of violating a primitive taboo, that overwhelmed me and made me flinch. To be sure, I was blinded momentarily by the sight of what I ought not to have seen, when O-kumi let her arms and legs wave about, and the black, naked parts of her anatomy appeared from under her dressing gown. I heard a thundercloud rumble and shake the house with its anger. I fled as fast as I could into the adjoining room, and slamming the sliding door behind me, groped for the wall and held my breath—only to find an equally petrified Bunzō standing beside me, the thick, bluish lenses of his glasses dancing on the bridge of his nose, as he shook with fear.

"What in the hell...? O-kumi, what do you think...?" Hikosuke's voice fluttered for a moment like a bird taking wing and changing direction. Then it turned into a painful moan.

"Oh, no. She's gone. Come quick. Come help me."

When we slid open the door, Hikosuke was bent over, breathing heavily. Locked in his arms was the half-naked corpse, its head thrown back, its disheveled hair sweeping the floor. From a corner of the sagging mouth ran a thin line of saliva, as milky and white as water in which rice is washed. It ran down behind an ear caked with dirt and left its stain on the unwashed cheek.

Bunzō and I busied ourselves, by rushing off to get the neighbor doctor, or the mortician, but our scurrying about was not dictated entirely by necessity. The house seemed to expel the living from its interior.

When we returned, we found Hikosuke standing barefoot by the well. He had stripped down to his drawers, and with a broom and bucket in hand, he stood there clicking his tongue as though contemplating what to do next.

"What are you doing?"

"I haven't been able to get a bit of cleaning done ever since O-kumi took to her bed. It's been bothering me no end because you know I'm not the type who can stand to see dirt around the house."

Despite his general lack of resourcefulness, Hikosuke was handy with tools. When it came to installing a shutter or a door, or packing up belongings, he would leap at the opportunity, undertaking the task with great pleasure. He was about to tackle cleaning the house with the same enthusiasm. But when we made our displeasure known at the inopportunity of his decision, the lip under his sober looking moustache seemed to lose its nerve and start to quiver.

"Where's O-kumi?"

"I left her like she was."

"Oh."

"I went ahead and put clothes back on her, but I thought I'd wait for the doctor before I did anything else. I've got water boiling."

"You're going to burn that lumber?"

"That's right," he said, laughing as though embarrassed. "They turned off the gas last month."

Hikosuke had a makeshift fireplace made from a pile of bricks that he had stacked beside the wall of the well, and by hanging a bucket over the fire he could cook a meal of boiled greens or noodles. He was stripping the broken garden fence of the last of its cypress-bark slats and throwing them on the flames. The bark began to spit white puffs of smoke, and the soot-covered water in the bucket started to boil. We stood there in a dumb silence. Rain clouds filled the evening sky. The dampness of the night breeze made our shirt collars stick to our skin, our necks wet with perspiration.

Finally the doctor arrived, and we entered the house. Hikosuke had returned O-kumi to her bed, covering the body with a quilt, and the face with a white cloth. He knelt beside her, his posture appropriately formal, while Bunzō and I sat down on the edge of the veranda. The doctor's manner was businesslike, and in no more time than it took for us to look away, he finished his examination, quietly slipped into his shoes, and started out the door. Outside it was getting dark.

An overhead light was turned on, and Bunzō and I installed ourselves, one on either side of the deceased, like two wooden statues, a pair of immovable objects. The coffin arrived late that night, but other than helping Hikosuke slide the body into the adjoining three mat room, we had nothing to do but sit and contemplate the endless wall of time that stood before us.

Meanwhile, Hikosuke gave the body its last bath. His breathing became labored, and each time he wrung out the towel, he repeated the phrase, "You poor thing, O-kumi. You poor, poor thing." But no sooner had we attributed the repetition of this plaintive litany to a final show of affection than he would chide the corpse for not assuming its proper position.

"No, no, that won't do. Don't stick out like that," he said, and taking the stiff, recalcitrant limb, he snapped the bone in two.

The popping sound, like that of the rain dripping drop by drop from the eaves, resounded louder and louder, drumming at the tympanum of my ear with mounting intensity as the night wore on. The hour grew late, and my mind became unpleasantly numb, boxed in, as though pressed between two boards, on account of the cheap liquor that the three of us sat drinking. Not only did the alcohol fail to have effect and let my thoughts take wing, to make matters worse I felt grounded to the spot as though I were a moth impaled on a pin. Bunzō and I were both caught in this unhappy business, and when I looked across at him leaning against a pillar, I saw the soft glow of the electric light falling across his shoulders. It seemed to smolder and envelop him in a cloud of poisonous yellow dust.

The only one enlivened by the alcohol was Hikosuke, and though from time to time he seemed to hesitate on account of O-kumi's presence in the adjoining room, still he went on and on.

"She really was a poor soul, when you think of it. Sold into geishahood as a girl, and after such an ordeal, what does she have to show for it? We're not even giving her much of a wake. Except for the one tenant from the house out front, no one else has come to express his last respects.

"Yes, sir. It was the morphine that did it. And then there were the stomach spasms. Of course, it all started with the mother. She's the one to blame. She's the one. But now they're both dead. I know I ought to take the ashes back to the country and bury them in the cemetery at the family temple, but given the financial straits I'm in, the old woman's are still up there on the cabinet shelf. It's terribly depressing to think I'll be putting another urn next to it tomorrow.

"On the other hand, this is a great weight off my mind. Now that O-kumi's gone, my brother will probably treat me better, but more than anything else, once O-kumi got hooked on morphine, there wasn't any way I could keep up with her. The long and the short of it is, I'm feeling relieved. Let's all drink to that. There's not much here, but help yourselves to what there is. Go ahead. Drink up. Drink."

As Hikosuke grew less coherent, his hands fumbled, and he spilled his glass on the table.

"I shouldn't have allowed myself to get this way."

He knew he had had enough, but it was nearly daybreak before, keeling over, he went down, one side of his bloated face hitting hard against the top of the table. Drops of liquor dripped from the hairs of his moustache, and he began to snore gently. Meanwhile, Bunzō and I had slumped over and were nodding off, looking very much as if we would rot away along with the old, tattered mats.

"Telegram. Telegram for Mr. Tabe."

Someone was rattling the front door, trying to rouse us. The sky was completely clear, and the sun already quite bright as we jumped up. It was a little after nine.

Hikosuke, who had gotten to the door first, was pacing back and forth barefoot on the dirt floor of the entryway. He clutched the telegram in his hand.

"What am I going to do? Now I'm really in a bind. What do you think I should do?"

"What's it say?"

"My sister's on her way to Tokyo."

"From Katsuura?"

"It says she'll be arriving at Ryōgoku Station at eleven this morning and wants me to meet the train. I bet it has something to do with the children. The young one has a bad leg. His old man had tuberculosis, and the germ must have settled in the kid's foot and deformed his ankle. My sister says she has to take him to the hospital and have a cast fitted to his leg. At least that's what she wrote in a letter a couple of days ago. This is something I must help her with."

Hikosuke appeared ready to head out the door.

"What about O-kumi?"

"That's what I meant when I said this was a mess. This is terrible."

While we were well aware of the servile attitude Hikosuke adopted toward his brother and sister, we felt irritated by this latest tizzy.

"What mess? The first order of business is to take O-kumi to the crematorium. Your sister will understand when you explain it to her. She'll be able to find her way around even if you can't get to the station to meet her."

"That's true, but ... "

"Look, it's nonsense, going over and over in your mind what you ought to do."

"Of course, I'm going to take care of O-kumi. First, I'll go to the crematorium, and after that, to the hospital. My sister..."

"What's happened to the mortician?" asked Bunzō. "The hearse ought to have been here by now. Maybe I'd better go see if I can hurry it along."

Hikosuke glanced uneasily about the room as he opened the wardrobe and pulled out a freshly laundered cotton kimono.

"Huh. That's strange...," he said, rummaging through the bottom of an old wicker hamper.

"What's wrong now?"

"There ought to be a vial of morphine hidden in here. You know my sister's husband was a doctor, and she asked me to store a number of things, including some bottles of medicine. Most of the medicine is a pain killer called Pantopon, and I hid it in here because I didn't want O-kumi getting into it. There was also a small vial of morphine powder marked with a skull and crossbones. Because I never knew what O-kumi would do next, it was too dangerous to leave around. I kept it here with the other bottles.

"Do you suppose I could have left it in Kurumazaka when we moved back? We certainly left there in a great hurry, didn't we? Oh well, no point in worrying about it now. I'll look for it when I have the time."

CHAPTER TEN

NO SOONER had Hikosuke returned from the crematorium and put the urn of ashes on the cabinet shelf, installing it next to the one from the previous year, than he announced he was off to the hospital. Bunzō and I headed home, taking the train from Nippori to Ueno, and then walking from Ueno Station to Kurumazaka. We made our way in silence.

In the course of our friendship we had developed a dislike for idle conversation and had come to scorn small talk for small talk's sake in much the same way we abhorred the act of eating as shamefully unbecoming. It was partly because of this habit that we said nothing to one another, but more than anything else there was nothing to say. Generally speaking, people at the the center of a maelstrom have little time in which to perceive the enormity of their predicament. In fact, the more irregular the event, the less they seem to have to say. Why, then, should we as witnesses to the death of a housewife work ourselves into a frenzy of grief? Certainly it would not reflect any depth of emotion on our part.

Of course, even an ordinary crisis may seem a catastrophe to the person caught in the spray of its gusty turbulence, but we need to remind ourselves that this flesh of ours, the epidermis forever exposed to the hot and cold currents of the earth, does not tear easily. Our hides are tough, and that we should know this fact reflects neither the achievement of any special enlightenment nor even dullness of the senses. In short, it is something acquired as a matter of practice.

And speaking of bad practices, just as Bunzō and I had drunk away the night last evening, and every evening prior to that, we now found ourselves standing on a streetcorner, covered with the dust of the city and looking the worse for wear from lack of sleep. This state of affairs came as no surprise, however, for it is how we always behaved. What is more, there under the burning sun, we wore the faces of happy boulevardiers.

—Ah, ah, look at these mugs, these faces! Whatever does a face say? One looks in a mirror with the hope of finding in its reflection some profundity of thought, some delicacy of feeling, a protean visage, but what does one see? For barring the intervention of only the most elaborately constructed conceit—for example, a looking glass designed to flatter and deceive its owner—one is likely to be disappointed. What he is likely to rub his nose against is a rubbery mass, a whole lot of cheek as it were, inflated with self-importance but none too high in intelligence.

Indeed our faces are flat, complacent, and without real change, lacking even the daily drama as seen in the impassive rocks on the shoal over which the tide washes in and out, or the transition to and from gray when the sky clouds at dusk and then clears in the morning. The grimace, the tear-stained cheek and the happy smile are really one and the same, masks exchanged hastily from one occasion to the next. Struggle as we may, we cannot escape this single layer of skin. Trapped behind its exterior, we can make all the claims in the world about possessing content and having fine ideas, but what does it matter? For anyone to take a good look at his face is to send a chill down his spine and bring on a fit of pique.

At such times, where, oh where, is the heavenly visage, the beatific smile, that makes my heart beat, that gently rocks my soul with the soft and distant tinkle of its bell? Oh, my bodhisattva, you who dwell in beauty far above the earth.... Oh, Yukari, Yukari....

No sooner had I uttered her name than I swooned and everything became gray and indistinct. I grew so tired and listless that, even if some kind soul had taken hold of me from behind and snapped me back into shape, I should have been unable to respond to his attempts to revive my spirits. I longed only for my bed with its worn-out mattress. But when we reached the lodging house and stepped inside, a square-faced man sitting at the bottom of the stairs stood up and seized Bunzō by the arm.

"You'll have to come with me to headquarters."

Who knows why, but Bunzō had inherited a certain weakness in the chest, and a few years past he began to cough blood. Moreover, his smallish head and the pallor of his complexion made him appear of slight build. Yet in point of fact, strip him to the waist, and he revealed a large and sturdy frame. Whenever he drank and began to heatedly debate a topic, he became a veritable myrmidon, behaving like a paid claque shouting at a rally. He bellowed, his chest swelling, its hairs bristling, his fist banging on the table as if—"Here, here"—he were hammering out the particulars of an agreement. To all appearances, he looked perfectly fit, and no one could have guessed how badly ravaged his lungs were. Perhaps it was his way of challenging the disease, of throwing down a gauntlet in the contest for his health, that he raved with fury, spewing out words, and at the same time, shellacing his lips with yet other coat of rouge lipstick. At any rate, this bit of foppery had become Bunzō's unshakeable habit since the onset of his illness. If, as one French critic wrote, Chopin alone had the trappings of a true consumptive, surely Bunzō's vitality was such that, as I have often told him, he stood at the opposite end of the spectrum as the world's only genuinely "fake" consumptive. Even now he pulled himself together, throwing his head back with a look of pride, and swept aside the hand that sought to hold his arm in its vice-like grip.

"What do you think you're doing?"

"I'm from the police."

"What do you want?"

"It doesn't matter what it is. Just come along."

"I don't recall a reason for me to be involved with the police."

"In that case, you have nothing to worry about. Come along peaceably. You'll be home in no time. Let's get going."

I was completely taken aback by the abrupt turn of events.

"What's gone wrong?" I asked Bunzō.

"I don't know, but it can't be serious. At any rate, I'd better go and find out."

Bunzō and the square-faced man went out the door, and I was left standing in the entryway. When I turned around, perceiving that someone was behind me, I saw Yasuko peering around the corner of the shōji.

"What's going on?" I asked.

"I don't know. Well, not exactly.... You'd better come in here, where we can talk."

I seated myself by the hibachi in the downstairs room.

"Please listen to what I have to say. It has to do with Bunzō's sister."

"Yukari?"

"You know, what with her being in trouble with the law. I haven't said a word until now because I didn't want to have you worry, but the police have been coming round to check on the house from time to time. They said Bunzō wasn't in trouble, but he *is* Yukari's brother, after all.

"Yesterday the man who makes the rounds—yes, the one who was just here—came, and while we were talking at the door, the postman arrived with a special delivery letter. He couldn't have picked a worst time. The letter was addressed to Bunzō, and on the back of the envelope was a man's name written in a man's handwriting. The policeman took the letter and opened it. Would you believe it? It was from Bunzō's sister."

While I was vaguely aware the police were keeping an eye on us, I did not pay much attention because I knew Bunzō was not connected in any way with the political movement his sister was involved in. Interrogating Bunzō would not reveal anything; the police would probably take his name and let him go. There was little reason to be worried for his sake. My concern was for Yukari.

"What did the letter say?"

"I was hardly in a position to read it, but I did get a peek before the man stuffed the letter into his breast pocket. There was one phrase that caught my eye. It said, 'Tomorrow'—that means today—'at 7 p.m., Shinjuku Station.' That was it. Or at least all that I could see. I wonder if Bunzō is going to be all right. The man kept coming to the house all day yesterday and today. He told me I was to inform him as soon as Bunzō came in. I wasn't to say a word to you, either."

There was but one thought in my mind as I collapsed on the bed in my room: How was I to save Yukari from impending disaster? Now that the police had seen the letter, it was inevitable that they would watch the station and wait for her to come out of hiding. It was just as clear she would fall into their hands, the rendevous at the station having become a trap. Its trick door would swing open, and she would land in jail. There was no way to contact her, and it would be seven o'clock in a matter of hours. Aside from tossing restlessly on the bed, I did not have the faintest notion what to do and nothing seemed to suggest itself. What was needed was action, not ideas, I told myself. I had to throw myself into the fray and see what happened. I got up, and rooting through my wardrobe, I found a musty suit I had shoved away in a corner. I pulled out a khaki-colored jacket—what had passed for mountain-climbing gear used in hiking about the countryside—and an equally tired pair of woolen knickers. I got dressed quickly. Concerned that my identity might be known to the authorities through my association with Bunzō, I donned a hunting cap and pulled it down over my face. I put on a pair of dark glasses to keep the dust out of my eyes, and from a wicker suitcase I produced an old pair of cleated shoes. Holding them in one hand, I crept down the stairs, slipped out the door unnoticed and unchallenged by Yasuko, and was off to Shinjuku.

In order to kill time while the sun was still high, I entered a bar near the station and tried to relax with a scotch. Inwardly, I was beside myself. How to determine from where, and by what means, Yukari would appear at the appointed hour? Would she come by train, streetcar, or taxi? Would she use the station entrance, the ticket gate, or the lobby? Not only would it be impossible to distribute myself about a station kept under tight surveillance, but to be seen loitering in a strange getup was likely to arouse suspicion.

What would Yukari do? No, what would *I* do in her situation...?

For a person on the run, nothing is more fearful than an inquiring eye, and no vehicle safer in public than a taxi. Yet to sail up to the curb of the station in a cab involved an element of danger. One would have to proceed with caution. First, have the driver stop nearby. Next, study the area from the inside of the car. Yes, that's it. Have the driver stop alongside the streetcar tracks directly across from the station, on this side of the thoroughfare, and then.... Or so I theorized. It was a strategy of sorts, but everything depended on luck—and luck in generous measure. I had nothing more to rely on than a calculated guess, and I resigned myself to the considerable likelihood of failure. For want of something to turn to, I lifted my eyes toward heaven and looked at the ceiling. A large chandelier hung overhead. Because it was still early in the afternoon, it had yet to be lit.

"My bodhisattva, my Samantabhadra, I do not presume to know in what manner you look upon the writhings of the creatures of this earth, or what you will think of this latest bit of nonsense on my part. But let my say in my defense, my constant prayer has been that I might find Yukari one day, and in so doing, obtain in her the slightest resemblance of yourself—yea, even a petal of the flower of your august being—as your shadow moves, its presence virtually undetected, amidst the dust of the earth.

"Yet here I am, asking you to countenance, and by your leave, grant success to a smart-alecky scheme of a rescue operation impetuously conceived in the brain of the mere mortal that is myself. Alas, I am too foul with the stench of this life to stand before you. I beseech you to forgive me, to pass by, rendering me only, with eyelids heavy and eyes downcast, the Buddha's quiet look of compassion.

"In truth, the reason I have called upon you, the bodhisattva of *prajñâ*—of wisdom in action—and you alone is . . . no, my shame is almost too great to say it . . . is because I am a lovesick fool."

And what appeared to me as I studied the ceiling—what came crashing down about my head, nearly knocking me from my stool— was a lump of flesh, or fat, an object that bore no similarity whatsoever to a heavenly flower. It was Yukari's body, the sum of the parts of which I had dared only to have a glimpse. Indeed, in the past whenever I had occasion to think of her, it was her face that I envisioned, and even that was cast in a dim light. Just as one avoids speaking of a sensitive topic and resorts to generalities, in the same way I had allowed the area about her breast and torso to be veiled in a haze. As for the smoldering of her loins, it remained unseen, or deliberately ignored.

But the apparition I now saw was of Yukari transformed into an enchantress, a lascivious sorceress, whose naked flesh seemed to glow with a wet, sticky look; whose head, disembodied, floated in the air, the blood pumping forth in great spurts, effusive as the elephantine laughter of Gaṇeśa, the deva of glee. Yukari's stifling limbs reached out to seduce me. Their saccharine beauty penetrated even to my underwear, ate into my flesh, and raced through my body. Her pure white arms melted like candy over my neck and shoulders.

Yes! Wasn't this precisely what I had been searching for? Had I not been in danger of denying myself a peerless nutriment, of excluding the element of the flesh from my vision of Yukari, and in the process, of losing the real person altogether? What a waste to let this woman be thrown in prison to have her flesh rot in chains.

How absolutely vital it was that I get to her first—to seize her, to cling to her, to suck at her bosom—for to do so is to know the taste of this earth and be nourished by its fruit.

In this instant when my bodhisattva seemed so far away, hovering over the misty perimeter that divides this world from that, I rose to my feet, tottering but leaving in time to be at the station by six-thirty. I crossed the streetcar tracks and took up a position on the far side of the square. I was hardly visible in the twilight.

The spot I chose was near the entrance to the station, and I stood there with what I told myself was the resolve of a Perseus who, rising radiant from his ablutions in the sea, is prepared to slay a dragon. But to every set of eyes that coldly returned the scrutiny I administered to the face of each and every passing woman, no doubt I hardly looked the part. No mythic hero, no Perseus was I; to the contrary I must have seemed a mere philanderer, a wayward son, who, strolling along prostitutes' row, gawks at the pretty girls.

Although the sun set late at that time of year, it was a cloudy night, and even for an overcast sky, it seemed unusually dark. Also this hour of the day witnessed the heaviest traffic through the station. The crowds made it easy to hide, and though I was inconspicuous behind a pillar, when I peeked about I could see here and there—by the entrance, beside the telephone booths, near the policebox—men in business suits who were obviously police dressed in street clothes. They gave themselves away by their isolation from the crowd or the intensity of their vigilance.

Were it not for the thought of Yukari, even the Yukari of a decade ago, never should I have operated so independently or with such brazenness in the face of a police dragnet. Yet so certain was I that the slightest suggestion of her, the barest trace of a shadow, had only to present itself, and though I were surrounded by a crowd of ten million, my entire being would come alive as though charged by lightning. More readily than any hunting dog, I would sniff her out.

—Ah, ah, if only Yukari will appear, I shall rush to her side even at the risk of my life. Holding my breath and standing on tiptoe, I strained to catch sight of her riding in one of the taxis moving to and fro along the intersection across the way. Ten minutes, twenty minutes, thirty minutes...

It was a little past seven by the large clock on the side of the station roof, when the traffic signal changed and out of a line of vehicles backed up at the light, a lone taxi began to advance in the direction of the station. It glided to the curb stopping only a few yards from where I stood, and I caught sight in the car window of a couple, a man and a woman, leaning forward on the back seat of the cab. That was when I saw, unmistakeably despite the waning light, under the shadow of a narrow brimmed hat, the line of her eyebrows, her nose, her . . .

Ah, Yukari! The memory of her shot through me, and like a bird taking wing at the sound of a gun, I rushed to her, and the door of the taxi.

"Yukari! It's not safe. Get away from here as fast as you can."

Just as the man stuck his booted foot out the door, and was ready to alight from the vehicle, Yukari looked up at me, her face emerging for the first time from behind the man's broad shoulders.

—Ah, ah, what hapless issue! How cruel these ten years had been! What devil had put his disfiguring hand to her visage? The outline of her features was unchanged, but her skin was leatherish and yellow, dark spots now staining its surface with the mark of a heartless disposition. Greed burned in her eyes, and her lips were contorted into a permanent curse. So undone was I by the sight of this she-demon, this *yakṣa*, and by the white heat—the fulminating hellfire—of a hatred for all mankind she spewed with a hiss in my direction, that my cry "It's not safe!" became a mere gasp, hardly, if at all, audible.

"Damn."

The man, who was observing the station from inside the cab, swore and pushed Yukari back into the seat.

"Stay still."

Without a glance at me, or concern for my welfare, he leaned forward and clamped his hand on the driver's shoulder.

"Head for Nakano. We're in a hurry, understand? I'll make it worth your while."

The door was slammed shut in my face, and I was thrown back from the car. I stood there, dumbly rooted to the spot, choking on the exhaust of the taxi as it sped away. For my troubles on Yukari's behalf, I received no reward whatsoever, not so much as a nod of recognition, or a word of thanks to cling to.

Now that the taxi had vanished, I was like a stake that stood out, a signpost hammered into the ground. So helpless was I that an hour, even two—perhaps an eternity—may have elapsed before I began to move. My feet, at least, seemed to have perceived the fact I had fallen into the startled view of one of the plainclothesmen who was now pressing toward me through the eddies of the bustling crowd. My little drama with the taxi had unfolded in a matter of seconds, but that was no reason why it should have escaped his vigilant eye. His eyes now rested squarely on me.

"What shall I do? What shall I ...?"

I dashed down the side alley to the rear of the station. I cut through the people moving outside the gaudily lit eating and drinking establishments that lined the way, bumping into them and catching their angry shouts of surprise, but I paid no attention and ran oblivious to everything. When I reached the street that runs east and west in front of the Yodobashi Post Office, I turned right, and like a fish gasping and leaping as it climbs the rapids, I made my way against the current of automobiles and horsedrawn wagons, their horns blaring, the traffic clattering to a halt. As I hurried along, the shoes barely remaining shod on my feet, I broke into a great open space. I had shot down a narrow sluiceway and been released into a great sea, so dazzling was the expanse of sky that arched overhead. I had reached the intersection where the street enters the highway that runs north and south, connecting Shinjuku and Ōkubo.

My head began to reel, but I held my breath and crossed to the other side. From there a maze of narrow alleys led to the red-light district. I slowed my pace, unable to bear the pain of running further. To avoid drawing attention to my disheveled appearance, I tried to walk slowly and calm the pounding of my heart. I looked behind, and as luck would have it, there was no sign of my pursuers. I heaved a sigh of relief, but perspiration began to flow from every pore of my body. My parched throat burst into flame, and involuntarily, I stumbled in the direction of a small bar on the street.

"Don't I know this place?"

It was the bar where Moichi had taken me the other night. I parted the curtain at the entrance and stepped inside before I realized it. The bar had yet to fill up with customers, and there were unoccupied seats to the rear. I collapsed on a stool, and turning to the young girl who worked at the counter, I spat out the one word I could still manage to say:

"Sake!"

"Well, fancy seeing you here."

I looked to see who was speaking to me. There was Moichi sitting beside me.

"Where've you been? Out for a little hike in the woods, I suppose?"

Because he was drunk, his eyes bloodshot, and his eyelids drooping, he failed to notice the flushed and extraordinary appearance of my face.

"I've been drinking since noon," he announced, slurring his words as he spoke.

"Things must be going pretty well if you can afford to celebrate so early in the day."

"Not really, no. In fact, they've gotten out of hand. A little while ago Hikosuke showed up at my place. Oh, I almost forgot . . . I hear it's all over for poor old O-kumi. But what can you do? When your number's up. . . . "

"Of course, people may say that," he continued, "but I know better. There's a more down-to-earth reason why O-kumi got hooked on morphine. And it's a hellava lot saucier than the one Hikosuke tells about stomach cramps being the cause. You know about it?"

"No, nothing."

"What I'm saying is that once a person like O-kumi gets hooked on drugs and runs short, she's no better than a piece of junk. Something that's ready for the dump yard. But give the girl a shot, and I hear she was something else again. Get my point? I'm willing to bet ole Hikosuke himself was the one who relaxed the rules every now and then and gave her an injection."

Moichi's broad hints and smutty innuendoes were like specks of lint that one wanted to brush away. I was doubly nauseated and about to light into him, when perceiving my annoyance and the growing shortness of my temper, he changed the topic.

"At any rate, Hikosuke appeared at my place with his sister and kids. He said he had to talk to me about the hospital in Shinano-machi. The hospital wouldn't have the cast ready until the following day, and since his sister wanted it put on before returning to Katsuura, would I mind if she and the children spent the night? Now it's not the first time this has happened. 'Here we go again,' I thought to myself, but I didn't feel I could object. 'It's all right. Go ahead and stay,' I told them.

"Well, as I was about to leave and turn the place over to them like a gentleman, the sister tried to hand me some money. I refused. It's not necessary, I said, but she insisted. She claimed they had inconvenienced me so many times she wouldn't feel right until I took the ten yen. True enough. They never bat an eye at the thought of imposing on me whenever they come to Tokyo. I figured I was entitled to let her do me a favor.

"I should have known better, though. It was all too good to be true. Something smelled of a rat, and would you believe it, Hikosuke came running after me as soon as I was out the door. 'Hey, Moichi, I'll take half of the money.' I could hardly believe my ears, him pulling a stunt like that. Whoever heard of such nerve?

"'I feel bad,' he says, 'because I can't take you out for a drink. My sister expects me to go with her to the department stores.'

"'What has this,' I asked him, patting the ten-yen note in my pocket, 'got to do with money for your booze?' 'Well, nothing,' he says, but then he started to complain about how he didn't have the cost of carfare or how he couldn't keep relying on his sister. So I said, 'Look, I can't give you half because I have to find a place for myself tonight. Here, take this one yen coin.' He was off in a flash.

"It's a damned mess. Don't you agree? The whole thing left such a bad taste in my mouth I came straight here. I was drinking by myself until you came in .... Hey, look who else is here. It's O-tsuna."

The sight of O-tsuna emerging from the back of the shop reawakened the stabbing pain of an earlier wound, and though I tried to shift stools and move away, I found myself hemmed in between her and the wall to the rear. There would be no escaping her. She pressed her body against mine.

"I'm so glad to see you. You didn't forget after all, did you."

I was struck by the light green color—the color of new foliage— that flashed past my eye as she flipped over the sleeves of her kimono and put her arms about my shoulder. She gave me a shaking much the way one would hug a petulant child to make him feel better. Then, pulling up one of her sleeves, she reached for the serving bottle and poured a cup of sake for Moichi.

"This one's on me."

"Hey, hey!" he said, as though to thank her. "Just come in to work?"

"Hm. My, but you're in a good mood."

"Not really. That's what I was just telling him. Hikosuke has ... "

"Never mind. I overheard the whole story from the kitchen in the back of the shop."

"Well, of all the ... By the way, when I went to visit to you-know-whom ..."

"Don't even mention him. I don't want to have anything more to do with the man." By now O-tsuna had pulled up a stool and was sitting beside me.

"Moichi, I want you to stop going to his house and saying a lot of things you shouldn't."

"Now I've done it. I knew I had said the wrong thing. Anyway, I may not know what's going on between the two of you here, but you don't have to hang all over him to make it obvious. No matter where I go today, there's something peculiar in the air. And that applies to *you* too." Moichi was speaking to me.

"Yes *you*, you're as much to blame as she is. Sitting there cool as can be while someone else's woman dallies with you."

I felt as if my skin was about to be rubbed raw, caught as I was between the animosity Moichi revealed in the terseness of his smile and the heat generated by O-tsuna as she pressed against me. Fearful, moreover, of staying any longer in the vicinity of Shinjuku station, I raised a silent cry to heaven and was about to kick over my stool and leave, when four tough-looking characters entered the bar.

They appeared to be drunk as they stumbled in and shouted noisily "Sake! Sake!" but they were not so intoxicated as to fail to look in our direction. They exchanged a knowing glance among themselves. I saw Moichi blanch, and as the color drained from his face, I had the terrible feeling—it passed through me like a shot—that I had no idea what to do next. It was too late to try to leave the bar.

One of their number had his eye trained on Moichi. He spoke in a voice loud enough for everyone to hear.

"Hey, you over there, that kisser of yours looks awfully familiar. Aren't you the fellow who gave us a display of his fancy footwork the other night? Come over here and join us. It's not like we're perfect strangers, is it?"

Before we had time to gulp and realize he belonged to the gang that had come barking after us the night at the brothel, he was moving down the bar, headed in our direction. Perhaps it was my outfit, but he ignored me. It was as though I were a total stranger.

He bumped against Moichi, prodding him with his shoulder, and reiterated his demand that Moichi join him and his friends. There was an insistent tone to his voice, as he tried to intimidate Moichi.

"Come over here where we can see that kisser of yours, and we can have a drink together."

The veins stood out in sharp relief on Moichi's forehead. He got up, knocking over the stool.

"Who do you think you're pushing around? Don't underestimate me, buster. You think you scare me?"

That Moichi should begin to rave like a madman was a sign, the pained howl, of a person unfairly cornered. By now the three toughs at the front end of the bar had stood up.

"Who the hell does the bastard think he is? Tell him to step outside. Hey, you. Step outside. We'll beat the crap out of you."

"What's going on? Stop it now, everybody. Moichi, I said stop it."

O-tsuna spoke in a high pitched voice, but her plea that Moichi quiet down and not get involved in a fight was all but drowned out by the sound of scuffling feet. Moichi, nearly exploding with rage, marched toward the door.

In the split second it took for me to stand up and turn to join him, I recognized several faces in the crowd that had gathered on the street as belonging to men involved in the stakeout at the train station. I retreated to the rear of the bar as fast as I could, and taking refuge behind a curtain that hung in the kitchen doorway, I looked about the unfamiliar surroundings, wondering what to do next. O-tsuna was beside me.

"You leaving?"

"Is there a way out the back?"

"Umh. It's over here. What a nuisance, those boys getting into a fight. Let's both leave."

Going out the kitchen door, we groped our way along the dark, cramped space where the eaves of the bar and the adjoining establishment created a narrow passagway. It led to a busy side street lined with coffee shops and bars. I leapt out just in time to catch a taxi that came whizzing along, and as I hopped in, O-tsuna jumped in too. She acted as though it was the most natural thing in the world, and bouncing on the rear seat of the cab as it pulled from the curb, she produced a compact and proceeded to powder her nose.

CHAPTER ELEVEN

HAVING PILED one fabrication on top of another in telling this tale, I now find myself in the maddening predicament of being unable to fabricate yet another lie. I am like a mountain climber who has lost his grip or a detective without a clue. Surely no one but myself is to blame for this state of affairs, yet I cannot help feeling overwhelmed with regret and chagrin when I think it has all come about because of Yukari.

Now, as never before, let me be totally candid and tell you why I stuck the tip of my pen into the trash heap of history and used it like a hook to pick through the rubble and unearth the carcass of Christine de Pizan, to truss it up and tie together the loose ends of the life of this wrinkled old woman. It was because I was stirred by a secret plan, namely, that of finding a link, of detecting a trace of a connection, between the life of Christine's Joan of Arc and that of my Yukari. Alas, this karmic connection, this casting of a flower upon a mandala in an *abhiṣeka* ceremony designed to identify one's bodhisattva, has become a tissue of lies, a figment of my imagination, having neither truth nor fate to support its validity. This fabrication—a palimpsest of my own devising—was the product of a silly infatuation, of a heart haunted every minute, whether awake or asleep, for the last ten years by the vision of Yukari, of a tormented mind that sought through a process of superimposition to reshape her image into the likeness of the Maid of Orléans. Yet what I produced in my endless tracings, in the prolix and petulant limning of my troth, was but a pale imitation, a portrait of Yukari that bares little resemblance to Joan of Arc. What I have written is nothing more than the record of a lovesick idiot.

That I failed in this undertaking was due, was it not, to the fact that the most important part of Yukari's identity, the whole body and not merely her face, had been shrouded in mist? And was it not on this account that my manuscript was destined from the start never to see the light of day? And why, in turn, I felt doubly compelled to press forward with it?

So much for excuses and explanations. It should come as no surprise that I let the days slip idly by and the blank pages of my manuscript lie white on my desk. To be lazy was bad enough, but I compounded matters by coming to rely more and more on my bodhisattva, expecting Samantabhadra's transcendent powers to be the source of my salvation. I borrowed a shaft of his otherworldly light, and taking advantage of its mistlike properties, used it to surround everything in my life—my manuscript, my work, my philosophy, my feelings—in an aura of mystery.

Of what condition, what pathology, do we speak in my case? What brought on this fever, this fiendish activity in which I expended so much time and effort drawing analogies and trying to overcome the contradiction—indeed the self-delusion—inherent in polishing and applying yet another layer of interpretation to the life and legend of Christine de Pizan, especially when I never intended for anyone to read this tale?

By the same token, I never set out to defraud or deceive anyone, no matter how many lies I may have told in the course of fabricating this story. So that, just as I made known my complaint about Yukari's nebulousness—the outline of her form being indistinct whenever I called her to mind—in all fairness I must also confess that inwardly there were nothing more delightful, nothing more likely to send galvanic shivers of glee through my entire being than those moments when I sat at my desk and sought to flesh out her image, to conceive of Yukari in her corporeality. How my head would spin! I was like a madman who stomps round a sacred tree brandishing an axe but, restrained by an unseen force, is unable to touch the hallowed branches.

And though I am given to inflating the nobility of my labors, prepared at a moment's notice to expand at great length on such topics as "The Writer and His Instrument as the Steward of

Reason," in point of fact, as I sat before the blank page of my manuscript, my pen was merely growing horny and itching for relief. The farce I had created, the fraud I sought to perpetrate, was no first-class subterfuge, no tour de force of showmanship. To the contrary, it was the product of the basest and most despicable laxity of the human spirit.

When I think of Yukari now, I experience an almost intolerable pain. The vision of her that I had been denied, and that has remained pale and nebulous for so many years, suddenly became a nightmare that relentlessly assailed me and gave me no peace however hard I tried to exorcise the horrid image from my mind. Those eyes burning with greed, the contorted lips, the splotchy complexion.... Surely I would not care had the transformation been confined to changes in her appearance—a nose fallen off, a missing eye, the sloughing away of a burned cheek—for Yukari had always been more of an idea than a face. But what was unbearable was the metamorphosis of her soul. The Yukari who had been the object of my every prayer had become another woman completely, changed beyond recognition. Her physical being was now inhabited by a different soul, one devoid of any affinity to the original.

—Ah, ah, what mad swan-maiden myth was this? In the twinkling of an eye my swan had molted and become a fire-eating emu that hopped into a taxi and drove away, leaving behind only a trail of fumes.

Yet what is truly extraordinary about this tale—indeed fabulous in the truest sense of the word—was that I detected as I breathed in the gas and the whorl of dust and dirt blown in my face, the presence of that which, although hardly moving, made its presence known by its shadow and its subtle fragrance.

Rather than a partaker of the sorrows of this world, the earthly woes that rend the hearts and souls of the weary and downtrodden, this pale, redolent being takes its pleasure in giving joy to all mankind. It sought to breathe mirth—the joyousness of Ganeśa's laughter—into bodies gasping their last breath, and by letting it shake them to the core of their existence, resuscitate them and bring them back to life. Doubtless its fragrance was of the flower that is not of this world, and its countenance of the Majestic One endowed with the eighty minor and thirty-two major signs of a Buddha. Surely it was my Samantabhadra, a bodhisattva who no longer made his revelations in dreams and visions, but having incorporated himself into the ripe limbs hidden beneath Yukari's dress, finally burst forth from this guise and, like a fire burning with a singular brilliance, revealed himself in his true form. When the flames had burned away, all that remained was an abandoned shell, the dross of Yukari's body.

In the end it was Yukari's insubstantial form that had become the temporary seat of Samantabhadra's manifestation, and try as I might to thank Yukari for making this miracle of the avatar possible, I cannot express my gratitude enough. For me to offer my appreciation after having spoken ill of her may seem too much of a switch. All I can say is that my feelings are genuine, and there is no way I can state them without their sounding strange or out of place.

What a wonderful chronicle of the life of the bodhisattva Samantabhadra this tale might have been if, in the instant his heavenly rays pierced my body, I had, as I lived, cast off the mantle of my putrid hide and been born again as his heaven-sent child. But even as I stretched my hands impatiently toward the skies and reached for the promise of a better reincarnation, alas, my feet were caught in the grinding jaws of a monstrous dragon, and I could not escape this life. I could only writhe, struggling in vain to free myself, here upon my bed.

(In point of fact, no sooner had I escaped the dangers that had threatened my life last night in Shinjuku than I foolishly allowed myself to accede to O-tsuna's overtures and had the taxi take us to a cheap hotel in the suburbs. Now, after having spent the night with her, I have awakened to find the morning sun pouring in through the window. In its light, I appear a vile and filthy thing.)

Here, in bed next to O-tsuna—her body, her hair, her sweaty, greasy flesh, her white, painted face caked with powder—rests the feckless soul that is myself. Would that I might cling to the flower of Samantabhadra's diadem, but I have lost all means to obtain his grace.

"The gods are constituted not unlike ourselves," says Alain, the French essayist. "Nay, let me be more emphatic. They are constituted, as are we, from beasts."

Does this mean, Samantabhadra, that—like this nobody that is myself and this shameless hussy sleeping next to me—you too belong to the verminous ranks that crawl upon the earth? Or are you a thing apart? Are you unlike the foreign gods of whom Alain speaks, and having severed all ties to this world, set in the sky like a rare and marvelous crystal formed from elements unknown to this terrestrial plane? The path before my eyes clouds over, and unworthy, I am unable to behold your true and perfect form. I entertain no hope that you will deign to look upon me, and by your presence prove the reality of my existence in some small corner of your consciouness. Moreover, whatever prayer I may hope to offer is about to be stiffled by the beasts of which Alain speaks. Despite my efforts to resist their screeches and cries, they have raised a vehement protest and are seeking to take control of my voice, to use my throat as the conduit for their clamorous shouts. All that is left to me is to repeat the novelist's complaint—

> I am sick, and what on earth is the good
> of it all?
> What good to them or me, I cannot see!

—Ah, ah, I cannot see the point of it all!

I propped myself up in bed and gave O-tsuna's naked shoulder a hard shove. She rubbed her eyes and moaned softly as she stretched in bed.

"What time is it? Are you awake already?"

I brushed aside the arm she extended to encircle my neck.

"Don't touch me, you whore!"

Her body gave off a powerful odor as she sat upright in bed.

"What did you say? I dare you to repeat it."

"I said I was sick and tired of the state I perpetually find myself in."

"Well, you'd better be more careful how you talk to me. What do you mean, 'whore'? Just remember I don't let you pay me."

She grabbed my wrinkled jacket from the foot of the bed and swung it about like a piece of rope.

"What have we here? And what's in the pockets? I wonder. You put on this dirty old rag and parade about in it so proud of the fact you don't give a damn what people think. But tell me just what it is you can do? Actually, you're the type who needs money to make him interesting. But wouldn't you know, you haven't a sen to your name."

How right she was. I was totally broke. O-tsuna had offered a rude reminder of my pennilessness. And just as abruptly I was reminded to everything that had happened yesterday. The memory came rushing at me and hit me with a thud. What, I feared, had become of Bunzō? No, more than that, what had become of me? By now the authorities had determined my identity, and given the wiles of the police in this harsh land, there was little likelihood they would stand casually by and let me slip through their hands.

What good would it do to imagine a hypothetical situation in which I got away scot free, or even more improbable, in which I succeeded in pulling off a plan of escape? Whether I speak of this hotel room or the lodgings at Kurumazaka or the circle of friends at Nippori, the whole of my life is a dark pit, an underground cellar, so it mattered little what form of incarceration awaited me. What was the point of allowing myself to get upset, since the choices were all one and the same? Yet I could not but wonder if there was not something more to life.

Such things, say, as azure skies, limpid seas, gentle zephyrs, mountains crowned with trees, meadows filled with flowers gently waving in the sunlight. . . .

—Ah, ah, settings so serene yet so remote from my daily life! How desolate and dreary my day-to-day existence! Suddenly these things became vitally important, urgent even to the point of pain. In order to grasp the most ephemeral moment of peace, I was like a swimmer who steps to the end of the diving board and is ready to take the plunge. Poised on the brink, I leapt and flew into the air. And as I rose through the fragrant blue, flapping my arms like wings, I wanted to shout as loud as I could, unleashing my pent-up cry.

Had I been my usual self, I should have looked upon the sight of such a fellow with utter distaste. I would have called him a fop, a person lacking in character, a case of nervous prostration, a man incapable of surviving in the dust and dirt of the city. I would have laughed a loud and haughty laugh, ridiculing his lyrical paeans to lofty peaks and crystal waters as just so much silverplate— superficial emotions and sentimental poetry unworthy of a true man and artist.

But let there be no mistake. My cri de coeur was nothing frivolous. It came from the very depths—the inner chemistry—of my being.

Yes, that's it! Board a train! Board a ship! Embark on any vehicle that, sounding the whistle of departure, is leaving at top speed.

I jumped out of bed and ripped the jacket from O-tsuna's sweaty hands.

Now, where shall I go? And what about money?

Any hope of raising cash lay solely with Sakagami Seiken, but I had not submitted a manuscript of late. He would be difficult to approach.

What of it? I shall press my case. In no more time than it took to get my clothes on, I had made up my mind.

"So you're running out on me?" observed O-tsuna who sat in bed smoking a cigarette and watching me closely as I got dressed.

Me? Run away? Like a coward? What a boorish opinion! No, I have no choice but to follow the dictates of my inner chemistry. To believe in the sources of my own vitality has become my motto, my article of faith.

"I can see how you'd think my running off is a disgrace. All right, it is. You'll have to chalk it up to a defect in my character—and debit my account for the loss you've sustained. But something extraordinary has exploded inside me, and it tells me that questions of how much I owe you, or you owe me—all the additions and substractions on the balance sheet of human relations—don't matter. It says to kick them aside. Sorry, but I can't help myself. I've got to get out of this place."

Knocking over the chairs and table that seemed to reach out and clutch at me like things possessed, I moved toward the door.

"Well, do as you damn well please."

I fled down the corridor with the sound of O-tsuna's insults ringing in my ears. As I stepped outside, the wind that rustled through the bushes hit me squarely in the face. I thought I would faint, and my world would go dark, as I headed down the garden path.

CHAPTER TWELVE

"THAT POSES a problem for me, you know. Especially since you say it has to be right away. You always march in here with the wildest schemes."

Leaving the hotel, I rushed to the office of *Political Debate* magazine in Toranomon. Seiken tried to be noncommittal and brush aside my request for money that, plucking up my resolve, I had dared to put to him.

"No, it has to be now," I said, determined to have my way. "You only have to come up with two hundred yen. I tell you I have the material for a long article lined up. I can write it in no time."

"I don't understand why you need the money all of a sudden."

"That's what I told you. I'm leaving town. I want to get away as soon as I leave this office. I'll do the article when I get to where I'm going."

"I have no objection to your going on a trip. But I don't see why it has to be today."

"It does, that's all. The condition of my health, yes, my health requires that I go. Besides, I'm a little behind on the rent for my room, and Kuzuhara has to be paid. She's not having an easy time of it either."

Although I had done nothing more than let slip the truth about my rent being in arrears, the mere mention of Yasuko's name caused Seiken to squirm uneasily in his seat. The chair creaked under the weight of his big belly.

"Well, that's for certain.... No, I meant to say you have your reasons for leaving town, but..." A look of apprehension flickered behind the thick lenses of Seiken's glasses.

"It's difficult for me too, you know. I met Miss Kuzuhara once or twice after you brought her here on that business about the scrap metal, but the arrangements on her side have yet to fall into place. If you say the advance is absolutely necessary, I'll go along with you, but before we go any further I want you to know my association with Miss Kuzuhara is only the most casual..."

Seiken's words trailed off into an incoherent mumble. It appeared he was feeling more insecure than I. My mind was stirred by the thought of something unpleasant about his relationship with Yasuko. Actually, my suspicions were not new, but dated from the day when Yasuko's manner had suggested as much.

Yet because I considered conjecture along these lines distasteful—a veritable soiling of the mind—I did my best not to think about Yasuko and Seiken. Certainly there was no point in wasting time on them, yet I could not help feeling pity, however superficially, at the discovery of a certain faintheartedness lurking beneath the surface of Seiken's stubborn exterior.

"For the moment, it's not Kuzuhara I'm worried about. You needn't trouble myself on that score," I said, trying to find a means to smooth things over. "What's important is the trip."

"What's the absolute minimum you can manage with?"

"The amount I just asked for."

Seiken heaved a weary sigh as he hiked up his vest and thrust his hand into the secret pocket of the bellyband he wore underneath his shirt.

"This is all I have on me at the moment." he said, producing a billfold and fishing out five or six ten-yen notes.

"You'll have to agree to make do with this. I can send you more later. I'll forward it to where you're traveling."

"Fine. Whatever is convenient for you...."

"Good. We're agreed. Now there's the matter of what to do about your landlady, but damn it, I'd appreciate it if you stopped bringing up the name—'Kuzuhara, Kuzuhara.' As far as I'm concerned, she and I..."

Normally I should have said nothing and let Seiken's remarks pass without comment, but the pain of this redundancy, the repetition of his complaint, became more than I could bear. My ears were overly sensitive, burning as they were from the blood that had rushed to my head, so that the enunciation of each sibilant in the recitation of "Kuzuhara, Kuzuhara" was like the sting of a bristly caterpillar, and I, like the man stung by its barb, unleashed a howl of pain.

"So? What about her?" I shouted, my body shaking with rage. "I was talking about preparing a manuscript for you, and it has nothing to do with her. I was asking for an advance against work and not a thing more. Don't think you're offering me hush money to keep quiet about your private affairs."

Once unleashed, my voice grew louder and shriller; my face puffed out and turned bright red.

Oily beads of sweat began to form on Seiken's forehead. "Now what are you talking about? Haven't I done what you asked me to do? I don't see why you have any argument with me."

"The way you've treated my request is an insult."

"Insult? Do you think I'm going to put out good money only to be told I'm being insulting? I refuse to have anything further to do with you."

"And that's how I feel about you. Everytime I think of the money, it calls to mind too many filthy associations."

"What are you calling 'filthy'?"

"The fact that this conversation has degenerated to a level where two people are shouting at each other shows how sordid the whole business is."

"Then shame on you for coming in and asking for money in the first place."

"Yes, damn it, I realize what a terrible mistake I've made."

"Why don't you stop talking like a smart aleck and get out of here."

"I will."

The sound of Seiken standing up and banging his big, hairy fist on the table coincided with my slamming the door as I rushed out of the office and into the corridor.

I was almost to Karasumori Shrine before I started to come to my senses. I had walked oblivious of trolleys, automobiles, pedestrians—the whole spectacle of the city as it unfolded before me—during the time it took to walk this far. Doubtless I was punchdrunk, reeling from my argument with Seiken, yet I felt exactly the opposite. It was as though I bore a dead weight, my soul seeming to drain to my feet, and bleeding out the soles of my shoes, soak into the ground. I was terribly depressed. Perhaps it was the result of a great fever that, having hotly enveloped me like a farmer's straw rain cape, made my skin steam and left me feeling limp and lifeless. I was still standing on two feet, but I might have well been in a coma.

Would anyone, I wondered, understand that the true source of my depression was the punctilious attitude I had adopted in speaking to Seiken—an attitude so self-righteous as to be comical. But then, too, I was beginning to feel a twinge—admittedly a mere smidgen—of regret at not having taken his money.

As a general rule, the giving and receiving of funds is invariably complicated by mixed feelings, the joy of being either the giver or the recipient alloyed by an unrefined sentiment, the sort of precipitant that sinks to the bottom of a bottle of fine wine or clouds the last of the sake drawn from a cask. It is rare to feel otherwise, and as a result, we are often at pains to find a rationale that lends an official explanation to exchanges of money.

Such public statements are vacuous, but they have a logic that is apparent to all, since maintaining a certain tidiness in human affairs is an important part of the design for living. The formalities become the finishing touches, so to speak, the tidy adjustments that gloss over small injustices, that set aside minor irritations, that cause us to hide our small physical aches and pains, because we know what the world wants to see is the polished exterior of an unruffled disposition. One hardly needs to be told people find it easier to be smart and operate along practical lines rather than let an ache in the backside, or the proverbial pain in the neck, get the better of them and become the source of an unwarranted headache. This is the natural law of adulthood, and it is how grownups get on with the everyday functions of life, with the living and breathing of each day. Yet here I was, acting ever so much the small child, who waving his arms and kicking his feet, cries in bed. My carrying on was, of course, no more significant than the buzzing of a fly caught under glass, but how powerfully it shook the microcosm in which I lived. What's more, it was not behavior befitting a man, or patriot, but tell me, just what does it mean to draw distinctions and say one man is heroic, and the other is not...?

—Ah, ah, were I a heroic type, I'd have no need for this non-sense, this running on and on at the mouth. Instead, wouldn't I, with a clap of my hands and a high, dry laugh, find myself transported to far broader and more transcendent paths? What does it say of me that, after having donned the sackcloak of self-reflection, my thoughts continued to dwell on the sheaf of ten-yen notes in Seiken's pocket? Let people point their finger at me as an example of everything that is base and ugly. Let them call me a maggot. Why should I care? I certainly don't plan to protest, because I have nothing to say in my defense.

Very well, a maggot is a maggot, and it does as maggots do. Likewise, I am a mere human being, a man, and no matter what else I may pretend to be, there is no altering the fact that I am not of exalted birth. I do not have mystical powers at my disposal, and I shall not be able to summon forth the clouds.

Yet even a maggot must have his say. The one thing I want known is that my current state of depression does not arise out of any lingering attachment to funds that might have affected my personal gain. It has its origin in the sense of loss I experience at the thought of having done irreparable damage to my long-standing friendship with Sakagami Seiken. Perhaps to say this now sounds empty, and I may be thought a nervy, insensitive type for having said as much, but the facts prove otherwise. For were I truly brazen, Seiken's sheaf of bills would be snugly tucked in my breast pocket. My regret is not for the cash. My concern is solely for Seiken.

Sakagami Seiken! Kind friend and senior in years! Was it not you, and you alone, who took an interest in me, you who showed concern for the impoverished but freewheeling student of life, you who bought his trifling manuscripts, you who over the years saw to the supply of his larder? Whatever wrong could you have committed, my friend, that I should put you to shame, that I should drive you to anger and sadness, that I should heap abuse upon your name and give your heart pain?

Yes, what is it that I claim you've done? What does it matter, this game of catchball between you and Yasuko? Why should I find it unpleasant? What made the blood rush to my head as it did? And what, pray tell, did a vulgar display of bad manners on my part have to do with my so-called aspirations to the practice of the way of Samantabhadra? Why, nothing, of course. . . .

Go ahead and say it: What bodhisattva practice? Tell me where in my behavior has anyone detected a scintilla, a single glimmering reflection, of Samantabhadra's wisdom?

—Ah, ah, whither, my bodhisattva? In what distant sky? As I stopped in my tracks and sighed out loud, a passing couple stared at me with an incredulous look. Stumbling forward, I ran the remaining distance to Karasumori Shrine. "Yes, this was the place." I muttered to myself as I recalled the chance meeting I had there with Jinsaku and O-tsuna.

But the face that floated before my eyes was neither of O-tsuna wildly imbibing the elixir of life, sucking the world dry of its vitality, nor of Jinsaku groping hopelessly about as he struggled to find his way out of the confining web of human sentiment. No, it was something else, and it advanced at a terrible speed, shunting aside my images of O-tsuna and Jinsaku and relegating them to the status of distant specks on the horizon. It was as cold and white as sheets in a sickroom, and lying face up like a corpse on its deathbed, it finally revealed itself to be none other than the face of Hisako, her eyes staring fixedly at the ceiling, her complexion the color of solidified wax. Feeling as though some device had hoisted me into the air, I turned around, and hurriedly retracing my steps to Toranomon, I set off for Atagoshita.

As the narrator of this tale, I suppose I am obliged to supply the reader with a suitably serious and convincing explanation as to why my feet should change direction so abruptly. Unfortunately for you, I have abandoned any remaining shred of a claim to being a skillful weaver of plot. I've said as much previously, and because both by nature and habit I am inclined to do as I please, and to avoid what I dislike, inevitably my work has suffered from an unevenness, a kind of chiaroscuro effect.

Yet in this instance I really have gone too far. Once again I have allowed my story to be foolishly swayed by my preferences, which like a pair of scales, swing violently back and forth, hopelessly out of balance. And just as one of the pans inevitably will tumble and fall from the beam of the scale, I too have cast aside the wisdom of keeping a level head, and a body grounded in reality. All that remained to me were my two feet which moved of their own accord. More than anything else, I wanted to entrust the tiresome business of devising a handy rationale for my erratic behavior—an interpretation capable of convincing even myself—to someone else.

My guess is that, like everything else, feet have a life of their own and do as they damn well please. At any rate, as they raced along they left me short of breath and wondering where this impulsive act might lead. Whatever meaning would it have in my life? What fruit or flower would it bear? None, no doubt; and, alas, before I had time to utter a word of regret, I felt a lump form in my throat at the queer sight of the apparition that Hisako had become, and I found myself standing in front of the house in Atagoshita.

The shōji at the narrow vestibule of the entryway had been thrown open to reveal a screen with irises painted on a silver background, and from behind it emerged, as she came to the door, not the maid but Hisako herself. She was about to go out. Both her formal dress and the look on her face spoke of cheeriest and most unclouded of dispositions.

"What a delight! How nice of you to stop by."

I stood there with a dumb expression on my face. I felt utterly stupid, as though I had been seen through and made to look the fool.

"I want you to know I'm completely recovered. I'm about to go out to the Kabuki theater. With friends. Won't you come in? Jinsaku is here."

"Well, I . . ."

"Oh, please do."

"I think not."

The curious turn of events left a bad taste in my mouth, but I tried to swallow my feelings.

"Congratulations on your speedy recovery," I said almost in a whisper, as I struggled to think of something appropriate to say. "Please don't hesitate for a minute to go on living in the very, very best of health."

Hisako stared at me, puzzled by the peculiarly stilted and almost sarcastic tone of my greeting. The horrific vision I had seen of her had vanished, and I turned to leave. Just then Jinsaku appeared at the door and insisted that I come in.

"Hisako is about to go out, but I'm here watching the house. Why don't you keep me company?"

I was returning to my senses, and insofar as I continue to abide in this vale of tears with my fellow man, I felt an obligation to join Jinsaku in seeing off Hisako who, like a fish diving in a pond, gaily flicked her skirts and sailed out the door. Jinsaku led me to his study on the second floor.

"I've been on my best behavior yesterday and today," he began proudly. "I don't know whether that's the reason, but as a result,

Hisako's condition began to improve immediately. Amazing, isn't it. I mean, the way a woman's mind works. Stay home a day or two, and in no time Hisako's fever breaks and she's back to normal."

"You can't complain if playing the faithful husband works miracles."

"Incidentally, I used the time to write an original play for the Nō stage. I call it *Tobikura—The Miracle of the Flying Storehouse.* It's based on the legend of the priest who lived on top of Mt. Shigi and who used a flying begging bowl to collect rice for his temple. The protagonist is a woman, and the deuteragonist, her younger brother the priest. The play begins with the sister traveling from Shinano to Yamato in search of her brother, and . . .

"Well, here, take a look at it for me. I'm especially interested in your reaction to the opening lines in which the sister describes her journey."

"So you haven't been round to Shinjuku lately?" I asked in time to check the movement of Jinsaku's hand as he reached for the newly bound copy of his play. His face registered a look of surprise.

"No, I haven't. Because, well . . . ," he said, hesitating. "I thought I could forget by not going over there, but as a matter of fact, I had a phone call from her a few minutes ago."

"From O-tsuna?"

"Yes."

"I see."

"She was very apologetic. She said there were a number of things for which she felt very sorry. She sounded terribly contrite. She said she really wanted to see me, and that she would be waiting at the Ginza. I was pretty harsh with her, but since she was being conciliatory, who am I to be a stickler about pride and reputation? Besides, Hisako was going out, so I thought I'd go to the Ginza and. . . ."

Jinsaku turned a fixed and intent gaze on me, his eyes hot and feverish. He inched forward on the tatami until our knees almost touched. Though I tried to back away, his head was practically in my lap when he bowed formally.

"I'm really quite the fool. I apologize for all the silly, shameful talk you've had to listen to. Dismiss it as the nonsense of a man who's lost his head over a woman. I simply lost control. Go ahead and laugh at me if you like."

Perhaps his forced smile—the tragicomic mouth with the turned-down corners, the histrionics made to echo about the room—attested to an inner joy that Jinsaku sought to suppress just as it struggled to escape its bonds and break forth in song. Because his delight at being in love again was buffeted by waves of excessive tenacity, by the fear of getting involved too deeply, he felt a need to confirm, by announcing the idea to someone else, the worth and pleasure of his romantic intoxication. Furthermore, it was apparent he had chosen me as the unfeeling rock, the heart of stone, upon which to dash his joy and thereby sound out his true feelings. I hardly knew how to deal with him, but I was able to sit there, neither placating nor ridiculing, silent as the rockface I was meant to be, because suddenly a powerful emotion had shot through my being and made it hard to the core.

Jealousy! Yes, let's put it down to jealousy. I could think of nothing but O-tsuna's voluptuous body. If after having been dropped from Yukari's heavenly ladder I happened to land on O-tsuna's navel, then hand me Shih-te's broom and let me sweep, for what better foothold could I ask for to find my way back to the Great Path of Samantabhadra?

—Ah, ah, O-tsuna of the sweet and ignorant flesh! You are my Joan, my own Jeanne Duval, lover of the immortal poet Baudelaire. How could I allow this rare, earthly gem to pass into Jinsaku's coarse hands? I drew a deep breath, and as a new sense of vitality awakened and moved through me like a tremor, I rose to my feet, champing at the bit of my resolve.

"You have things that you must do," I said, adopting a superior tone of voice. "What's more, I suggest you throw yourself into them with all the strength at your command. To hell with what others think. Do what you want to do. A real challenge will give me something worth fighting for too. Goodbye."

I left Jinsaku totally dumbstruck and marched out of the house. And like a carrier pigeon that girts the sky in a grand loop and then zeros in on its target, I turned singlemindedly toward Kurumazaka—and the task of destroying what I had created there.

What need have I to be concerned about arrest or imprisonment? If I am to embark on a journey to recapture O-tsuna, the enterprise will have to commence with the rejection of everything that Kurumazaka represented. Should I allow myself to be oppressed by the rotten smell of that fathomless pit, my life will be transformed into one long, empty whine that, reverberating endlessly in the air, wanders off in the universe. I shall sell every book, every bit of rubbish stained and sullied by that luckless place. Today! Now! This instant!

But where shall I go?

—Ah, ah, if only I knew.... But because each reflexive act— action taken at random and without forethought—contains its own order, and more importantly, the seed of the next act to be carried forward on behalf of the order of things yet to come, we must never shirk from undertaking them. I may not succeed in what I do next, and if in the final analysis my actions bear no fruit, then all that need be said is they were the end of me. To speak of arrest, vagabondage, or death by the wayside is to speak of a departure so sweeping, of a resolve so unshakable, as to admit no room for second thoughts. The choice is both paramount and irrevocable. Without a doubt it is upon acts such as these that one stakes his life.

"But what about Iori Bunzō?"

That was the question I asked myself the moment I put my hand to the latticework door of the lodging house, only to find Yasuko clattering frantically down the stairs, the hem of her kimono in disarray, the color draining from her cheeks, her bare feet treading on the dirt floor of the entryway. Finding me at the door, she clung to my arm, gripping it in fear, and gasping, her breast heaving in a desperate effort to catch her breath, she could hardly answer my questions.

"What is it? What's happened?"

"Bunzō has..."

"Bunzō has what? What about him? Is it the police?"

"No, no. He got back minutes ago."

I felt a shock akin to electricity shoot through me, and pushing aside Yasuko's hands as she clutched at me, I flew up the stairs. The sliding door was partially open, but as I was about to step into Bunzō's room, I ran headlong into a wall of air at the threshold. It repelled me with the force of a steel door.

I staggered back into the corridor, my legs shaking and unsteady, for Bunzō's once powerful frame lay draped across the bed, and though it was hidden and only dimly visible in the shadow of the shōji, it appeared to glow, burning with an ardent fire. Perhaps it was this ardency, but it enjoined an unspoken interdiction, prohibiting the trespass into his quarters of anybody who reeked of intercourse with the living.

And in the instant I was held in abeyance, what arrested my eye were the two articles that had slipped through his fingers and fallen to the floor. The sight of these two things, this odd pair of objects, seared through my brain and branded it with an indelible image. There, scattered on the tatami, were Bunzō's bar of rouge, the lipstick he had always used, and the single blossom—a heaven-sent flower—of a small, purplish vial marked with a skull and crossbones.

CRITICAL ESSAY

The Art and Act of Reflexivity
in The Bodhisattva

NEAR THE end of a long interior monologue in chapter 11, the first-person narrator, *watashi*, addresses the bodhisattva from whose name the title of the novel derives. He wonders if Samantabhadra is "a thing apart ... set in the sky like a rare and marvelous crystal formed from elements unknown to this terrestrial plane" (XI:258).[1] Not for a second should we, the readers, be deceived this sudden supplication of the deity represents a true expression of the narrator's feelings. To the contrary, he has argued consistently, even vehemently on one occasion, that a bodhisattva "does not reside solely 'above the clouds'" (VI:215). Certainly not Samantabhadra, who is the incarnation of *prajñā*, or the intuitive wisdom of Mahayana Buddhism as it translates into worldly action.[2] Had not *watashi* witnessed "the miracle of the avatar" (XI:257) only hours before? It appears the author has taken liberties with his material, and we are asked to wonder why.

For the moment, however, let us exercise a bit of license and appropriate *watashi*'s diamond-in-the-sky metaphor for Samantabhadra as an apt description of this novella. For not only does *The Bodhisattva* scintillate with a special iridescence, from the mirrorball-like imagery of its opening line to the burning ardency of its closing scene, but also the work is constructed of elements not customarily associated with the Japanese novel. One scans the horizons of a literature characterized by psychological, episodic, and aesthetic emphases to find other works, by other recognized masters, that rival *The Bodhisattva* in its heightened use of language, especially style; its tongue-in-cheek humor; its paradoxically random, and in what in this essay is defined as "reflexive," ordering of plot. If heretofore the novelty of Ishikawa's writings has resulted in their being considered anomalous, the evolution of our understanding of what constitutes modern and postmodern literature helps us to recognize this work as an important bridge in the development of avant-gardism between the pre- and postwar eras in Japan and to see how its "rare and marvelous crystal" illuminates by contrast what has been traditionally defined as contemporary Japanese literature. It points the way to a less conservative and more inclusive—or shall we say enlightened?—definition of the field.

SWEEPING GESTURES

IN THIS seminal work of 1936, Ishikawa Jun not only set the pattern for his development as a writer of what he subsequently called *jikken shōsetsu*,[3] or "experimental novels," but also created, by anticipating trends in world literature, an early example of metafiction in Japanese literature. In metafiction, the means of the narrative are their own ends; and as the narrator *watashi* tells us in the opening paragraph of the novel, they are special: fiction is not of this world; it has its own logic, mobility, and the power to transform mundane objects. The sweet and gentle breezes emanating from its quarter bear the promise of relief from the fetid odors and gusty turbulence of everyday life. To escape our surroundings, we need only make the *sweeping* gestures of "scorning the earth" (*chi o harau;* 1:163; 11:173)[4]—to employ the narrator's metaphor for his pen as both broom and magic wand—and let our imaginations soar. The concept of fiction as saving grace is developed, first, through its being identified with the "flower" of creation, namely, the *hana* of the *hana*-vs.-*chiri*,[5] the blossoms-vs.-dust antithesis, that provides the architectonic structure of the novel. It is augmented by multiple images of flight and transcendence, either as similes of birds taking wing or poets bursting into song. Finally, it coalesces into *watashi*'s agonized awareness that "*words* . . . are [his] true bodhisattva" (VII:223).

Indeed the most graphic expression of this novel's glorification of fiction, and its "fabulous" (XI:257) powers, lies in the words themselves—the verbal tour de force that Ishikawa puts on for us to read. While not entirely free of an occasional uneven and overly experimental passage, on the whole, breezy descriptions alternate with impromptu, if not staccato, dialogues which, in turn, alternate with quasi-philosophic orgies followed by indirect speech, or a blend of two or more of the above modes, the pace interrupted only to offer the reader a familiar aside ("Now...") or a bit of epigrammatic advice ("As a general rule..."). Verbs are strong action words; characters are forever running, leaping, soaring—*hashiru, haneru, hassuru, chi o harau, hishō suru*[6]—in a Sisyphean effort to overcome the leaden weight of terrestrial reality. Events happen suddenly, almost always at random and often serendipitously: one exhausts a thesaurus searching for sufficient equivalents for the numerous precipitant adverbs, *tossa ni, totan, tachimachi, totsuzen, yaniwani, iuyori hayaku.*[7] At times the speed at which the tale is told is almost breakneck. It is as if the powerful compression of ideas and images unleashes a kinetic energy that drives along the garrulous text with its long sentences, minimal paragraphing, and direct speech buried in the narrative. Ishikawa gives full range to the agglutinative features of Japanese word order, to frequent use of compound verbs to express double meaning, and to complex word play: e.g., the pun on teeth, *ha,* and fitted dentures, *ireba:* "[Bunzō's] brawny arms flew back looking white and forlorn in the air *as freshly pulled teeth* [*nuketa* ha *no yō ni*] ... no matter how much strength [he] might have once possessed, there no longer existed any task to which he might *indenture* his hands, and by putting them to work, get a *grip* on life again [*ika ni chikara o ireyō to shite mo chikara no* ireba *ga naku*]" (VI:215).

Yet there is something unorthodox and contradictory about the continuity and play of the narrative. At the same time that Ishikawa creates a sense of flow and permits his narrator moments of virtuosity, he also sets about undermining *watashi*'s authoritative voice through the liberal use of sentences giving "false scent": "To be approached in public by a beautiful woman, by one so conspicuously well dressed, and in terms so cordial, was...an embarrassment" (V:203); or reversing conjunctions (*shikashi, shikaru ni, so itte mo*) coming in rapid succession; by fracturing tense and time through the introduction of a novel-within-the-novel that curiously links and juxtaposes bohemian life in Tokyo in the mid-1930s with France in the tumultuous days of the Hundred Years War; and by a habit of twisting the narrative: "I have even thought of jumping ahead" (II:175); or interrupting it: "since she has gone to the trouble to remind me of her existence by putting in an

unsolicited appearance, it becomes my turn...to back up a bit"
(v:201). The overall effect is to strain the reader's credulity and to
suggest the narrator and/or author is operating out of control. By
maintaining an underlying thread of a story line while creating a
heightened sense of acceleration and imminent instability, Ishikawa
prepares the reader to accept dissimilar groups of reference and
metaphor as well as sudden reversals of meaning.

Thus, at the same time that Ishikawa honors the spirit of fiction
and revels in the uses of language, he maintains a surprisingly ironic
and anarchical attitude toward his material. Once again, this detach-
ment is apparent from the beginning—in the cavalier attitude of
the narrator in the opening paragraph: "'Whoever said [Tarui
Moichi] was interesting, anyway?'" (1:163), he quips;—and is
maintained throughout the work by an admixture of elegant and
vernacular diction: "the impoverished daughter...peddling as
wares the belles lettres of her avocation as a lady" (11:171). By the
end of the novel, *watashi* has become so devil-may-care about his
role as to abrogate it altogether.

> As narrator of this tale, I suppose I am obliged to supply
> the reader with a suitably serious and convincing explanation
> as to why [I] should change direction so abruptly. Unfortu-
> nately for you, I have abandoned any shred of a claim to
> being a skillful weaver of plot.... I have cast aside the wisdom
> of keeping a level head, and a body grounded in reality. All
> that remained to me were my two feet which moved of their
> own accord....My guess is that, like everything else, feet
> have a life of their own and do as they damn well please.
> (XII:264–265)

This is not the first time we encounter *watashi*—especially his
legs—behaving involuntarily, and the story carried off in a new
direction. To be sure, Ishikawa is powerfully in control of his
material no matter how much he has his narrator dissemble or
stagger.

Because what is written tongue-in-cheek is ironic, it is difficult
to detect (Is this serious?), and moreover, to assess for meaning
(What justifies the nonsense?). Consequently, the reader is depen-
dent upon clues—the secret winks communicated to him from the
writer—to learn what is afoot, as it were, in the author's mind.
Indeed, before the end of chapter 3, we are twice cautioned about

how we perceive what we read. The facts of historical inquiry are not what they appear to be (II : 174) nor can "sincerity" be accepted at face value (III : 181). Both are to be taken with a large grain of salt, or as the Japanese circumlocution *mayutsuba-mono*[8] has it, with one's eyebrow wetted down with a touch of spit. Again, in chapter 6, *watashi* writes suggestively that,

> in responding to the call [of the petty affairs of the world] . . . I have continued to let my story run astray. Someone might see an artful bit of camouflage in this tendency of mine, and no doubt there is ample evidence for such an opinion. (VI : 209)

The facetious tone of the novel alerts us to the possibility of alternate readings and hidden meanings. Although *The Bodhisattva* is narrated in the first person, and at a glance appears to resemble an "I-novel" in the manner of the Japanese naturalistic school of writing, in fact it is parody of the genre as we shall come to see: a *watashi shōsetsu* written in contradistinction to the *watakushi shōsetsu*.[9] Furthermore, it is well-meaning takeoff—perhaps an accolade offered by Ishikawa to André Gide, his mentor in the art of modernist fiction—of Gide's *Paludes* (1895). This now-forgotten *sotie* on the monotony of salon life in Paris is the story of a young writer who, situated in his ivory tower in the midst of a great "swampland," writes a parody about writing a parody. It was a work that Ishikawa was to cite years later as having an influence on his early fiction.[10]

The Bodhisattva is something else again. It is also allegory, and the predicament *watashi* describes in being "enveloped by the stuffy affairs of the world . . . gasping for air in the midst of a swirling cloud of dust" (IV : 220) goes beyond the struggle to create a parnassian prose in the midst of noisome circumstances. Through *watashi*, Ishikawa depicts the very real and poignant dilemma of the writer who posits the right and preeminence of fiction, or any countervailing myth to state the matter differently, at a time when his surroundings hinge on capitulation to absolutism—whether in the form of a slavish acceptance of reality, an unquestioning view of life and literature as solely naturalistic, or a dogmatic adherence to a political system considered divine and inviolate. *The Bodhisattva* ranks as one of the few anti-establishment—indeed resistance— novels to have been written in Japan between the seizure of Manchuria in 1931 and the invasion of China in 1937. Although understated in comparison with the defiant tone of *Marusu no uta* (The Song of the War God),[11] Ishikawa's short story published in January 1938, and immediately banned by the authorities, a close reading of *The Bodhisattva* reveals a veiled critique of a society that, unable to confront its seriously troubled nature, looks to a *deus ex machina* solution, in the form of either an imperialist state or a proletarian revolution, as the means to its salvation.

What to do, then? *Doko e?*—"Where to?" asks *watashi* repeatedly and rhetorically, only to deliver a plaintive sigh—"Ah, ah"—of mounting despair at the realization there will be no escaping the realities of "this sordid landscape . . . this land, an imperial realm no less, in which such mindless breeds prevailed and proliferated" (1:170). *Watashi*'s struggle is largely interior. He wrestles with contradictory feelings of self-hate and affirmation, of wanting to write but also to jettison his career, and of wishing to die—his ambivalence about life illustrated through the subplot involving his friend and alter ego, Bunzō. He knows his influence over the course of current events is hopelessly circumscribed, but he seizes the single opportunity to defy the powers that be "with the resolve of a Perseus" (x:250) and sets out to save Yukari. Though the result of this reflexive act is to be confronted with an ugliness more hideous than the face of the Gorgon Medusa, he is not so traumatized by this reversal so as to fail to see the irony of his predicament. Throughout the novel, *watashi* maintains sufficient levity to recognize that, however transcendent fiction may be, with its ability to lift us temporarily out of the mundane, it also has its limits. He does not fall into the error of thinking it a panacea for the world's ills. Moreover, he has no interest in having it explain life, or in promoting the myth of himself as omniscient narrator. By not losing sight of this point, he remains true to the relativistic attitude inherent to his metafictional posture.

Rather than straightjacket life with an absolutist view, *watashi* believes in what happens spontaneously and at random, as his reflexive style of narration also suggests. One might even see *The Bodhisattva* as a manifesto of literary and philosophical anarchy: a work written in praise of the gay abandon of living and writing recklessly, and of the serendipity that comes when life is allowed to order itself at random. At the end of the novel, *watashi* offers his final counsel on the oxymoronic, no-exit situation in which he and his fellow countrymen are living. Viewed in light of the period in which Ishikawa wrote these words, they border on sedition.

But where shall I go?
—Ah, ah, if only I knew.... But because each reflexive act—action taken at random and without forethought—contains its own order, and more importantly, the seed of the next act to be carried forward on behalf of the order of things yet to come, we must never shirk from undertaking them. I may not succeed in what I do next, and if in the final analysis my actions bear no fruit, then all that need be said is they were the end of me. To speak of arrest, vagabondage, or death by the wayside is to speak of a departure so sweeping, of a resolve so unshakable, as to admit no room for second thoughts. The choice is both paramount and irrevocable. Without a doubt it is upon acts such as these that one stakes his life. (XII:267)

Surely Ishikawa's employment of the phrase "reflexive act" (*mubō naru kōi*) is a play upon the words "*acte gratuit*" (*mushō naru kōi* as he rendered them in his translation of Gide's novel) taken from *Les caves du Vatican* and that enjoyed currency in Europe as a shibboleth for iconoclastic behavior[12] in the years that witnessed the collapse of the nineteenth-century social order after World War I. In this instance the narrator is not manipulating the text but is dead set on taking action as dictated by the instincts of his "inner chemistry" (XI:260).

the whole of my life [was] a dark pit, an underground cellar, so it mattered little what form of incarceration awaited me. What was the point of allowing myself to get upset, since the choices were one and the same? Yet I could not but wonder if there was not more to life....

But let there be no mistake. My cri de coeur was nothing frivolous. It came from the very depths—the inner chemistry—of my being.

Yes, that's it! Board a train! Board a ship! Embark on any vehicle that, sounding the whistle of departure, is leaving at top speed (XI:259).

Watashi may not know where his recklessness will lead him, but to remain within the status quo is to be buried alive.

If, as an exercise in metafiction, *The Bodhisattva* is vitally concerned with issues of narrative style, at the same time it is a social and political document, especially given the times in which it was written. For behind its celebration of language for language's sake—the smokescreen thrown in the face of the authorities, the cloud of dust kicked up by *watashi* to stifle the "the beasts... seeking to take control of [his] voice" (XI:258)—lurks its all-important satirical, even subversive, message. Thus, in order to better understand both the "flower" and the "dust" of Ishikawa's creation, let us turn briefly to a discussion of the story, its overlay of Buddhist and other imagery, and finally, Ishikawa's theory of "automatic living and writing." It is from the careful arrangement of the helices and axes of these elements that its rare crystal is constructed. The brilliance of Ishikawa's writing in *The Bodhisattva,* and subsequent novels, lies in his special ability to order multiple levels of parody, allegory, and satire into an intricate whole.

YUKARI: IN SEARCH OF "AFFINITY"

AT ITS most obvious level of appreciation, *The Bodhisattva* is an evocation of life in the back alleys, cafes, and bars of Tokyo—and in the original, of the intonations and nuances of Tokyo dialect as it was spoken in the first decade of the Shōwa era. Hailing the ever-present taxi, the narrator takes us on a tour of the city as he ventures from his lodgings in Kurumazaka to Nippori, Toranomon, Shinjuku, and Atagoshita. Settling into the comfort of the back seat, he regales us with his story. For those who know Tokyo, he covers familiar, nostalgic territory.

Set in early June 1936, in the last of the good weather before the onset of the rainy season, the novel presents us with five days in the life of its first-person narrator. He is identified only as *watashi* (first-person, informal male pronoun for *watakushi* in Tokyo speech), but he is strikingly similar to his author. He aspires to a career as a writer, in this instance composing for his own edification a biography of the early French poet and feminist writer Christine de Pizan (1363?–1431?). While Pizan seems an unlikely topic, Ishikawa's choice speaks of his erudition and his desire to draw linkages across cultures. One might even see it as a reflection of his intuitive sense of future directions in literary scholarship. With the rise of Women's Studies in the last two decades, there has been a revival of interest in this neglected figure of Renaissance literature, especially her vision of a feminine utopia as depicted in *Le livre de la cité des dames* of 1405.[13]

Watashi would prefer to devote his energies to such esoterica, but in order to make ends meet, he must turn out copy for *Seiron* (Political Debate), a journal of contemporary issues. He is unhappy with this work, and his unhappiness is compounded by his circle of acquaintances—the hapless Tarui Moichi; the luckless Tabes, Hikosuke and his wife O-kumi; the avaricious Kuzuhara Yasuko. Each is driven by the same grinding poverty that haunts him, impoverishment having turned each one into a caricature of his true self. Take, for example, *watashi*'s erstwhile friend Moichi, who works for "Mutual Finance" and who, characteristically enough, is forever in need of someone to lend him a watch, a room for the night, or to stand him the cost of a round of drinks. Or take the case of Kuzuhara Yasuko, simultaneously inspired by the small economies she realizes on household expenses and her big plans to make a killing in the commodities market by purchasing and reselling five thousand tons of *tetsukuzu*, or scrap metal—the word "scrap" (*kuzu*) echoing the sound of her surname; and Yasuko, the cheapness of her soul. Her success is assured if only *watashi* will help her, she insists, appearing repeatedly at the sliding door to his room.

Surrounded by such bothersome types, *watashi*'s sole source of comfort and inspiration is Yukari ("Affinity"), the sister of his former college classmate and best friend, Iori Bunzō. Because of her involvement with the political underground, *watashi* has not seen Yukari for a decade, his unrequited love fueled only by his vision of her as all that is pristine and ideal. In short, she is a latter-day version of the providential *tennin* "angel," or otherworldly creature in *Taketori monogatari* (Tale of the Bamboo Cutter), *Hagoromo* ([The Goddess in] The Feather Robe), and other early classics of Japanese literature.[14] To possess Yukari is to experience paradise on earth. But she is wanted by the police, and the climax of the novel comes, ending almost as precipitiously as it begins, when *watashi* rushes to Shinjuku Station to save her from falling into their trap. That this self-styled "bookish intellectual" (v:204) succeeds in reaching her first and thereby outwitting the police is almost immaterial, however. What is important is how the incident epitomizes, by pulling together the subplots tangential to it, the hero's resolve to act on his instincts, and how this reflexive act leads to the destruction of what he calls his "swan-maiden myth" (XI:257), namely, the apotheosis that he has made of Yukari.

MITATE: GLORIFIED ANALOGIES

THE BODHISATTVA would be a thinner, more transparent piece of writing were it not for the amplification of the text that Ishikawa achieves through mitate,[15] a technique reminiscent of the conceits of seventeenth-century English metaphysical poetry. In ordinary Japanese parlance, mitate refers simply to identifying like-sets: comparing objects, diagnosing a disease, or parodying a topic. Often it is a game, played at a geisha party perhaps, in which customers are likened to flowers, animals, or prominent names in history—Is the guest a plum or a cherry? A zinnia? Or a cosmos? Who is the tall, perceptive giraffe? And who, the plodding elephant? In the art of renga, or linked poetry, it becomes a complex process of adopting images from preceding lines and recasting them in different contexts as parallel or analogous topics.

In kyōka,[16] the comic form of Edo-period poetry that Ishikawa studied and practiced, mitate becomes the amalgam of the parlor game and the practice of linked verse: not only does it draw analogies and link images, but more specifically, it identifies lesser, even ignoble, subjects with higher and more illustrious levels of being. Similarly, its companion operation—yatsushi,[17] which refers originally to a highborn person travelling incognito—implies an aristocratic, noblesse-oblige descent into the plebeian. As members of what might have been called the underground literary establishment of Edo, the kyōka poets of the Temmei era (1781–1789) gathered in coteries in which, by renaming themselves with humorous sobriquets, e.g., Yadoya-no-Meshimori ("The Inn's Ample Servings"), or Shikatsube-no-Magao ("The True Face of Seriousness"),[18] they set aside rigid distinctions in rank and education and acted as social equals. In so doing, they created a setting in which they viewed their fellow participants as the "Undiscovered Genjis" (Yatsushi Genji) and "Glorified Komachis" (Mitate Ono-no-Komachi) that they immortalized in countless kyōka verses, and ukiyo-e and surimono prints.[19]

Through the use of mitate, Ishikawa is able to lift the events of his story out of spatial and temporal confines and give them a historic, even global, context. In chapter 2, the novel-within-the-novel moves from its setting in Japan to a cataloguing of the principal events in the life of Christine de Pizan, who shortly before her death composed the first and only contemporary literary account of the exploits of Joan of Arc. Joan's story is, of course, the tale of the innocent maiden who, in France's hour of peril, rallied its armies and restored its honor. Not only do Christine and Joan constitute a matching pair for *watashi*, he also sees them as an abstraction of an inherently interdependent and indivisible relationship between older woman and young girl, authoress and heroine, feminist and feminist ideal. Taken together their lives symbolize the extremes of female experience—with Christine representing the downtrodden and oppressed status of her sex, and Joan, its triumphant leader. He recognizes Christine's vision of Joan is no more substantial than the dust to which all matter and mortals return, but it comes into being and prevails as a powerful image because of the poet's determined and—at Christine's late age—almost bone-crushing devotion to the beatification of Joan. Put in terms of *watashi*'s respective references from the symbolist theories of Paul Valéry and Arthur Symons, the poet succeeds because of her "unending efforts" (VII:221) to make "flowers bloom on paper" (VI:214).

Moreover, he is attracted to the possibilities in the superimposition of an analogy taken from the pages of French history as applied to Asian tradition. He sees the symbiotic relationship of Joan and Christine as a mirror image of the legendary Chinese hermits and objects of Zen iconography, Han-shan and Shih-te (Jp: Kanzan/Jittoku).[20] Han-shan is the eccentric T'ang-dynasty poet of "Cold Mountain" fame; Shih-te, "The Foundling," the lowly monk and sweeper of the kitchen at the Kuo-ch'ing monastery. Whenever Han-shan descended from his mountain lair, Shih-te had saved for him the few scraps gleaned from the kitchen floor. The two became inseparable friends and were often seen laughing, drinking, and cavorting about the temple grounds like a pair of long-haired simpletons. Legend grew that they were incarnations of Mañjuśrî (Jp: Monju) and Samantabhadra (Jp: Fugen), the bodhisattvas of wisdom and wisdom-in-action.[21] In Zen paintings, Shih-te is often depicted as wielding a broom by which he gathers scraps for Han-shan or—interpreted more figuratively—the gems of Mañjuśrî's wisdom. Han-shan is shown reciting his verses in a state of intoxication.

By *watashi*'s admission, his analogy is a "slightly lame metaphor" (II:173)—perhaps because the reader is tempted to identify Christine with Han-shan since both are poets?—but the concept is not as impaired or farfetched as he fears. (We need only recall, for example, Kerouac's *Dharma Bums*, of 1958, in which members of his Zen coterie are likened to Han-shan; "Japhy Rider" and "Alvah Goldbrook" also serve as *kyōka*-like pseudonyms for the.poets Gary Snyder and Allen Ginsberg.) Moreover, the diachronic alignment of Mañjuśrî and Samantabhadra with the synchronic combination of Joan and Christine is reinforced by the imagery of the aforementioned dichotomy of flowers vs. dust. In particular, the introduction of the floral "garland" or "wreath" (*hanawa*) to describe *watashi*'s "protean visage of womankind" (II:173) ought to give us pause and call to mind the "Flower Ornament" or *Avataṁsaka Sûtra*, the principal scripture of Hua-yen (Jp: Kegon) Buddhism.²² Among Buddhist texts, this sutra singles out Samantabhadra as chief of the bodhisattvas and gives special prominence to his vows and practices. The narrator of *The Bodhisattva* intends for his reader to identify Christine with Shih-te, and in turn, with Samantabhadra; likewise, Joan is to Han-shan as Han-shan is to Mañjuśrî. For *watashi* the triumvirate of Christine, Shih-te, and Samantabhadra is the agency by which the collective glory and wisdom of Joan, Han-shan, and Mañjuśrî is brought into the world. In the chaos of the Hundred Years War, did not Joan manifest herself as France's bodhisattva? And in applying the deft touch and tidying sweep of her pen to her heroine's tarnished reputation after the ignominious trial and execution at Rouen, did not Christine become Joan's Shih-te, and her Samantabhadra?

Watashi extends the parallel even farther. As he confesses in an offhand remark (IV:193), Joan of Arc is actually an analogy for Yukari—and by tacit extension—Christine, for himself. If Joan had been the liberator of her country in its difficult hour, surely through her commitment to revolutionary ideals, Yukari becomes the symbol of his chiliastic dream that someday the world will be "turned on its end" and a "Buddhaland" established here on earth (VI:214; II:173). Or so he fantasizes. The connection is so tenuous that he himself can hardly believe it, and this fact explains in large measure why Yukari remains throughout the novel a nebulous figure—"glimpsed through rifts in pristine clouds" (VI:218)—and why *watashi* experiences great difficulty in fleshing out his vision of her. Nonetheless, he longs for Yukari with almost religious devotion, and he assumes the task of beatification as his "practice" in the Way of Samantabhadra. As he asks in his forlorn prayer, delivered to the unlit chandelier in the bar near Shinjuku Station, to obtain Yukari is to know even a particle of the divine. To tell her story, and to rush to her side, are his attenuated means of linking himself to a movement that will "upset the normal order of things" (VI:214) and alter the state of affairs in the land/ kingdom/ imperial realm as the word *kokudo*[23]—Ishikawa's metonymical way of referring to Japan—must be variously translated.

The novel is shot through with analogies; in fact, the correspondences and mirror-imaging of its characters and ideas are not unlike the reflections of the myriad jewels of Indra's Net, a central metaphor in Hua-yen Buddhism, in which every facet of reality is seen as radiating with every other image. It is interesting to note, that, whereas the ordering of relationships among characters in most Japanese novels is by means of "the eternal triangle," or not atypically, triangles within triangles, in *The Bodhisattva* it is achieved by pairs and chains of analogies. Likened first to "a bead of water"(I:163), Tarui Moichi, for example, soon degenerates into "an ordinary pot finding [its] mate" in Tabe Hikosuke and becoming one of the set of "two vases that, breathing with one accord, absorb the air of each other's mediocrity" (III:175); only to be linked to Terao Jinsaku, a teacher of Nō chanting, through the "off-color" arrangement (V:202) of sharing the rent on a room at the Benihana Apartments. Thus it is that this rolling stone and former errand boy for the vaudeville theater in Asakusa performs his amateurish rendition of Shih-te in tandem with Hikosuke's, or Jinsaku's, role as Han-shan. Or, again, an implicit parallel is drawn between Kuzuhara Yasuko and Shih-te when *watashi* recognizes that her penuriousness arises out of a childhood spent as a "scullery maid" (IV:198). "Monomania was her normal state of mind" (IV:197), he intones, failing to see how Yasuko's obsessions hardly differ in extent from the "high degree of excitability" (III:180) that afflicts him; or just about all of the characters for that matter.

The analogies and pairings assume, finally, a metaphysical dimension in the exercises of verbal rubbery carried on between *watashi* and Bunzō—the dialogues that Hikosuke calls "*konnyaku mondō"* (VII:221).[24] Although not without a suicidal impulse himself, *watashi* becomes the advocate of life and the vitalistic power contained in words, and he uses his pen in the manner of the symbolists to turn a black hole into a flower. By contrast, Bunzō has written himself off as a "defect" (VI:212). By abusing alcohol, he seeks to take his life. Life and death war within the breasts of both men, but it is Bunzō who yields to self-destruction. In the final scene, the trademark of his myrmidon-like vitality, his bar of rouge, lies abandoned alongside the purple vial marked with a fatal X.

AWASEKAKŌ: ART OF THE PALIMPSEST

IF THE poetic device of *mitate* makes it possible to embellish or "glorify" the narrative and give it greater density of interpretation, Ishikawa also strikes upon the concept of the palimpsest of medieval European letters as further means to amplify the text. Palimpsest (literally, "scraped again") refers to a parchment or tablet that has been erased in order to inscribe a new text and, by extension, to a multilayered approach to writing. Accordingly, for Ishikawa it becomes the *locus classicus*, so to speak, of *mitate* in western literature. A palimpsest possesses the fascination of a double-exposed photograph, a painting revealed to be rarer by the discovery of a second layer of composition, or an archeological dig that uncovers the site of an earlier level of inhabitation. It is, in Baudelaire's phrase, a fitting metaphor for the human mind.

> What is the human brain, if not an immense palimpsest? My brain is a palimpsest, as yours is too, reader. Innumerable layers of ideas and feelings have fallen one after another on your brain, as gently as light. It seemed as if each were swallowing up the previous one. But in reality none has perished.... Forgetting is only momentary therefore; and in such solemn circumstances, in death perhaps, and generally in the intense excitement generated by opium, the whole immense, complicated palimpsest of memory unfolds in an instant, with all its superimposed layers of dead feelings, mysteriously embalmed in what we call oblivion.... Just as every action, thrown into the whirlwind of universal action, is in itself irrevocable and irreparable, an abstraction of its possible results, so each thought is ineffaceable. The palimpsest of memory is indestructible.[25]

In this century, the uses of the multitiered construction of the palimpsest fired the imagination of the Imagists, e.g., H. D. and Ezra Pound; more recently, it has been the key concept employed by literary critic Gérad Genette in *Palimpsestes: La littérature au second degré* and his analysis of the novels of Marcel Proust as "surimpressionism."[26] It is through techniques Genette calls para- and hypertextuality, bricolage, transformation, and transvalorization that Ishikawa may also be said to enrich his text.

Ishikawa does not use the word palimpsest per se, there being no equivalent in Japanese; nor does he attempt to turn it into a paronym, as is often the case when Japanese borrows from a foreign tongue. But the idea is everywhere in evidence, judging from the deliberate and patterned alignment of characters (*Orurean no shōjo to Poashii no rōjo to o* awasekakō *to suru;* 11:172), analogies (*watashi no shukō ni kakaru* mitate *Kanzan Jittoku;* 11:173), transparencies (*Yukari no omokage o kono tōki yo no shōjo ni* sukiutsushite; XI:255), and lacquerings (*kakumade* uwanuri *no tesū;* XI:256). He employs it in the "shadow play" (VII:234) of having Jinsaku dance like a stick figure before a curtain of dust; or in having *watashi* read in O-kumi's dying face "the Buddhist depiction of the nine stages of the decomposition of the flesh" (IX:239). Just as the palimpsest is a product of the literature of Europe's Middle Ages, the superimposition (*hensō no utsushi-e*)[27] employed in this scene derives from the thought and art of Japan's medieval period. It is through these subtleties that Ishikawa substantiates his use of analogy and links cross-culturally images that lack traditional associations.

T'IEN-LUNG: "THE ZEN OF ONE FINGER"

THE OVERLAY of Buddhist images in the narrative notwithstanding, *watashi*'s stated belief in nothingness is anarchic rather than Buddhist, for by no means does the novel advocate the propositions of institutional religion. To the contrary, *watashi* is sarcastic: leave the rigors of the monastic life to others; his notion of religious zeal is Taoist "pure inactivity" (XIII:224). Still he does not hesitate to appropriate Buddhist terminology in order to call his novel a *rishōki,*[28] i.e., a chronicle of the miraculous works of a bodhisattva. In his view, there is value to the "mumbo jumbo" (*uroji muroji;*

VI:214)²⁹ of Buddhism, but only if and when it can be translated into his own idiom.

It was stated previously that the narrator draws upon the paired images of *hana* (flowers) and *chiri* (dust). The words occur regularly, and in a variety of forms as *hanawa*, wreath; *hitohira no hana*, single blossom; *hyappō no hana*, the hundred treasures of the Lotus; *chirizuka*, heap of dust; *sajin*, grit and grime; *zokujin*, worldly affairs, etc., dust also being closely associated with *kuzu*, scrap; *hogo*, trash; and *ori*, dregs.³⁰ As a metaphor for glory and evanescence, the imagery of flowers and dust is often employed in works of Japanese literature, most notably the *Heike monogatari* (Tale of the Heike);³¹ but in this case its appearance has special significance. The novel's reference in chapter 8 to the ninth-century Chinese Zen master, T'ien-lung (Jp: Tenryū; VIII:224) alerts us to the source and meaning of Ishikawa's particular reasons for employing the image. Religious tradition has assigned to T'ien-lung the role of creator and teacher of the nonverbal lesson of "The Zen of One Finger" that appears in the koan text of *Pi-yen lu* (Jp: *Hekiganroku* [1128]).³² More importantly, the story is prefaced by the epistemological question of how-one-knows-prior-to-knowing:

A speck of dust rises in the air: it contains the whole of the earth. A single flower blooms: the world gives issue. Yet before the speck appeared, and the flower blossomed, how did we behold them? And set our eyes upon their glory?³³

These well-known lines from the Buddhist literature set the stage for the story of the monk Chu-ti (Jp: Gutei) who, when he sought to learn the fundamental law of Zen, was shown by T'ien-lung who simply raised a finger. Chu-ti was enlightened by this act, and thereafter, "whenever anything was asked, [he] would just raise one finger."³⁴

The world is an unspoken whole; likewise, the query that prefaces the story of T'ien-lung and Chu-ti is a brilliant encapsulation of the doctrine of universal interdependence fundamental to Huayen Buddhism. It is the concept illustrated by the aforementioned reflecting jewels of Indra's Net; of the "Treatise on the Golden Lion" of Fa-tsang (643–712), in which the sect's patriarch cites a single hair atop the head of lion as containing the hairs of all lions;³⁵ of the many parallel references to worlds-within-worlds in the *Avataṁsaka Sûtra*, especially its final chapters, the *Gaṇḍha-*

vyūha (Jp: *Nyūhokkaibon*) section on "Entering the Realm of the Reality."[36]

More often treated as a literary text than a religious one, the *Gaṇḍhavyūha* relates the story of the youth Sudhana (Jp: Zenzai dōji),[37] and his journey throughout India in quest of enlightenment. Advised by Mañjuśrī to seek his teachers among people from all walks of life, he travels the land, visiting monks, nuns, lay Buddhists, nonbelievers, wizards, and night spirits. He encounters Maitreya, the Buddha of the Future, who leads him to the "tower of the treasury of adornment" where he sees "innumerable similarly adorned towers, each as extensive as space, yet not interfering with each other."[38] Finally, he returns to Mañjuśrī, and through his intervention, seeks the counsel of the chief of the bodhisattvas.

> Observing Samantabhadra, [Sudhana] sees in every pore every feature of the mundane and spiritual worlds, and finally he sees himself in Samantabhadra's being, transversing infinite realms, coursing in a sphere of endless, inexhaustible knowlege.[39]

It is the perfection of *prajñā* (Jp: *chie*), knowledge or wisdom— but meaning, specifically, wisdom translated into action—that symbolizes the workings of Samantabhadra, and it is this particularly activist orientation toward bodhisattvahood that sets him apart. In the name of enlightenment for sentient beings, he is prepared to assume any form, be it male or female, kitchensweep or prostitute, as suggested by the legend of Shih-te, or other stories such as the one told in the Nō drama *Eguchi*. (Caught in a sudden downpour on the road to Eguchi, the poet-priest Saigyō [1118– 1190] sought shelter at a brothel but was denied admission by a courtesan who discloses she is an incarnation of Samantabhadra come to save him from going astray.[40]) It is the air of protean spontaneity and unpretentiousness that attacts *watashi* to this bodhisattva. He chooses him as his guardian spirit, and in calling himself a disciple of Samantabhadra's way (*Fugen-gyō*),[41] he seeks to use words "to take the gem of Mañjuśrī's wisdom, and sundering it like a diamond into tiny chips and pieces, translate its essence into … ordinary speech and publish [it] throughout the land" (II:173). Samantabhadra is his bodhisattva, he tells Bunzō, precisely because he does not reside "above the clouds" (VI:215).

HOTOKE NI NARU:
DEATH AND TRANSFIGURATION
IN THE VERNACULAR

WATASHI CHAMPIONS the argument that a bodhisattva is a manifest and this-wordly being. He is able to speak unabashedly of his visit with Moichi to the brothel in Shinjuku, he tells us, because "such places are not unknown to Samantabhadra" (II: 174). He announces that, though the presence of his bodhisattva may go undetected by the "clairvoyant eye" (*tōkan no me*)[42] of a follower of Zen, as one attuned to recognizing the divine in the mundane, he need only "use his nose to sniff [it] out" (VIII: 224).

Bunzō adopts the role of devil's advocate with regard to this proposition. For him, *watashi*'s beatification of Samantabhadra constitutes the latest fabrication in a long line of fictions and self-deceptions. "How can you possibly be proud of yourself? Think how silly you look, kneeling at your desk and listening to your pen scratch away at the composition of a dirty old mandala" (VI: 214). Moreover, his definition of a bodhisattva reflects the vernacular interpretation—one that substitutes *hotoke*, a close yet not identical synonym for buddha (Jp: *butsu, butsuda*) or bodhisattva (*bosatsu*).[43] As Hikosuke prepares to clean the house after O-kumi's death, Bunzō asks, quite literally, "Where's the Buddha?" (*Hotokesama wa;* IX: 241). Of course, he is speaking of the corpse, conferring instant buddhahood upon it as in the common expression *hotoke ni naru* (to become a bodhisattva; to die)[44] and elevating O-kumi to a degree of sanctity she had not enjoyed in this life. As the Latin expression *De mortuis nil nisi bonum* (and its English derivation, "Ne'er speak ill of the dead") suggest, the canonization of the deceased arises out of feelings of reverence—and dread, namely, the primitive avoidance of any ill will or vengeance likely to be wreaked upon the living. This is the interpretation that Bunzō opts for: "Only by dropping dead...[does] a man become a bodhisatt-va." For him, bodhisattvas reside outside this world. "And what will you do," he says poking fun at *watashi*'s views, "when I hop on a cloud and take off to the heavens?" (VI: 214–215). He laughs a high, dry laugh—the laughter that is heard whenever the characters in the novel take themselves too seriously.

Watashi is often reminded of the ludicrous situation in which he finds himself. Typically his frustration is directed at the petty machinations and maneuverings of Moichi or Yasuko, yet he knows that their behavior is symptomatic of a larger problem. They, and people like them, make "no distinction between the world of the living and the realm of the dead ... seeing the dust that dances about their heads as the flower of their lives" (VIII:225). He equates most of Japan with this "mindless breed" (I:170); and, referring to an inability to establish anything but the most superficial rapport with Jinsaku, he laments that Jinsaku and he are the latest generation "of rara avises born on this barren island, a land too sterile to water and nourish the seeds of a taste for naked sentiment or directness of speech.... Words lose their meaning, and what is left is the empty shell of formality. Indeed they become useful only to fumigate the air." (VIII:232). The country is populated by pimps and prostitutes, usurers and their henchmen in dark glasses, publicists and right-wing parvenus such as Sakagami and Yamanoi of *Seiron* magazine, intellectuals like Jinsaku whose true thoughts remain indecipherable.

KUMO NO UE: "ABOVE THE CLOUDS"

IT IS a kingdom imperiled, a land sorely in need of the intervention of a Joan of Arc but whose leader, like Yukari (although she represents the opposite end of the political spectrum), can only be glimpsed "above the clouds." *Kumo no ue*[45] is a well-known phrase from the classical lexicon that refers to the emperor and the lofty status of the imperial court. We need only recall that at the time when *The Bodhisattva* was written, the Japanese emperor was considered divine, and his subjects forbidden to look upon his person. "Above the clouds" appears often in the novel, although initially in connection with the fragrant but unseen presence of Yukari or Samantabhadra. In *watashi*'s dialogue with Bunzō, however, a subtle shift occurs. For the first time a veiled contrast, rather than analogy, is drawn between the seeming nebulousness of a bodhisattva and the invisibility of temporal authorities.

> If you think Samantabhadra resides only above the clouds, in some sort of imperial palace in the sky, you're dead wrong, and what's more you're looking in the wrong direction. I can't make myself clearer on this point: it is because my bodhisattva manifests himself here on earth that he is a true bodhisattva. (VI:215)

At this point Buddhist imagery ceases to be employed for textual
amplification and is put to allegorical and satirical uses that verge
on the subversive. Bunzō cautions *watashi* immediately against
loose talk, and we know that *watashi* himself is cognizant of the
possible consequences of lèse majesté from the passage concerning
Jinsaku's proposed revision of the Nō drama *Semimaru,* a work
banned from the repertoire for its suggestions of immoral conduct
on the part of an emperor and subsequent discontinuity in the
imperial succession.[46] After the unhappy rendezvous with Yukari,
and the destruction of the "swan-maiden myth" through Samantabhadra's use of Yukari as "the temporary seat of [his] manifestation" (XI:257), all pretense is dropped, and at the risk of introducing extraneous material into the narrative, *watashi* makes his point
explicit. In a translation from the French, he quotes the essayist
Alain: "The gods are constituted not unlike ourselves. Nay, let me
be more emphatic. They are constituted, as are we, from beasts."
Once again, the implications are too volatile to let hang in the air,
and the frame of reference of Alain's *Les dieux*[47] is narrowed to
include no more than "foreign gods" (XI:258). It is at this point
watashi inserts the dissonant and dissembling reference to Samantabhadra as a "crystal-in-the-sky" that is cited at the beginning of
this essay.

If *watashi* had found through his investigations into the life of
Christine de Pizan that mythmaking, like fiction, is possessed of
meliorative uses for beautifying history, he also comes to the sober-
ing realization of its fallacious applications. As a result of Yukari's
metamorphosis into a *yakṣa*[48]—the "miracle of the avatar" that
transforms a comely swan into a "fire-eating emu" (XI:257)—he
recognizes that neither she, nor a nodding Buddha, nor an emperor
residing above the clouds can "turn the world on its end" (VI:214)
and change the existing order. He dismisses his glorification of
Yukari as the product of "a lovesick idiot" (X:250; XI:256). The
error of his ways lies, he finds, in having allowed himself to think
Yukari might have altered the course of his life or the situation in
which he finds himself.

> I had borrowed a shaft of [Samantabhadra's] otherworldly
> light, and taking advantage of its mistlike properties, used it
> to surround everything in my life—my manuscript, my work,
> my philosophy, my feelings—in an aura of mystery. (XI:256)

Mystification has its fair uses as a technique of fiction for soften-
ing the sharp edges of reality, or concealing what one dare not say
in public. Yet it must be handled with care, as *watashi* recognizes
only too clearly, because of the dangers inherent in its misapplica-
tion. And if this lesson is valid for the realm of fiction, how much
more true for real life!

Watashi's world is filled with gloom at the despair he perceives
on every side. "I cannot see!" (xi:258), he shouts, citing lines in
English from D. H. Lawrence's "Last Lesson of the Afternoon"
(*Rhyming Poems*, 1913), a poem in which a teacher regrets that
his "pack of unruly hounds"—shades of the pimps "barking at
[the] heels" (1:169) of Moichi and *watashi* in the back alleys of
Shinjuku—are eager only to give chase to the sound of the dis-
missal bell. It is a lament probably familiar to Ishikawa from his
own short-lived career as a high-school teacher,[49] but more importantly, it is charged with the frustration he experiences at the
thought his readers may fail to note, or even care about, the point
he seeks to convey. It is "the novelist's complaint," he says.

> I am sick, and what is the good of it all?
> What good to them or me, I cannot see! (xi:258)

Although Ishikawa quotes only two lines, Lawrence's poem expresses more fully the thought that weighs on *watashi*'s mind:

> So shall I take
> My last dear fuel of life to heap upon my soul
> And kindle my will to a flame that shall consume
> Their dross of indifference; and take the toll
> Of their insults in punishment?—I will not—
> I will not waste my soul and my strength for this,
> What do I care for all that they do amiss!
> What is the point of this teaching of mine, and of this
> learning of theirs? It all goes down the same abyss.

Moreover, *watashi* perceives that the pervasive darkness is
identified with larger forces. It is not simply a personal matter of
"the crepuscular light dividing life from death" (viii:233) that
wars within his breast. More importantly, it is the crisis that hangs
over the land in the form of the ominous thunderheads he sees
from O-tsuna's window after their hour of lovemaking. The scene
is both beautiful and bittersweet. One of the rare quiescent mo-

ments in the novel, it is a plaintive statement of what is happening to the country.

> There, at the heart of the metropolis and its great roar, all that I could see on the horizon was the shadow of desolate clouds piled one on top of another. . . . As I sat there looking out the window, I felt utterly oppressed by the darkness that hung so heavily, layer upon layer, over the lights of the city. I felt crushed by the weight, pinned down and unable to move. The woman slept silently beside me, covered in a light quilt that assumed the contour of her woman-flesh, adorning it with an array of fans scattered across a turquoise back-ground. But I was filled with shame. So great was my humil-iation, and so hard did I bite the nail of my thumb out of frustration, that it turned an incandescent blue and white, burning like the hottest of flames. (v:208)

The mood is almost one of *mono-no-aware,* a rarity in Ishikawa's writing, and it is precisely the seductive feeling of powerlessness associated with Japanese-style pathos that *watashi* fears most. How tempting, how all too easy "to heave a great sigh of relief and entrust one's life to the hands of fate" (v:208). He cannot rest blithely unconcerned, however. Otherwise, to what purpose have human beings been created and set apart from "paving stones, or the stand of trees across the way?" (v:208).

SEISHIN NO UNDŌ: THE PRAJÑÂ OF THE SPIRIT

IT IS will (*ishi*), or spirit (*seishin*),[50] he decides, that gives mankind his unique capacity. And the lack of it, why *watashi*'s life—like the imaginary diary entry he records in dubious imitation of Tolstoy (VII:222)—is so spiritless. The will to be otherwise remains the last bulwark against acquiescence to absolutism. The conscious exercise of words is one form of resistance—already we have noted the frustration *watashi* experiences at the way words either are "empty shells," or, in his conversations with Bunzō, threaten to become unintelligible (even though these dialogues are rich in suggestion for the novel). How much easier communication had been a decade earlier when he and Bunzō had devised a language of "aeroplanes" and "fireworks" (III:183) and conveyed an entire body of thought via a single utterance. *Watashi*'s tongue is always on the verge of losing control—the novel uses the pejorative verbs *shaberu* (to chatter) and *kuchibashiru* (to run at the mouth),[51] to describe undisciplined talk. It leads him to commit "blasphemy" on one occasion when he speaks ill of O-kumi's mother as having died "a dog's death" (IV:191). He is ashamed of himself, but at times he permits this license because "prattling" is, he says, the only way to verify the fact of his existence. It is a defense against silence, or being silenced; and it is an alternative to the irresponsible know-nothingism that has become fashionable in certain intellectual circles. He believes in the vitality inherent to words—even as it manifests itself ironically in the phrase "I shall die!" (VII:223)—and he sees words as his raison d'être and his praxis in the way of the bodhisattva. It is for this reason that he chooses to "brush from [his] wings the dust of the floating world and the dregs of human sentimentality" (I:163) to become a novelist.

Therefore by definition, the act of writing is a far different operation from living and talking. In the initial conversation between Bunzō and *watashi*, these "literary youths" (*bungaku seinen*)[52] agree as to what writing is not: it does not consist of working in a "prescribed form or shape," nor is it a matter of having the right "equipment." Under no circumstances is it to be equated to an "overwhelming proliferation of words" as represented by the "mountain of trash" produced by Balzac, for example. They also attempt to define the topic in constructive terms by speaking of the importance of maintaining a high level of creative energy ("Tell me, why is it a writer takes up his pen at the precise moment he decides to relax his powers of concentration?"), and a vague notion of "totality" that dictates the nature of a work of art ("It is for the sake of the larger design that the individual branches are sacrificed.... that men become artists;" III:181), but their dialogue does not lead to the articulation of a theory of prose, and the novel never really returns to the subject in a substantial way. Only later, when *watashi* is stymied by his inability to work, he remarks, "As a general rule, the inspiration to write derives not from anything anterior to the act of writing but the act itself" (VII:217). The implications of this laconic aside are not explored, but the passage contains the germ of a theory of vitalistic prose that resonates with *watashi*'s sharply delineated views on the nature and importance of reflexive acts.

It was not until the publication of *Bungaku taigai* (All About Literature)[53] in 1942 that Ishikawa articulated his modernist philosophy of vitalism concerning the two concepts of automatic living, *seishin no undō* (the action of the spirit) and automatic writing, *pen to tomo ni kangaeru* (thinking with my pen).[54] In this collection of essays, he posits the existence of a level of consciouness—a Bergsonian élan vital, a Taoist *ki*—that he calls "spirit" (*seishin*) and distinguishes from the ordinary workings of the mind. The task of the novelist is to shut out "psychology" so that "spirit" comes into play and creates something new, something that advances—"even if only one ten millionth of a second divided into more infinitesimal units"[55]—faster than quotidian reality. Like the concept of *prajñā* that informs the bodhisattvahood of Samantabhadra, Ishikawa's spirit derives from an intuitive, almost unconscious, wisdom or energy that translates itself into action.

> This is to think with words on the very perimeters of language. Neither is it to pause, to flash upon a clever idea and transpose it to paper with a look of self-satisfaction; nor is it to think first in slovenly fashion and then shore up one's thoughts in consultation with Reason. The author's effort always originates in the yet unknown. What new worlds are to be created if he intends to pull into a work the flotsam and jetsam of what he knows already? I cannot salute the notion that one should write by beaming a flashlight on reality and reproducing it before the batteries fail. All that writers need comprehend before putting pen to paper is that the road ahead is utter darkness. Truly, this is the only experience open to us.[56]

HAN-SHIZENSHUGI: ANTI-NATURALISM[57]

THE UNARTICULATED target of Ishikawa's polemic is the *watakushi shōsetsu*, or I-novel. As mentioned previously, it is the object of parody and satire in *The Bodhisattva*. For Japanese naturalist writers, the novel was an unadorned depiction of reality experienced subjectively by a first-person author who, out of a commitment to realism, and especially an attitude of "sincerity" vis-à-vis his reader, expunged any hint of fabrication from his writing. This naturalist prescription dominated Japanese letters during the first third of this century. Ishikawa was among the first of a young generation of writers, particularly those influenced by postnaturalist French fiction, to respond to the call raised by the critic

Kobayashi Hideo (1902–1983) and others, who argued on behalf of the "pure novel" (*junsui shōsetsu*).[58]

In *The Bodhisattva*, Ishikawa targets "sincerity" (*seijitsu;* III:181; *seii;* VI:211)[59] as the salient and troublesome feature of Japanese naturalist fiction. Indeed, it is this notion that separates Japanese naturalism from French and American, the idea reflecting perhaps the overweening value attached to displays of interpersonal and group loyalty in prewar Japanese society (and to the related issue of "face," about which this novel also has something to say). Ishikawa's rejection of a "sincere" approach to literature is expressed in his flagrant use of fabrication—what he calls "lies" (*uso*)[60]—and *watashi*'s denunciation of the hypocrisy that underlies the naturalist style.

> How is it possible for the flower of sincerity to burst forth if the greasiness of the hand that holds the pen—the blue vein standing out on the author's forehead, the drop of sweat hanging on the tip of his nose, the anger in his shoulders, in sum, the whole fetid smell of his body—is transmitted to the tracings on the page? What a dreadful farce! One proceeds to read a novel but ends up seeing instead the big, fat face of the author. (III:180)

That one person's sincerity is another's infidelity is the point suggested, for example, by the difficulties that ensue between Yasuko and her patron, Tsuruta: "So long as 'sincerity' remained untranslated into its true meaning of hard cash, there would never be an end to their jockeying back and forth over the question of who was truly sincere" (VI:211). *Watashi* takes care, therefore, to have us understand that, although conceived in the first person, his story is neither a naturalist novel nor what passes as its counterpart in Japanese literature, namely, "the novel of manners" (*fūzoku shōsetsu;* IV:192).[61] Given the plethora of detail in *The Bodhisattva*, and a public conditioned to read for setting, *watashi* makes a point of interrupting the episode of the old woman's wake to say he has no interest in treating his material in a mannerist way. Such a "*wazakure*" (IV:192)[62]—a display of virtuosity that amounts to no more than showing off one's talents—is not his intent. In his first published short story, *Kajin* ("The Beauty," 1935),[63] he had appended a similar, more extended message. This testy apologia is the oft-quoted manifesto of Ishikawa's anti-naturalism.

Having written this much, let me put my pen aside. It would not have been an impossible task for me to transform this narrative into a novel. I believe I have the skills to dress up the plot; certainly I do not lack for material calculated to touch a man to the quick. I am oppressed with it. Yet as least this time it appears I will not be able to develop this *récit* into a novel; otherwise I should have finished the tale of the old woman mentioned in the opening lines.

Perhaps someone will be sarcastic and ask if this is the best I can do. Let me say I write what I feel compelled to write. One starts by pulling the cork to get at the sake stored in the cask. It just so happens that my particular keg laps with the acrid talk of the utter loathesomeness of the world. But if for a moment I thought I had created even the slightest impression that I am resting quietly, feeling smug about my myself and my ability to spread a sheet of paper over life and trace on it a pastiche in imitation of the naturalist novel, then I would snap my pen in half and abandon this profession forever. Better to be out on the streetcorner drinking my share of rotgut with the local hooligans.[64]

NANI GA SŌ, NANI GA RŌ: ASKING WHAT HEROIC MEANS

AS ALWAYS, Ishikawa's use of fictional techniques is deliberate, skillfully roundabout, and very much in evidence. Take, for example, *The Bodhisattva*'s sense of dramaturgy. Often it is Kabuki-esque, as when Moichi enters a bar, or O-kumi makes her first and last appearances. There is a fascination with the burlesque and the ghoulish, and the story unfolds using the theatrical effects of natty costumes, exaggerated gestures, lifts, and eerie lighting—in short, letting out all of the stops employed by Grand Kabuki. At other moments, the novel becomes the epitome of the classical French stage by way of its tableaux vivants and windy declamations.

Nonetheless, *The Bodhisattva* ends on an anti-climatic—or as *watashi* would say, "unheroic" (XII:263)—note. A "maggot does as maggots do," he says disparagingly of himself (XII:264). He has only the instincts of his "inner chemistry" to reply upon, but at least for now his feet are planted on the ground, or as his facetious remark has it, on "O-tsuna's navel" (XII:266). As the name suggests, O-tsuna ("Rope") ties him to reality. Whenever she is near, the etheral Yukari and Joan have been forced from his mind. After the vexing encounter with Yukari, *watashi* decides to abandon once and for all not only his chiliastic dream of salvation conferred from outside this world but also the self-loathing and death wish attendant on its loss. By the end of the novel, he is quite convinced a bodhisattva is not a lofty, supernatural being who deigns to intervene upon occasion in human affairs. Rather its nature is on the order of Shih-te, humble sweeper of the earth, who attempts to order reality as best he can and broadcast wisdom in random, inexplicable ways. Ideals are illusions, and there will be no *deus ex machina* solution to the problems that bedevil Japan. In the untenable situation in which *watashi* finds himself, what remains to him is the power of reflexive gestures. It is unclear, perhaps even moot, where his potentially subversive behavior will lead him, but he has no interest in what his times define as heroic or patriotic: "Tell me," he asks, "what does it mean to draw distinctions and say one man is heroic, and another, not? [*nani ga sō, nani ga rō*]" (XII:263).[65]

In its provocative questioning of literary, social, and philosophical concepts and styles, *The Bodhisattva* can also be seen as a satirization of the Japanese intelligentsia of the mid-thirties. On the one hand, there is Bunzō who represents the case of the burnt-out *tenkōsha,*[66] or volte-face writers, who have cast aside the radical aspirations of their youth as a result of government suppression of left-wing thought. Meanwhile, Jinsaku portrays the apolitical dilettante who devotes himself to forms respected as traditional, yet lacking viability as modern art. *Watashi* finds himself tottering precariously, "like a pair of scales" (XII:265), between these extremes. He is in danger of falling into a state of abulic self-pity like Bunzō or retreating into meaningless erudition like Jinsaku. He resists these temptations; finally, his inner chemistry saves him from either pitfall. For the present, he can only laugh at himself and the world in which he lives. He chooses to partake of the breath of Samantabhadra and the mirth of "Gaṇeśa's laughter" (X:249, XI:257),[67] for they promise to revitalize body and soul, and like the cackle heard echoing throughout the novel, restore a semblance of sanity. This "karmic connection" (XI:255)—the product of a dubious *abhiṣeka* ceremony[68]—in which *watashi* casts his lot, as well as the flower of his art, upon the face of his patron bodhisattva is, finally, ironic and humorous.

As the novel ends, Ishikawa focuses our eye on Bunzō's bar of red lipstick and the purple vial of morphine—the paired symbols of *hana* and *chiri,* the petal from Samantabhadra's diadem and the compassionate droplet from his water bottle. At the same time, he superimposes a final image. Like Joan of Arc burned at the stake, or Yukari who is ready "to go up in flames at any moment" (VI:212), in his self-immolation Bunzō glows with a faint light. Time is up in the great "wrestling match" fought by the divided halves of his soul and "measure [d] out in a thin column of smoke." But the "dying ember" (VI:216) of his once fair face emits a final ardency. Bunzō has become a bodhisattva in his own right. And a tale that began with nothing more than a scintillating drop of water ends as a burning flame.

Notes to the Critical Essay

1. Passages quoted from *Fugen* are identified in the critical essay by chapter (roman numeral) and page number (arabic numeral) as they appear in Ishikawa Jun, *Ishikawa Jun zenshū* (Complete Works of Ishikawa Jun) (Tokyo: Chikuma shobō, 1974), 1:161–268.

The principal critical materials in Japanese on this author and his novels are: Aoyagi Tatsuo, *Ishikawa Jun no bungaku* (Tokyo: Chikuma shoin, 1978); Izawa Yoshio, *Ishikawa Jun* (Tokyo: Yayoi shobō, 1961); and, Noguchi Takehiko, *Ishikawa Jun ron* (Tokyo: Chikuma shobō, 1969). For materials in English, see William Jefferson Tyler, "The Agitated Spirit: Life and Major Works of the Contemporary Japanese Novelist, Ishikawa Jun," Ph.D. diss., Harvard University, 1981. Also Lucy Tian Hiang Ko Loh, "The World of Ishikawa Jun's Fiction," Ph.D. diss., Princeton University, 1986.

For translations of Ishikawa's works into English, see "Asters" (*Shion monogatari*, 1956) in Donald Keene, *The Old Woman, the Wife, and the Archer: Three Modern Japanese Novels* (New York: Viking, 1961), pp. 119–172; also "Moon Gems" (*Meigetsushu*, 1945) in *The Shōwa Anthology*, V. Gessel and T. Matsumoto, eds., W. Tyler, trans. (Tokyo: Kōdansha International, 1985), 1:45–62.

Although "reflexive" (and "reflexivity") as a critical term in this essay derives first and foremost from the fact that it is used as a key word in the novel in the form of "reflexive acts" (*mubō naru koi;* XII:267), it also relates to the use of the term in the literary and cultural anthropological writings of Victor Turner. See Victor Turner, "Liminality and the Performance Genres," John MacAloon, ed., *Rite, Drama, Festival, Spectacle* (Philadelphia: ISHI, 1984), pp. 19–41.

2. *prajñā* (Skt; Jp: *chie,* 智慧), wisdom, or specifically, wisdom put into action or practice. "True wisdom or understanding, beyond the discriminating intellect and conventional truth, that emerges from the actualization of True-mind; the power and functioning of enlightened

Mind." Philip Kapleau, *Zen: Dawn in the West* (New York: Anchor Press/Doubleday, 1980), p. 296.

Samantabhadra is identified in the novel as the "bodhisattva of *prajñâ*" (*chie no bosatsu,* 智慧の菩薩) in chapter 8. Also see note 21.

3. *jikken shōsetsu,* 実験小説.

4. *chi o harau,* 地を拂う. The verb *harau* is used in two senses: to sweep as with a broom, and to vacate or drive away.

5. *hana,* 花, or 華, meaning flower; *chiri,* 塵, dust.

6. *hashiru,* 走る, to run; *haneru,* 跳ねる, to kick or splash; *hassuru,* 発する, to depart; *chi o harau,* 地を拂う (cf. note 4); *hishō suru,* 飛翔する, to soar.

7. *tossa ni,* 咄嗟に, on the spur of the moment; *totan,* 途端, just as, no sooner than; *tachimachi,* 忽ち, instantly; *totsuzen,* 突然, suddenly; *yaniwani,* 矢場に, immediately; *iuyori hayaku,* 云うより早く, before one can say a word.

8. *mayutsuba-mono,* 眉唾物. Literally, "things having to do with eyebrow spit." Just as a speaker of English will wink as a gesture to indicate facetiousness with regard to what he says, or to caution a listener against duplicity on the part of third party, a Japanese will wet the tip of a finger with his tongue and then brush the finger along the edge of his eyebrow. Often the gesture is abbreviated to the motion of raising the hand to touch the eyebrow.

9. *watashi shōsetsu,* わたし小説, as opposed to, or a parody of, *watakushi* (or, *shi-*) *shōsetsu,* 私小説, the term in Japanese for an "I-novel."

10. In an essay entitled *Jido mukashibanashi* (Once upon at time with André Gide), Ishikawa wrote in 1951: "In addition to *L'immoraliste,* I was especially fond of *Paludes.* I still like it. As a matter of fact, it is probably Gide's masterpiece. What galvanized me was a vision of the dual potentiality within this author: starting with *Paludes,* what events could we expect to see occur within the setting of the novel? And what manner of terrestrial existence would this young writer create for himself?" (*Ishikawa Jun zenshū,* 11:155).

11. *Marusu no uta,*「マルスの歌」. Published in *Bungakkai.* The magazine was ordered to suspend sales of the January issue and to cease publication temporarily. Ishikawa was arraigned in Tokyo District Court and fined ¥30, along with the editor Kawakami Tetsutarō, who was fined ¥50. Kikuchi Kan, president of the Bungeishunjū Publishing Company, covered the fines. The outspoken nature of the piece is evident even in the opening paragraph:

> There it is again...that song. How shall I describe the feeling it evokes in me? It is twilight. I sit in my room alone. To my ear comes the clamorous sound of the popular refrain. It has its origins in the madness of the streets, its frenzied crescendo rising to a fever pitch to assault my window. It is "The Song of the War God" of which I speak.
>
> > In this realm with gods somnolent
> > Where the voice of wisdom has fallen silent,

> utterly silent
> What will ensue in the hour when you, Mars, stand
> and gird for battle?
> "How bold!" "How valiant!" they say.

The chorus of voices becomes a tempest. Like a smoldering fire bursting into flame, it spits forth an acrid smoke, the blackness of its soot blanketing every household, its grime penetrating into every nook and cranny, there to wither city arbors and asphyxiate backyard fowl and household pet. There, in the gaping mouths raised in song, one sees the malaise of our times, open and suppurating like a large, fetid wound.... I rise from my chair, and turning in the direction of the popular refrain as it echoes down the street, I shout "NO!"
(*Ishikawa Jun zenshū*, 1:283–284)

The title and strong antiwar message of this piece is reminiscent of Alain's *Mars ou la guerre jugée* (1921).

12. *mubō naru kōi,* 無謀なる行爲, a reflexive or reckless act; cf. *mushō naru kōi,* 無償なる行爲, Ishikawa's translation of Gide's term, *acte gratuit*. Again, in "Once upon a time with André Gide," Ishikawa writes:

Hōōchō no nukeana [Ishikawa's Japanese title for his translation of Gide's *Les caves du Vatican*, 1914] appeared in a pocket edition from the Iwanami Publishing House in 1928 thanks to the help of Hayashi Tatsuo. I still like the "play" one finds in this work. One French critic wrote that Gide had the "privilege of play." For literature to develop, I think we need to recognize this right. Though Lafcadio's *acte gratuit* became a popular phrase even in Japan, what good is it as just a device in a novel? (*Ishikawa Jun zenshū*, (11:157–158).

For information on the currency that this phrase enjoyed in Europe as a byword for iconoclastic behavior, see Germaine Brée and Margret Guiton, *The French Novel from Gide to Camus* (New York: Harcourt, Brace, 1962), p. 27.

13. See Charity Willard, *Christine de Pizan—Her Life and Works* (New York: Persea Books, 1984).

14. *tennin,* 天人. An "angel" or otherworldly female creature. The most famous examples are *Kaguya-hime,* "the Shining Princess," in *Taketori monogatari* (The Tale of the Bamboo Cutter, c.950), and the heavenly being who descends to earth by means of a feather robe depicted in the Nō drama, *Hagoromo* (The Feather Robe).

15. *mitate,* 見立.

16. *Temmei kyōka,* 天明狂歌. The style of comic or "mad" *waka* verse that flourished among poetry circles in the city of Edo during the Temmei era (1781–1789). Later, it became a term for *kyōka* verse written in imitiation of this style. See Donald Keene, *World Within Walls* (New York: Holt, Rinehart, and Winston, 1976), pp. 512–524.

17. *yatsushi,* 俏し, or 窶し. Derives from the verb *yatsusu,* to diguise or masquerade.

18. Yadoya-no-Meshimori, 宿屋之飯盛; Shikatsube-no-Magao, 鹿都部之真顔. Note that the *meshimori* were women who worked as waitresses and prostitutes at wayside inns; hence, more correctly, "The Inn's Ample Server," or "Full (Pro)portions."

19. *yatsushi* Genji, 窶し原氏; *mitate* Komachi, 見立(小野之)小町. Genji is "the Shining Prince" and principal figure in Murasaki Shikibu's *Genji monogatari* (Tale of Genji; c. 1005); Ono-on-Komachi is one of the thirty-six great poets of the Heian Period; also, reputedly the greatest beauty of the period. Townsmen and courtesans from the pleasure districts were often portrayed as contemporary versions of Genji and Komachi in the *ukiyo-e,* 浮世絵 or pictures of the floating world, produced during the Edo period. *Surimono,* 摺物, constitute a special style of print within the larger woodblock print tradition and were frequently embellished with *kyōka* verses. See Richard Lane, *Images from the Floating World* (Secaucus, N.J.: Chartwell Books, 1978).

20. Han-shan (Ch; Jp: Kanzan, 寒山) and Shih-te (Ch; Jp: Jittoku, 拾得). The story of Han-shan and Shih-te was first recorded by the T'ang dynasty Keeper of Records, Lu Ch'iu-yin, who sought out the two famous eccentrics at the Kuo-ch'ing monastery. For further details on this legend, see "Introduction," *Cold Mountain,* B. Watson, trans. (New York: Columbia University Press, 1970), pp. 7–14.

21. Mañjuśrî (Skt; Jp: Monju, 文殊) and Samantabhadra (Skt; Jp: Fugen, 普賢). Mañjuśrî is seated at the left hand of the historical Buddha, (*Shaka nyorai*), and Samantabhadra, the right. Mañjuśrî represents the Buddha's ultimate wisdom, while Samantabhadra represents that wisdom translated into practice. The former is usually depicted as seated upon a lotus mounted on the back of a lion; the later, on the back of a white elephant. When Samantabhadra rides forth on his elephant, the heavens are said to release clouds of incense and the holy sâla tree shower the earth with blossoms.

The introduction of Samantabhadra bodhisattva to Japan dates from the Nara period and the importation of the Hua-yen, or Kegon, sect of Buddhism, which was patronized by Emperor Shōmu (r. 724–749). Although the cult of Samantabhadra ceased to flourish after the Heian period, this bodhisattva continued to be the object of veneration among esoteric sects for his ability to confer long life as the bodhisattva of longevity (*Fugen enmei bosatsu,* 普賢延命菩薩). See Daigan and Alicia Matsunaga, *Foundation of Japanese Buddhism* (Los Angeles: Buddhist Books International, 1974), 1:94–98.

Samantabhadra is also the principal intercessor for women seeking buddhahood (*nyonin jōbutsu bosatsu,* 女人成仏菩薩). In Heian period paintings, he is often depicted in the company of ten "cannibal women," or *râkṣasa,* converts (*jūrasetsu'nyo,* 十羅殺女). In their worship of this bodhisattva, Heian ladies purportedly often likened themselves to these demonesses. See Katō Shūichi, "Kaisetsu: Ishikawa Jun shōron" in Ishikawa Jun, *Bungaku taigai* (Tokyo: Kadokawa bunko, 1955), p. 268; and *Butsuzō ikonogurafuii* (Tokyo: Iwanami shashin bunko, 1951), 42:27, 53.

22. Hua-yen, or Kegon, 華厳. A sect of Buddhism that developed in China. Its teachings derive from the *Avataṁsaka Sûtra* (Skt; Jp: Kegongyō, 華厳経). See Thomas Cleary, *Entry into the Inconceivable: An Introduction to Hua-yen Buddhism* (Honolulu: University of Hawaii Press, 1983); also Francis Cook, *Hua-yen Buddhism—The Jewel Net of Indra* (University Park: Pennsylvania State University Press, 1977). For a complete translation of this sutra, see Thomas Cleary, *The Flower Ornament Scripture: A Translation of the Avatamsaka Sutra* (Boulder and London: Shambhala Publications, 1984–1986), vols. 1–3.

23. *kokudo*, 國(国)土.

24. *konnyaku mondō*, 蒟蒻問答. An idiomatic expression describing a discussion that is amorphous in nature and that appears to have no conclusion or end; hence, "argument for argument's sake." *Konnyaku*, or devil's tongue, is a starchy tuber related to the taro family of potato and from which blocks or noodles of a gray gelatin are made and used in Japanese cuisine.

25. Charles Baudelaire, *Les paradis artificiels*, 1860. Cited and translated in Gérard Genette, *Figures of Literary Discourse*, A. Sheridan, trans. (New York: Columbia University Press, 1982), p. 228, n.59.

26. Gérard Genette. *Palimpsestes: La littérature au second degré* (Paris: Éditions du Seuil, 1982).

27. *hensō no utushi-e*, 變相の寫繪. The superimposition on O-kumi's face of the Buddhist depiction of the nine stages of the decomposition of the body: literally, "a copy of an illustration of the aspects of transformation," with specific reference to a *kusōzu*, 九相図, a Buddhist painting of the nine stages of decomposition of a corpse. Such scrolls were used in the practice of *kusō* (Jp; Skt: asubha-bhâvanâ), meditations on the nine types of corpses, designed to free the viewer from attachment to the life of the flesh. See *Japanese-English Buddhist Dictionary*, S. Iwano, ed., (Tokyo: Daitō shuppansha, 1965), p. 188.

28. *rishōki*, 利生記.

29. *uroji muroji*, 有漏路無漏路. The Vision of the Washed Few and the Illusions of the Great Unwashed: literally, the way (*ji*) that is tainted/"wet" with illusion (*uro;* Skt: sâsrava); and, the way that is without it (*muro;* Skt: anâsrava). Ishikawa uses the sound of this phrase to heighten the sarcastic tone of the passage; hence, the insertion of "the mumbo jumbo of their conundrums" in the translation. *Ibid.*, p. 190.

The other Buddhist phrases that Ishikawa refers to in chapter 6 of the novel are: *kyōge betsuden*, 教外別伝, "transmission of the teachings outside the scriptures," and, *nan'i ryōkō no ura omote*, 難易両行の裏表, "difficult and easy as obverse and reverse."

30. *hanawa*, 花輪; *hitohira no hana*, 一瓣の花; *hyappō no hana*, 百寶の花; *chirizuka*, 塵塚; *sajin*, 砂塵; *zokujin*, 俗塵; *kuzu*, 屑; *hogo*, 反古; *ori*, 滓(澱).

31. *Heike monogatari*, 「平家物語」. Flower and dust as a metaphor for glory and evanescence is found in the opening lines of this great classic of the rise and fall of the Taira family in twelfth-century Japan:

The bell of Gion Temple tolls into every man's heart to warn him
that all is vanity and evanescence. The faded flowers of the sâla trees
by the Buddha's deathbed bear witness to the truth that all who
flourish are destined to decay. Yes, pride must have its fall, for it is
as unsubstantial as a dream on a spring night. The brave and violent
man—he too must die away in the end, like a whirl of dust in the
wind. (*The Tale of the Heike*, H. Kitagawa and B. Tsuchida, trans.
[Tokyo: University of Tokyo Press, 1975], p. 5).

32. T'ien-lung (Ch; Jp: *Tenryū*, 天龍[竜]). Ch'an [Ch; Jp: *Zen*,
禅[禅]) master of ninth-century China, about whose life nothing is known,
except for several anecdotes concerning his teachings. The most famous is
"The Zen of One Finger" told in *Pi-yen lu* (Ch; Jp: *Hekiganroku*, 碧巖錄;
Blue Cliff Record) and *Wu-men kuan* (Ch; Jp: *Mumonkan*, 無門関; The
Gateless Gate), two collections of Zen *kōan*, or conundrums. See "Chu Ti's
One-Finger Ch'an," *The Blue Cliff Record*, T. and J. C. Cleary, trans.
(Boulder, Colo: Prajñâ Press, 1978), pp. 123–128; and *Two Zen Classics:
Mumonkan and Hekiganroku*, A. V. Grimstone, ed., K. Sekida, trans.
(Tokyo: Weatherhill, 1977), pp. 35–36, 197–198.

33. The original text in Chinese reads: 一塵擧大地収。一花開世界
起。只如塵未擧花未開時。如何著眼。(第十九則俱胝只竪一指) *Heki-
ganroku*, S. Ōmori, ed. and anno. (Tokyo: Bunkōsha, 1976), 1:144.

34. Chu-ti (Ch; Jp; Gutei, 俱胝). For a translation of the entire lesson,
see "Chu Ti's One Finger Ch'an," *The Blue Cliff Record*, T. and J. C.
Cleary, trans. pp. 123–128. The story of Chu-ti's encounter with T'ien-
lung is as follows:

Master Chu Ti was from Chin Hua in Wu Chou (in Chekiang).
During the time he first dwelt in a hermitage, there was a nun named
Shih Chi ("Reality") who came to his hut. When she got there she
went straight in; without taking off her rain hat she walked around
his meditation seat three times holding her staff. 'If you can speak,'
she said, 'I'll take off my rain hat.' She questioned him like this three
times; Chu Ti had no reply. Then as she was leaving Chu Ti said,
'The hour is rather late: would you stay the night?' The nun said, 'If
you can speak, I'll stay over.' Again Chu Ti sighed sorrowfully and
said, 'Although I inhabit the body of a man, still I lack a man's spirit.'
After this he aroused his zeal to clarify this matter.

He meant to abandon his hermitage and travel to various places
to call on teachers to ask for instruction, and had wrapped up his
things for foot-travelling. But that night the spirit of the mountain
told him, 'You don't have to leave this place. Tomorrow a flesh and
blood bodhisattva will come and expound the truth for you, Master.
You don't have to go.' As it turned out, the following day Master
T'ien Lung actually came to the hermitage. Chu Ti welcomed him
ceremoniously and gave a full account of the previous events. T'ien
Lung just lifted up one finger to show him; suddenly Chu Ti was
greatly enlightened. At the time Chu Ti was most earnest and single-

minded, so the bottom of his bucket fell out easily. Later, whenever anything was asked, Chu Ti just raised one finger. (p. 124)

35. Fa-tsang, 法藏. Third, and principal, patriarch of Hua-yen Buddhism. See *The Buddhist Tradition in India, China, and Japan*, W. T. de Bary, ed. (New York: Vintage Books, 1972), pp. 166–178.
36. *Nyūhokkaibon*, 「入法界品」.
37. *Zenzai dōji*, 善財童子. Also see Jan Fontein, *The Pilgrimage of Sudhana: A Study of Gaṇḍavyūha Illustrations in China, Japan, and Java*, (The Hague and Paris, Mouton, 1967). The thirty-fourth teacher that Sudhana visits, the night goddess, reveals herself to be a transformation of Samantabhadra (p. 11).
38. Thomas Cleary, *Entry Into the Inconceivable*, p. 6.
39. *Ibid.*, p. 9.
40. *Eguchi*, 「江口」. For a translation of this Nō play, see *The Noh Drama*, Nippon gakujutsu shinkōkai, ed. (Tokyo and Rutland, Vt.: Charles E. Tuttle, 1955), 1 : 107–124.
41. *Fugen-gyŏ*, 普賢行.
42. *tōkan no me*, 透關の目.
43. *butsu*, 佛(仏); *butsuda*, 佛陀; *bosatsu*, 菩薩.
44. *hotoke ni naru*, 佛(仏)になる.
45. *kumo no ue*, 雲の上.
46. *Semimaru*, 「蟬丸」. For a translation and commentary on this Nō drama, see Susan Matisoff, *The Legend of Semimaru, Blind Musician of Japan* (New York: Columbia University Press, 1978).
47. Émile Chartier (pseudonym: Alain), "Les saisons," *Les dieux*, 1934. "Les dieux sont composés, comme nous sommes...je dirais même composés de divers animaux, comme nous sommes."
48. *yakṣa* (Skt; Jp: *yasha*, 夜叉). One of the ugliest forms among the eight levels of existence, but also a protector of Buddha's law.
49. Ishikawa taught French language and literature at Fukuoka Higher School (*Fukuoka kōtōgakkō*) in Kyushu from April 1924 to March 1926. Radical left-wing thought was sweeping through institutions of higher learning, and the Ministry of Education sought to curb its spread. Ishikawa became known among students and faculty for his liberal views and his sympathies for the union movement that began to develop among coal miners in northern Kyushu. He was relieved of his teaching duties in September 1925 and asked to tender his resignation, effective in March of the following year. He resisted throughout the fall semester, demanding to be fired—a step that the school, fearing an embarrassing explanation to the Ministry, was reluctant to undertake. Only in December did he relent as a face-saving gesture for the head of the school's French Department.
50. *ishi*, 意志; *seishin*, 精神. *Seishin* as used in this context should not be confused with its more moralistic and nationalistic usages in Japanese. See Ishikawa's comment in the short story *Mujintō* (Vimalakîrti's Inexhaustible Light, 1946): "The public subjected words to the most fearsome abuse [during the war]. What depressed me almost to the breaking point was to witness the misappropriation and flagrant misuse of the one word

that I have always employed with the greatest of care." (*Ishikawa Jun zenshū*, 2:157).

51. *shaberu,* しゃべる; *kuchibashiru,* 口走る.

52. *bungaku seinen,* 文学青年. A term used to describe a young man, or men, with a strong interest in the arts and literature.

53. *Bungaku taigai,* 「文学大概」. *Ishikawa Jun zenshū*, 9.

54. *seishin no undō,* 精神の運動; *pen to tomo ni kangaeru,* ペンと共に考える.

55. *Ishikawa Jun zenshū*, 9:118.

56. *Ibid.*, pp. 210–212.

57. *han-shizenshugi,* 反自然主義.

58. *junsui shōsetsu,* 純粋小説. Also see Nakamura Mitsuo, "The French Influence in Modern Japanese Literature," *Japan Quarterly* (January–March 1960), 7(1):57–65.

59. *seijitsu,* 誠實(実); *seii,* 誠意.

60. *uso,* 嘘.

61. *fūzoku shōsetsu,* 風俗小説.

62. *wazakure,* わざくれ.

63. *Kajin,* 「佳人」.

64. *Ishikawa Jun zenshū*, 1:40.

65. *nani ga sō, nani ga rō,* 何が壮、何が陋. During the war years, the term *sōshi,* 壮(壯)士, was used as a word of praise for heroic soliders and patriotic supporters of Japanese militarism at home and abroad.

66. *tenkōsha,* 転向者. See Nakamura Mitsuo, *Contemporary Japanese Fiction:* 1926–1968 (Tokyo: Kokusai bunka shinkōkai, 1969), pp. 55–70.

67. Gaṇeśa, or Vināyaka (Skt: "one who removes obstacles"); Jp: *Kangiten,* "the deva of joy or ecstasy", 歡喜天). A Hindu deity and a tutelary god of Buddhism with the head of an elephant and the body of a human being. The figure is also depicted as having the elephant heads and entwined bodies of a male and female deva (Skt; Jp: *ten*), representing incarnations of Maō, the Devil, and of Kannon, the Goddess of Mercy. Known to both benefit and play tricks on human beings.

68. *abhiṣeka* (Skt; Jp: *kechi'en* [*kanjō*], 結縁[灌頂]). "*Kechi'en:* to make a connection. Before a person can receive the benefits of the Buddha, he must establish some kind of tie with [the Buddha]. In Shingon [Buddhism], this is done by means of *kechi'en kanjō*, a ceremony in esoteric Buddhism in which a layman tosses flowers at various images. The image on which the flower falls is then regarded as his own deity, with whom he has a special connection." *Japanese-English Buddhist Dictionary*, p. 166.

Other Works in the Columbia Asian Studies Series

MODERN ASIAN LITERATURE SERIES

Modern Japanese Drama: An Anthology, ed. and tr. Ted T. Takaya. Also in paperback ed. 1979
Mask and Sword: Two Plays for the Contemporary Japanese Theater, Yamazaki Masakazu, tr. J. Thomas Rimer 1980
Yokomitsu Riichi, Modernist, Dennis Keene 1980
Nepali Visions, Nepali Dreams: The Poetry of Laxmiprasad Devkota, tr. David Rubin 1980
Literature of the Hundred Flowers, vol. 1: *Criticism and Polemics,* ed. Hualing Nieh 1981
Literature of the Hundred Flowers, vol. 2: *Poetry and Fiction,* ed. Hualing Nieh 1981
Modern Chinese Stories and Novellas, 1919–1949, ed. Joseph S. M. Lau, C. T. Hsia, and Leo Ou-fan Lee. Also in paperback ed. 1984
A View by the Sea, by Yasuoka Shōtarō, tr. Kären Wigen Lewis 1984
Other Worlds; Arishima Takeo and the Bounds of Modern Japanese Fiction, by Paul Anderer 1984
The Sting of Life: Four Contemporary Japanese Novelists, by Van C. Gessel 1989

NEO-CONFUCIAN STUDIES

Instructions for Practical Living and Other Neo-Confucian Writings by Wang Yang-ming, tr. Wing-tsit Chan 1963
Reflections on Things at Hand: The Neo-Confucian Anthology, comp. Chu Hsi and Lü Tsu-ch'ien, tr. Wing-tsit Chan 1967
Self and Society in Ming Thought, by Wm. Theodore de Bary and the Conference on Ming Thought. Also in paperback ed. 1970

The Unfolding of Neo-Confucianism, by Wm. Theodore de
Bary and the Conference on Seventeenth-Century Chinese
Thought. Also in paperback ed.   1975
*Principle and Practicality: Essays in Neo-Confucianism and Prac-
tical Learning,* ed. Wm. Theodore de Bary and Irene Bloom.
Also in paperback ed.   1979
The Syncretic Religion of Lin Chao-en, by Judith A. Berling   1980
*The Renewal of Buddhism in China: Chu-hung and the Late Ming
Synthesis,* by Chün-fang Yü   1981
*Neo-Confucian Orthodoxy and the Learning of the Mind-and-
Heart,* by Wm. Theodore de Bary   1981
Yüan Thought: Chinese Thought and Religion Under the Mongols,
ed. Hok-lam Chan and Wm. Theodore de Bary   1982
The Liberal Tradition in China, by Wm. Theodore de Bary   1983
The Development and Decline of Chinese Cosmology, by John B.
Henderson   1984
The Rise of Neo-Confucianism in Korea, ed. Wm. Theodore de
Bary and JaHyun Kim Haboush   1985
*Chiao Hung and the Restructuring of Neo-Confucianism in the
Late Ming,* by Edward T. Ch'ien.   1985
Neo-Confucian Terms Explained: The Pei-hsi tzu-i by Ch'en
Ch'un, ed. and trans. Wing-tsit Chan   1986
Knowledge Painfully Acquired: The K'un-chih chi by Lo Ch'in-
shun, ed. and trans. Irene Bloom   1987
To Become a Sage: The Ten Diagrams on Sage Learning by Ti
T'oegye, ed. and trans. Michael C. Kalton   1988
*A Heritage of Kings: One Man's Monarchy in the Confucian
World,* by JaHyun Kim Haboush   1988
The Message of the Mind in Neo-Confucian Thought by Wm.
Theodore de Bary   1989

TRANSLATIONS FROM
THE ORIENTAL CLASSICS

Major Plays of Chikamatsu, tr. Donald Keene   1961
Four Major Plays of Chikamatsu, tr. Donald Keene. Paperback
text edition   1961
*Records of the Grand Historian of China, translated from the Shih
chi of Ssu-ma Ch'ien,* tr. Burton Watson, 2 vols.   1961
*Instructions for Practical Living and Other Neo-Confucian Writing
by Wang Yang-ming,* tr. Wing-tsit Chan   1963
Chuang Tzu: Basic Writings, tr. Burton Watson, paperback ed.
only   1964
The Mahābhārata, tr. Chakravarthi V. Narasimhan. Also in paperback ed.   1965
The Manyōshū, Nippon Gakujutsu Shinkōkai edition   1965

Su Tung-p'o: Selections from a Sung Dynasty Poet, tr. Burton
Watson. Also in paperback ed.   1965
Bhartrihari: Poems, tr. Barbara Stoler Miller. Also in paperback
ed.   1967
Basic Writings of Mo Tzu, Hsün Tzu, and Han Fei Tzu, tr. Burton
Watson. Also in separate paperback eds.   1967
The Awakening of Faith, Attributed to Aśvaghosha, tr. Yoshito S.
Hakeda. Also in paperback ed.   1967
Reflections on Things at Hand: The Neo-Confucian Anthology,
comp. Chu Hsi and Lü Tsu-ch'ien, tr. Wing-tsit Chan   1967
The Platform Sutra of the Sixth Patriarch, tr. Philip B. Yampol-
sky. Also in paperback ed.   1967
Essays in Idleness: The Tsurezuregusa of Kenkō, tr. Donald Keene.
Also in paperback ed.   1967
The Pillow Book of Sei Shōnagon, tr. Ivan Morris, 2 vols.   1967
*Two Plays of Ancient India: The Little Clay Cart and the Mini-
ster's Seal,* tr. J. A. B. van Buitenen   1968
The Complete Works of Chuang Tzu, tr. Burton Watson   1968
The Romance of the Western Chamber (Hsi Hsiang chi), tr. S. I.
Hsiung. Also in paperback ed.   1968
The Manyōshū, Nippon Gakujustu Shinkōkai edition. Paperback
text edition.   1969
*Records of the Historian: Chapters from the Shih chi of Ssu-ma
Ch'en.* Paperback text edition, tr. Burton Watson.   1969
Cold Mountain: 100 Poems by the T'ang Poet Han-shan, tr. Burton
Watson. Also in paperback ed.   1970
Twenty Plays of the Nō Theatre, ed. Donald Keene. Also in
paperback ed.   1970
Chushingura: The Treasury of Loyal Retainers, tr. Donald Keene.
Also in paperback ed.   1971
The Zen Master Hakuin: Selected Writings, tr. Philip B.
Yampolsky   1971
*Chinese Rhyme-Prose: Poems in the Fu Form from the Han and Six
Dynasties Periods,* tr. Burton Watson. Also in paperback ed.   1971
Kūkai: Major Works, tr. Yoshito S. Hakeda. Also in paperback
ed.   1972
*The Old Man Who Does as He Pleases: Selections from the Poetry
and Prose of Lu Yu,* tr. Burton Watson   1973
The Lion's Roar of Queen Śrīmālā, tr. Alex. & Hideko Wayman   1974
*Courtier and Commoner in Ancient China: Selections from the
History of the Former Han by Pan Ku,* tr. Burton Watson. Also
in paperback ed.   1974
Japanese Literature in Chinese, vol. 1: *Poetry and Prose in Chinese
by Japanese Writers of the Early Period,* tr. Burton Watson   1975
Japanese Literature in Chinese, vol. 2: *Poetry and Prose in Chinese
by Japanese Writers of the Later Period,* tr. Burton Watson.   1976
Scripture of the Lotus Blossom of the Fine Dharma, tr. Leon
Hurvitz. Also in paperback ed.   1976

Love Song of the Dark Lord: Jayadeva's Gītagovinda, tr. Barbara
Stoler Miller. Also in paperback ed. Cloth ed. includes critical
text of the Sanskrit.   1977
Ryōkan: Zen Monk-Poet of Japan, tr. Burton Watson   1977
*Calming the Mind and Discerning the Real: Fron the Lam rim chen
mo of Tson-kha-pa*, tr. Alex Wayman   1978
*The Hermit and the Love-Thief: Sanskirt Poems of Bhartrihari and
Bilhana*, tr. Barbara Stoler Miller   1978
The Lute: Kao Ming's p'i-p'a chi, tr. Jean Mulligan. Also in
paperback ed.   1980
*A Chronicle of Gods and Sovereigns: Jinnō Shōtōki of Kitabatake
Chikafusa*, tr. H. Paul Varley   1980
Among the Flowers: The Hua-chien chi, tr. Lois Fusek   1982
Grass Hill: Poems and Prose by the Japanese Monk Gensei, tr.
Burton Watson   1983
*Doctors, Diviners, and Magicians of Ancient China: Biographies of
Fang-shih*, tr. Kenneth J. DeWoskin. Also in paperback ed.   1983
Theatre of Memory: The Plays of Kālidāsa, ed. Barbara Stoler
Miller. Also in paperback ed.   1984
*The Columbia Book of Chinese Poetry: From Early Times to the
Thirteenth Century*, ed. and tr. Burton Watson   1984
*Poems of Love and War: From the Eight Anthologies and the Ten
Songs of Classical Tamil*, tr. A. K. Ramanujan. Also in paper-
back ed.   1985
The Columbia Book of Later Chinese Poetry, ed. and tr. Jonathan
Chaves   1986
Selections from the Tso Chuan: China's Oldest Narrative History,
tr. Burton Watson   1989
*Waiting for the Wind: Thirty-six Poets of Japan's Late Medieval
Age*, tr. Steven Carter   1989

STUDIES IN ORIENTAL CULTURE

1. *The Ōnin War: History of Its Origins and Background, with a
   Selective Translation of the Chronicle of Ōnin*, by H. Paul
   Varley   1967
2. *Chinese Government in Ming Times: Seven Studies*, ed.
   Charles O. Hucker   1969
3. *The Actor's Analects (Yakusha Rongo)*, ed. and tr. by Charles
   J. Dunn and Bungō Torigoe   1969
4. *Self and Society in Ming Thought*, by Wm. Theodore de Bary
   and the Conference on Ming Thought. Also in paperback ed.   1970
5. *A History of Islamic Philosophy*, by Majid Fakhry, 2d ed.   1983
6. *Phantasies of a Love Thief: The Caurapañcāśikā Attributed to
   Bilhana*, by Barbara Stoler Miller   1971
7. *Iqbal: Poet-Philosopher of Pakistan*, ed. Hafeez Malik   1971

8. *The Golden Tradition: An Anthology of Urdu Poetry*, Ahmed Ali. Also in paperback edition. 1973
9. *Conquerors and Confucians: Aspects of Political Change in the Late Yüan China*, by John W. Dardess 1973
10. *The Unfolding of Neo-Confucianism*, by Wm. Theodore de Bary and the Conference on Seventeenth-Century Chinese Thought. Also in paperback ed. 1975
11. *To Acquire Wisdom: The Way of Wang Yang-ming*, by Julia Ching 1976
12. *Gods, Priests, and Warriors: The Bhrgus of the Mahābhārata*, by Robert P. Goldman 1977
13. *Mei Yao-ch'en and the Development of Early Sung Poetry*, by Jonathan Chaves 1976
14. *The Legend of Semimaru, Blind Musician of Japan*, by Susan Matisoff 1977
15. *Sir Sayyid Ahmad Khan and Muslim Modernization in India and Pakistan*, by Hafeez Malik 1980
16. *The Khilafat Movement: Religious Symbolism and Political Mobilization in India*, by Gail Minault 1982
17. *The World of K'ung Shang-jen: A Man of Letters in Early Ch'ing China*, by Richard Strassberg 1983
18. *The Lotus Boat: The Origins of Chinese Tz'u Poetry in T'ang Popular Culture*, by Marsha L. Wagner 1984
19. *Expressions of Self in Chinese Literature*, ed. Robert E. Hegal and Richard C. Hessney 1985
20. *Songs for the Bride: Women's Voices and Wedding Rites of Rural India*, by W. G. Archer, ed. Barbara Stoler Miller and Mildred Archer 1985
21. *A Heritage of Kings: One Man's Monarchy in the Confucian World*, by JaHyun Kim Haboush 1988

COMPANIONS TO ASIAN STUDIES

Approaches to the Oriental Classics, ed. Wm. Theodore de Bary 1959
Early Chinese Literature, by Burton Watson. Also in paperback ed. 1962
Approaches to Asian Civilizations, ed. Wm. Theodore de Bary and Ainslie T. Embree 1964
The Classic Chinese Novel: A Critical Introduction, by C. T. Hsia. Also in paperback ed. 1968
Chinese Lyricism: Shih Poetry from the Second to the Twelfth Century, tr. Burton Watson. Also in paperback ed. 1971
A Syllabus of Indian Civilization, by Leonard A. Gordon and Barbara Stoler Miller 1971
Twentieth-Century Chinese Stories, ed. C. T. Hsia and Joseph S. M. Lau. Also in paperback ed. 1971

A Syllabus of Indian Civilization, by J. Mason Gentzler, 2d ed. 1972
A Syllabus of Indian Civilization, by H. Paul Varley, 2d ed. 1972
An Introduction to Chinese Civilization, ed. John Meskill, with the
  assistance of J. Mason Gentzler 1973
An Introduction to Japanese Civilization, ed. Arthur E. Tiedemann 1974
Ukifune: Love in the Tale of Genji, ed. Andrew Pekarik 1982
The Pleasures of Japanese Literature, by Donald Keene 1988
A Guide to Oriental Classics, ed. Wm. Theodore de Bary and
  Ainslie. T. Embree, third edition ed. Amy Vladek Heinrich 1989

INTRODUCTION TO ORIENTAL CIVILIZATION
Wm. Theodore de Bary, Editor

Sources of Japanese Tradition 1958 Paperback ed., 2 vols., 1964
Sources of Indian Tradition 1958 Paperback ed., 2 vols., 1964 Second
  edition 1988, 2 vols.
Sources of Chinese Tradition 1960 Paperback ed., 2 vols., 1964